MAUREEN

To Darlene – my
fellow writer

Mary E Trimble

Other Books by Mary E. Trimble

Sailing with Impunity: Adventure in the South Pacific

"If you're one of the millions of people who have dreamed of casting off everyday cares and setting sail for the South Pacific in your own 40-foot boat, this is the book for you! Mary and Bruce Trimble did what so many wish they could do. Her story will fire your imagination and fuel your fantasies. "
—*Robert H. Mottram, author of In Search of America's Heartbeat: Twelve Months on the Road.*

Tubob: Two Years in West Africa with the Peace Corps

"Trimble's honesty in describing her two years in Africa, both the trials and the triumphs, makes the book interesting and engageing. It provides a valuable view of The Gambia, while at the same time showing the strengths and weaknesses of the Peace Corps."
—*Story Circle Book Reviews*

Tenderfoot

"The explosion of Mount St. Helens is listed as the most devastating volcanic event in the history of the United States. There's plenty of romance and vivid descriptions of ranch life. And always in the background, the dangerous rumblings of a volcano threatening to blow its top. When it does, the book takes a thrilling life and death turn."
—*Skagit Valley Herald*

McClellan's Bluff

"The author proves her gift for confronting the complexities teens face as they learn to define their identities and establish independence as young adults. McClellan's Bluff comes very highly recommended."
—*Word Weaving*

Rosemount

"Rosemount is a wonderful young adult novel about teenage angst, deftly portrayed by Trimble's skill and perception. She succeeds in expressing the many uncertainties and attitudes of today's teenagers in a way that will invite understanding and acceptance."
—*Amazing Authors*

MAUREEN

ᴗ ᴗ ᴗ ᴗ ᴗ

A Novel

Mary E. Trimble

Maureen is a contemporary western novel. The characters, incidents, and dialogues in this book are products of the author's imagination.

Printed in the United States of America

Cover images & design © Bruce Trimble except:
Barn:© MH Anderson/Shutterstock
Woman:© Alliance Image/Shutterstock

Published by ShelterGraphics
Camano Island, WA USA

Author's Note

*I*n my first book, *Rosemount*, a Young Adult contemporary western, sixteen year-old Leslie Cahill rebels when her widower father announces he's sending her to a private girls' school in Spokane. A good student and musically gifted, Leslie loves her ranch life and riding her beloved Appaloosa, Polly.

In *Rosemount's* sequel, *McClellan's Bluff*, Leslie, then seventeen, is flattered when a neighboring cowboy, eleven years older, shows interest in her. He treats her like a woman, not just another kid. But danger lurks.

Throughout these two Young Adult novels, the Cahill housekeeper, Maureen Gardner, plays an important role in the family. In the years following *Rosemount* and *McClellan's Bluff* publications I have frequently thought about Maureen and how life was for her on the Cahill ranch. Her story was yet to be told.

In this novel, Leslie is seven when Maureen comes to the family; Leslie's brother Wade is seventeen. Their father John, still overwhelmed with grief from the tragic death of his wife and with the burden of managing the family, struggles to keep things running on their large eastern Washington cattle ranch.

Maureen covers a ten-year period. This is Maureen's story. Some of the events presented in *Rosemount* and *McClellan's Bluff* are revisited in this novel, but seen through Maureen's eyes, and written with an adult's perspective.

Dedicated to those who
have helped me along
the way.

*M*y heart stirred when I saw that help-wanted ad in the Seattle Times. Reading between the lines, I recognized despair. I knew despair.

> *Wanted: Housekeeper and care*
> *for 7 year-old girl on cattle ranch*
> *near Chewack, WA. Call evenings.*

It was clear to me now that I'd never have a child of my own, a deep longing I'd carried with me for as long as I could remember. I had a job, but I was just putting in time. Insurance was only mildly interesting.

Just that afternoon my boss at Safeco had approached me with the offer of a promotion as supervisor. He'd asked me to think about making this deeper commitment. Although I was honored to be asked, the idea of several more years in insurance made my heart heavy. Surely there was more to life than a career at Safeco. I craved adventure, something different, something away from sad memories and bitterness. In trying to make up my mind, I turned to the help wanted ads in the Seattle Times, really more to satisfy myself that I'd covered all the bases. That's when I saw the ad that tugged at my heart.

That evening I called the Chewack number. The rancher answered the phone. "Cahill."

"This is Maureen Gardner. I'm calling about your ad looking for child care and housekeeping."

"Have you had experience with children?" His deep voice sounded weary.

"Not my own, but I'm very close to my brother's and sister's children. I'm—"

"Do you mind my asking your age? Are you married? I'm only asking because Leslie, my little seven year-old daughter, is a pretty active kid. We need someone to be with her full time."

"No, not married. I'm forty and in good health."

"Are you familiar with ranching?"

"Not really. But I know children, and I'm a good housekeeper." He could have been no more surprised to hear that than I was to say it. Bragging isn't my style. For some reason, I knew this job was meant for me.

"Where do you live? Would it be possible for you to come to the ranch to meet us?"

"Seattle. I could come this weekend. Either Saturday or Sunday."

"It's about a four- or five-hour drive from Seattle to Chewack. How about coming Saturday, spending the night, or if you prefer I can get a hotel room for you. You don't have to decide that right now."

"That would be fine."

"If the arrangement is satisfactory, when could you start?"

"I'd have to give two weeks notice to my employer."

"Okay. Let me give you directions for getting here."

When I hung up, my mind flew in eight different directions. What had I just done? Well, it wasn't a commitment...yet. This guy didn't seem particularly friendly, just desperate. I wondered how many people he'd interviewed.

The following Saturday the drive over Stevens Pass to Chewack in eastern Washington seemed endless. My mind whirled and my stomach knotted. It wasn't too late to turn around, go back home. Back to the life I knew and my safe job. No. I couldn't do that. Too many reminders. I had to make big changes, make a new life. I kept driving. I tried to quiet the committee in my head by concentrating on the road.

Once in town, I called the ranch, per Mr. Cahill's instructions, to let him know I was close. I followed his directions to the Cahill ranch several miles out of town. I drove up the long driveway, dust billowing around my car on this hot June day. The drier climate in Eastern Washington always surprised me.

The ranch house looked inviting, but a little ne-glected, maybe forlorn. The gardens needed care, but if there were no Mrs. Cahill...

Mr. Cahill opened the door at my first knock. "Miss Gardner? Come in."

John Cahill was a handsome man, in a rugged way, but weariness lined his face. His hair was wet as though he'd just showered and his clothes were clean, but wrinkled. A tall, teenage boy, almost gaunt, came in from the kitchen, his hair slicked back, his clothes also clean. They apparently had made some effort to look presentable to me. Both father and son were in stock-ing feet.

"This is Wade, my son." The boy stepped forward and gave me a firm handshake, his smile shy. His coloring was much lighter, probably like his mother. His sharp blue eyes contrasted his father's almost black eyes.

The boy went back into the kitchen. "Come on, Leslie," he urged. "Don't you want to meet Miss Gardner?"

"No."

"Come *on.*" A young girl, led by her brother, hung back.

I smiled at the skinny little girl, trying to put her at ease. "Hi, Leslie, my name is Maureen."

"Hi." She looked at her brother with pleading eyes. The boy put his arms around her shoulders and drew her to him.

It was a family struck by tragedy. Barbara Cahill had been killed in a car accident about a year before. When Mr. Cahill spoke of it, his voice thickened and he looked away, breathing deeply. The loss was still fresh.

Mr. Cahill cleared his throat. "We haven't been able to make good arrangements for Leslie. My mother tried to help, but she's really too old to keep up with a little kid. We tried a daycare, but that meant one of us had to drive into town twice a day. Right now we have the hand's wife helping, but she's just a kid herself and has a child of her own. We're looking for someone who can stay here, take care of Leslie, cook, and manage the house. Wade is a big help, but he's still in school and we have a ranch to run. We've really gotten behind."

John sat on the couch, leaning forward, anxious, elbows on his knees, big, calloused hands clasped. "What kind of work have you done?"

"I took business classes in college, thinking I would eventually take over my father's insurance agency. I worked with him for about ten years, but then my mother had a stroke and needed care. That same year my father had a heart attack. We sold the business and I stayed home caring for them. After they passed away, I returned to work at a large insurance company. It's a good job, I'm a programmer/analyst, but the work isn't that interesting to me anymore. I need a change of pace, a change of scenery." I smiled, trying to put them at ease. I stilled my fidgeting hands.

Wade sat on a nearby chair with his sister on his lap. I admired his gentleness with the little girl.

The Cahills, all of them, showed me around the house. It was a nice house, cooled by air-conditioning, spacious, but it was obvious that its care had been neglected, that things had been pushed aside to make it look presentable.

"If you stay, I'd like you to have the master bedroom so you can have more space and your own bathroom. I'll take this room." He indicated a much smaller room. "The kids' bedrooms and bathroom are upstairs. Do you want to see them?"

"No, that's fine."

When I look back on it, I realize that John hired me pretty much on faith. They really didn't know much about me. Later John would say that the minute he saw me, he knew I belonged there, but he had been afraid their desperation showed, that they'd scare me off.

The sensible thing would have been to ask for references, but I couldn't bring myself to do that. As a matter of fact, Mr. Cahill didn't ask for my references either.

"What do you think?" he asked. His dark eyes bored into mine.

"I think it looks fine, Mr. Cahill." Surprisingly, I felt calm. My heart warmed to this family.

"Please call me John."

"Fine. All of you, call me Maureen."

"Would you care to spend the night, or I can make hotel arrangements for you in Chewack?"

"I'd be happy to stay here. Why don't I make myself useful the rest of the day? Tomorrow morning after breakfast, I'll head back home and start making arrangements there."

John Cahill's body relaxed as though a huge weight had been lifted. *I can't let this man, this family, down.* I, too, felt an unexpected lightness. In my heart, I knew I'd made the right decision.

John and Wade quickly left the house, leaving Leslie with me.

"Well, Leslie, can you show me where things are in the kitchen?"

Leslie silently went into the kitchen and opened the refrigerator door. Oh, my. Well. I couldn't start out by throwing things away, but some of the leftovers looked as though they'd taken on lives of their own.

"What should we fix for dinner?"

"I don't know," the little girl whispered.

"Okay, well, let's look around." I found a package of hamburger in the freezer, wrapped in butcher paper, a bag of potatoes, a lone onion. "We could make hash."

"I don't know what that is."

"I'll show you."

I set the hamburger out to thaw, and continued looking around.

Leslie began to thaw, too. "Next year I'll be in second grade! Mrs. Wilson will be my teacher."

"Second grade? Wow!"

"I love school. I have kids to play with there."

I found a loaf of bread in the bread box, eggs and milk in the refrigerator. "Leslie, do you have raisins?"

"We do!" She pulled a chair over to the cupboard, climbed up on it and pulled out an old box of raisins.

"How about cinnamon?"

She shrugged. "I don't know what that is."

"We'll find it. Every house has cinnamon." I opened another cupboard. "Here it is." The spice was probably at least a couple of years old; I'd be liberal with it. "Let's make bread pudding."

The little girl's eyes sparkled and she nodded, lips pressed together. I gave her the job of tearing the bread into bite-size pieces.

When John and Wade returned to the house, their eyes lit up with the promise of a good dinner. "Oh, boy!" Wade bent to wash his hands at the kitchen sink. "That smells good, Maureen."

As I was about to serve the meal, I had sudden qualms about where I should eat. Should I have set the table in the more formal dining room for John and the kids, then eaten in the kitchen? I didn't want to impose, yet I felt I was expected to eat with the family. I needed to clarify this issue.

"John, do you want me to join you here in the kitchen, or—?"

"Of course, Maureen. You'll eat with us, always."

We sat down to a beef hash, canned green beans, and biscuits hot out of the oven. The bread pudding was still warm from baking. Wade took two huge helpings.

John sighed in contentment. "Maureen, once you're here for good, I'll leave the shopping to you. The kitchen is yours."

"Can I go shopping too?" Leslie looked at me with huge, eager eyes.

"Of course, I'll need your help. Leslie was a big help with this dinner."

Leslie looked to her dad, then her brother, her little face smug.

John chuckled. "Leslie loves to be included, but we can't take her with us most of the time."

"I can ride a *horse!*"

"I know you can, honey, but there's more than just riding to do the work we do."

Leslie looked at me. "Can you ride?"

"I have, but it's been a long time. I'll bet you're a better rider than I am."

Wade perked up. "We have a gentle horse you could ride. When you come back I'll saddle up Dixie for you."

I was surprised how settled in I already felt with these people. And needed. That was a feeling I hadn't had in a long time. I hoped I wouldn't let them down.

I slept in the small room that would be John's. I say slept, but my mind whirled much of the night with unanswered questions. I wondered when the strangeness would dissipate. Would I ever feel at home here? I'd opened my window and the country silence soothed me. Seattle had gotten noisy with traffic twenty-four hours a day. I finally drifted off to sleep.

2

*L*ife had taught me that when something is meant to be, things easily fall into place. The department manager at work wasn't happy with my decision, but wished me well. My landlord was sorry to see me go, but had a waiting list of prospective renters.

Until I knew this arrangement would work out, I put some of my furniture and household goods in storage. When our parents died, we four siblings split up the treasures we wanted. Now I gave a few of those to my brother Roger and sister Sue.

Roger, the oldest, showed a bit of resistance to my plans. "We don't even know these people!"

Sue, my older sister, said, "I've never thought of you as a 'domestic.' But I have no doubt that you can handle it."

There were four of us siblings, Roger, Sue, and a younger sister, Diane. I was very close to Roger and Sue. Diane...not so much. I didn't care if I ever saw her again.

I heard them out, but stuck to my plans. "This is a family who needs me. Living on a ranch will be a good change of pace. I'll love getting away from city noise and traffic. They seem like nice people and they've had a rough time."

I couldn't remember much about the furniture in what would be my bedroom. I called John to ask if there was room for a small desk, and he encouraged me to bring it. I didn't mention it to him, but I also brought a small television, thinking I didn't want to intrude on the family's time together. Those two items and an occasional chair for reading were the only furniture I took with me.

My brother and sister helped me move. Roger hauled my stuff in the back of his pickup and Sue rode with me in my car.

We stopped to have lunch and look around the cute little town of Chewack. Another hot June day, it was amazing how the Cascade Mountain range could make such a difference in weather.

Following the directions that John had previously given me, we made our way to the ranch. I led the way, Roger followed. I was suddenly overwhelmed with apprehension. What in the world was I doing? My mind raced. My mouth felt dry. I forced myself to breathe evenly. I kept my thoughts to myself, not wanting to alarm Sue.

Roger swung the truck around with the back facing the house. We gathered at the truck. Roger nodded appreciatively. "Looks like a decent place."

The Cahill family came out to greet us. After introductions, John and Wade helped Roger carry my things into the house. John had cleared the master bedroom and adjoining bathroom.

Sue stood in the middle of the bedroom. "This is really nice, Maureen. It's like you have your own little suite." Relief surged through my veins. Sue's impression was important to me.

We made our way into the living room. Leslie tagged along. Wade turned to his sister. "Let's go out to the barn and give Maureen time with her family."

"No! I want to stay here."

John stepped in. "You can come back in awhile. Let's go." He took the little girl's hand, but met with resistance. He gave her arm a little tug. "Leslie."

As the little girl was being led out of the house, she looked back at me with pleading eyes.

I smiled. "I'll see you in a little while."

Roger, Sue and I walked around the house and for the first time I saw the kids' bedrooms. Their beds were made and the rooms looked as though they had been straightened. Back downstairs, we briefly stepped into John's office. Roger studied a map of Washington on the wall. "Look, the Cahill property is outlined on the map here. Wow, it's a big ranch."

In the dining room, Sue noticed a nice planter with dried out plants. "I think these are goners."

I nodded. "Mrs. Cahill was probably the gardener, inside and out. I wonder if I should just throw them out and replace them."

Sue nodded. "I think so, Maureen. John probably can't bear to do it, but having dead plants around isn't very cheerful, either. When you see stuff like this, just take the initiative and do it."

Roger laughed. "Remember what Dad used to say? 'It's better to beg forgiveness than ask permission.'"

We laughed. "He was good at that, too," I said as I led the way into the kitchen.

"This is super, Maureen," Sue said. "It looks really modern. Look at this huge window above the sink. You can see the world from here."

We joined her at the window. From there we could see the large barn, what I would learn was the calving shed, two pastures and the horse corral.

Roger nodded. "Nothing is going to get past you from here."

Sue hugged me. "Maureen, you'll have this place whipped into shape in no time. This is so exciting."

Roger nodded. "They seem like good people."

I walked out to Roger's truck with them. Sue turned to me. "We need to let Diane know you've moved."

I shrugged. "I don't know why. It's none of her concern."

"I don't want her to think I'm keeping things from her."

Roger, sitting behind the wheel, shook his head slightly, staring straight ahead.

I squeezed Sue's shoulder. "Do what you need to do. I just don't want her coming here. I've given her all I intend to, ever."

Roger leaned over to open the passenger door. "Come on, Sue. It's a long drive back."

I thanked them again for their help, and they drove off.

Although I was doing exactly what I wanted to do, I couldn't help feeling forlorn, out of my comfort zone, as I watched Roger's truck winding down the long driveway. *Wait. Wait! Maybe this isn't such a good idea.*

Leslie poked her head from the barn door, then ran toward the house.

"Leslie!" her dad called.

"It's fine," I called back, and opened my arms to the little girl.

* * *

18

The first morning after breakfast, John pushed his plate aside. "Thank you, Maureen. I really appreciate a cooked breakfast. Most mornings we've just been having coffee, or juice for the kids, and toast. Maybe a bowl of cold cereal. That's not enough for growing kids."

Wade helped himself to another piece of toast and soaked up the remnants of egg on his plate. "Sometimes you cooked breakfast on Sundays, Dad."

John shrugged. "Why don't you kids take off. I want to go over some things with Maureen."

After they left, John reached for a folder he'd put on the counter and took out a bank card. "I've set up an account with both our names on it. You'll need to sign this application. We'll call this our household account and it's what you'll use to buy groceries or stuff for the house. Pretty soon Leslie will need school clothes and I'll put more in for that. Let's see how this goes. I want you to speak up if you need anything. I'll pay you separately. This is just for household stuff. How does that sound?"

"It sounds fine, John. Very workable. While we're talking, would it be okay with you if I go through the house, the cupboards and closets, clean, and put things away?"

"Of course, I want you to feel that this is your home. The house is your domain. I'm afraid it has been neglected. Everything's a mess, I know. He shook his head and sighed.

"Maureen, the kids are to pick up after themselves, do their share of the work. I'd like you to give them chores to do, take out the garbage, that sort of thing. They need to learn that. Wade does a lot of the ranch work, now, but he should still make his own bed, pick up after himself. Leslie will need to learn how to do some of those things. We just haven't had time to teach her."

"I understand. What do you have for lunch? I've always heard that farmers have their main meal at noon."

"We're ranchers. Just sandwiches, maybe soup. Some days, if we're working far enough away, we'll take lunch with us. We have our main meal at the end of the day when everyone's home."

After John and Wade left the house, Leslie returned to the kitchen, dressed in pink jeans, a red stained tee shirt, hair in disarray and bits of egg in the corner of her mouth.

"Leslie, let's you get ready for the day."

"I am ready for the day."

"Let me show you what I do to get ready, okay?"

We went into the bathroom upstairs. "Show me how you brush your teeth."

I gave her a few tips on brushing all her teeth, then brushed her hair. She stood still for me, her eyes dreamy. I realized again how important human touch is. Warmth spread throughout my chest. I was fulfilling a need for this little girl.

"Do you want me to fix your hair in a ponytail?

"No, just straight." I did as she asked, then gave her a hug. Shyly, she hugged me back.

"I'll gather these towels while we're up here." I replaced the bathroom towels with clean, matching ones I found in the linen closet. "Let's go into your bedroom."

The room looked like a very lucky little girl's room. No doubt her mother had lovingly furnished it, probably made the curtains. "What a lovely bedroom."

Leslie beamed.

"Let's put these toys away, then change the sheets on your bed." I couldn't imagine when this had last been done. I put away what appeared to be clean clothes. "Leslie, I'll bet this striped tee shirt would look great with those jeans." While she changed shirts, I gathered dirty clothes, including the shirt she had been wearing.

"All right. This room looks tidy. Let's go into Wade's and do the same thing."

"I can't go in there. I'll get in trouble."

"Oh? Well, you can just stand in the doorway and watch." I changed the bed sheets and hurriedly straightened the room, then gathered dirty clothes that were heaped in a corner.

Returning downstairs, I glanced into John's bedroom, but it was tidy with a made bed and dirty clothes in a hamper. On his dresser was a framed picture of John and, I assumed, Mrs. Cahill sitting at a picnic table, both smiling. John's wife had been a pretty woman, about his age. She looked capable, like she was perfectly comfortable in her skin. A pang of envy shot through me. She'd had what I never would.

I dragged my mind to the present and began sorting clothes in the laundry room, just inside the back door. "Leslie, why don't you pull out all the white or light clothes. We'll wash them separately."

"When Wade washes our clothes, he doesn't do that."

Figures. "Well, he won't have to worry about it anymore. Separating them makes the colors last longer.

"We'll need to go shopping this morning. It looks like we're out of meat."

"Maureen, we have lots of meat in the big freezer."

"Big freezer?"

"I'll show you." Leslie led me to the attached garage and walked over to a large upright freezer that I hadn't noticed before. She opened the door. It was crammed with meat, mostly beef. Of course! This was a cattle ranch.

"Well, my goodness. You're right. We have lots of meat." Bins of butcher-wrapped beef were sorted by cuts as well as a big bin of pork, also butcher wrapped, and a few packages of chicken obviously purchased at a grocery store some time ago.

I took out a package of pork chops to thaw.

"But can we still go to the store?" Leslie asked.

"Sure, let's do that later this afternoon."

I spent the earlier part of the day doing laundry and cleaning kitchen cupboards. Much of the time Leslie sat at the kitchen table playing with her dominoes or coloring. She was good at entertaining herself, but I was rarely out of her sight.

At lunchtime John and Wade washed at the kitchen sink and sat at the kitchen table. I hesitated, but simply needed to ask.

"Do you suppose you two could wash either in the laundry room or bathroom? I really don't like the kitchen sink used for washing dirty hands."

Stunned silence followed as they gave each other furtive glances.

"Sure, we can do that." John glanced over at Wade, eyebrows raised.

Wade nodded. "Yeah, okay,"

"Thank you. That's important to me." I sighed inwardly. A small victory for me.

I served toasted cheese sandwiches and canned peaches for lunch.

"Wade," I said. "I went into your room to change your sheets, but Leslie just stood in the doorway because she didn't want to get into trouble. Would you prefer that I don't go into your room, or would it be okay for me to change the bed sheets and clean?"

Wade smiled, a little embarrassed. "I don't want Leslie playing in there, going through my stuff. But I'd like you to clean my room, Maureen. That'd be great."

"It's a deal. As we go along, I suppose we'll have a few things to work out."

John nodded. "Just speak up, Maureen, and we'll do the same."

My apprehension melted a bit. I expected give and take, and so far this family was giving me their cooperation, and appreciation.

After he finished his lunch, John stepped away from the table and noticed the package of thawing pork on the counter. In the briefest of motions, he signaled to Wade, something about Leslie, slanting his head toward the package of pork. I imagined working together so closely, perhaps in a noisy environment, they were able to communicate without speaking.

"Leslie," John said, "let's see what we can do to get your bike working again." The two of them went into the garage to look at the little girl's bicycle.

"Maureen," Wade said, "don't tell Leslie that we're having pork for dinner."

"Oh, why?"

He smiled. "We're eating Ruby. Mom loved pigs and Ruby was her pride and joy. She weighed over three hundred pounds. We had the sow bred and she had a litter of five piglets. Mom died before they were born, so she never saw them." His voice grew shaky, he cleared his throat, then continued. "We told Leslie to stay away from the pig pen, but she couldn't resist. One day she climbed into the pen to play with one of the baby pigs. I came along just as Ruby squealed and started after Leslie. I pulled her out by the seat of her pants. That's all it took for Dad to sell the piglets and have Ruby slaughtered. Leslie vowed she'd never eat Ruby. So when we eat Ruby we just don't mention that it's pork. So far it's worked."

I smiled sympathetically. "What a sad story. I'll work Ruby in with our dinners, disguising her as best I can."

Leslie burst into the kitchen. "Maureen, watch me ride my bike!" I stepped into the garage and she climbed on her small bike, circled the garage, steered through the open door, and down the cement driveway. The bike slowed as she ran out of concrete and onto the gravel, but she trudged on, made a wide turn, and returned to the garage.

"I'm impressed, Leslie."

She and I shopped for groceries that afternoon. It was strange buying food in large portions for a family. I bought cleaning supplies, too. And laundry baskets for the kids' bedrooms so they wouldn't have to throw their dirty clothes on the floor.

The store had an indoor plant selection and I bought three nice starters for the planter in the dining room.

"Can we go to Dairy Queen?"

Although I didn't mind her asking, I didn't want her to think that I was an easy touch. I'd learned from my nieces and nephews that children can easily get the upper hand. There was really no end to their asking.

"Tell you what, let's buy ice cream and we'll have it for dessert tonight. Why don't you pick out the flavor?"

"Can we get chocolate sauce?"

"Sure." Well, what's ice cream without chocolate sauce?

No matter what I cooked, it was appreciated, but it was soon apparent they preferred cooked vegetables rather than salad. Meat, preferably beef, was the mainstay of dinner, and they liked potatoes however they were fixed. Without fail, Wade's eyes lit up with dessert. "Oh, boy, apple pie!" "All right! Chocolate cake! Do we have ice cream to go with that?"

It might have been my imagination, but I think the three of them had a healthier glow.

On the first Sunday, I set the table for dinner in the dining room, thinking it would be a nice change of pace. John seemed surprised, but willing. For the first time he noticed the planter with fresh plants. "You got some new plants, I see."

"Yes. Is that okay?" I couldn't read his reaction.

"Of course. I just couldn't remember to water them. When they died, I couldn't bring myself to throw them out." He stared out the window, sighed, then glanced at me. "That's fine, Maureen, that's what I want you to do."

* * *

Around the second day at the Cahill's, I noticed a dog trailing after the three horses. I watched John, Wade and their hired hand Randy step down from their mounts, obviously weary, and walk the horses into the barn. The dog, looking just as weary, followed them. In a few moments I saw the three horses in the corral and watched as Wade put feed in their trough. The three men emerged, but not the dog.

Randy, their hired hand, a tall skinny fellow with a prominent Adams apple, slowly walked toward his house. John and Wade ambled into the house and washed in the laundry room. I always made sure there was a clean towel for them to use.

When they came into the kitchen, I asked Wade, "I see you have a dog. Where does he stay?"

"Yes, ma'am, Charley. He's a Blue Heeler, our cattle dog. He stays in the barn when he's not working with us."

"Even in the winter? Won't he get cold?"

"No, we have a place set up for him in the tack room. He's fine. He gets too dirty to have in the house."

* * *

While cleaning a hall cupboard, I found a hair-cutting set. On the first Sunday, I'd noticed the ranch work slowed down a little. It wasn't really a day of rest, but at least a bit more relaxed.

That late afternoon I mentioned my find. "'I can cut hair if anyone's interested."

John perked up. "You can cut hair?"

"I used to cut my dad's and brother's hair. Neither could bear to pay the price of a 'store-bought' haircut."

"It is expensive, but more than that, it takes too much time. If you don't mind, I could use a haircut."

We got a stool set up in the kitchen and I set to work. It seemed a little strange, touching him, but I was glad to do it. John had nice, thick black hair, receding a bit and graying at the temples.

It gave us a chance to chat without the rush of having to go somewhere. At first, I think it was awkward for John, as though it were too intimate, but I think we were both determined to act as though this was a normal thing.

Wade came in from outside and stopped in his tracks. "Wow! Could you give me a haircut too?"

"Make it shorter," John said.

Wade just grinned.

When it was Wade's turn, I asked him what he wanted me to do. Very specifically he described what he wanted and I complied, feathering the sides so it wouldn't "stick out." His dark brown hair was still a bit on the long side, but I heard no complaint about it from his father.

* * *

Gradually, I began to feel at home. Certainly the family made every effort to make me feel welcomed. During the day I kept busy and felt useful and needed. In the evening, I helped Leslie take her bath and wash her hair. She often asked me to read to her, and I was happy to do so.

At bedtime, she made her rounds to her father and brother, kissing them goodnight on the cheek, and then John went upstairs with her to tuck her in. I was touched by the tenderness her dad and brother showed her. It seemed to me that John was more available to Leslie now. I knew that my being there relieved him of a huge burden, and I silently rejoiced. I had made the right decision to come here. I was obviously needed and appreciated.

In the evenings, John usually read, mostly cattlemen's magazines. Wade flipped through TV channels and sometimes watched a program or two, but otherwise, spent evenings in his room, probably reading. Occasionally, I watched a program with Wade and sometimes John would join us. If it was a sporting event, I usually left them to it and went to my room. I love to read and my sister Sue and I often exchanged books.

On Friday nights Wade usually went out, casually mentioning to his dad where he was going, normally someplace with his friend Darrell. His curfew was one o'clock and from what I saw, he was always home by then, often earlier.

Once I climbed into bed, I fell asleep immediately. But, true to my habit, I often woke up, my heart feeling as though it had been hollowed out. A deep longing would almost suffocate me. Sometimes I climbed out of bed and walked around the room, thankful for its spaciousness, or read for awhile before going back to bed, hoping sleep would overtake me. Nowadays, more and more, it did.

3

The Fourth of July was the next week. "Do you do anything special for the Fourth?" I asked as we finished dinner.

"We used to," John said, "but didn't last year."

Of course. That would have been right after Mrs. Cahill died.

John sighed. "I guess I'd just as soon not do anything this year. If you want to visit your family, Maureen, go ahead. We can manage here."

"No, the Fourth has never been a big day with us. I just wanted to be prepared if you did something special."

John nodded. "Let's just have a barbecue, just the family. Maybe I'll bring my mother out."

Although he had been to town to visit his mother, I'd never met her. She apparently lived in a retirement community near Chewack.

Wade perked up. "Can I invite Darrell?"

"Sure."

Leslie chimed in. "Can I have Janelle over?"

"Okay. Maureen, can you call Janelle's mother?"

"Of course."

"Okay, guys, let's just leave it at that."

Wade spoke up. "We should ask Randy and Pearl though."

John sighed. "Okay, invite 'em." John looked at me. "Do you want to invite anyone?"

I laughed. "No, my family wouldn't want to drive over on a busy holiday. What would you want me to fix?"

"Let's barbecue steaks!" Wade said. "Dad does a great job with those."

John gave Wade a long, tired look, then nodded.

"I'll make a potato salad," I said, "and we can have corn on the cob, maybe a green salad."

Wade looked serious. "Pearl will want to bring something. Don't let it be complicated."

John chuckled. "Maybe she could bring rolls, the store-bought kind."

Apparently Pearl wasn't much of a cook. I barely knew the hired hand's wife; had only talked to her briefly on the phone.

They lived right there on the ranch, in a small house between Cahills and their long driveway. I'd passed it every time I left and returned to the ranch.

The next week Pearl called on me, bringing her baby girl, Karen. "I been wantin' to meet you, but didn't wanna bother you while you was settlin' in."

"I'm so happy you came. Will you have a cup of coffee?"

We sat in the living room, Pearl and Karen in a big chair, Leslie and I on the couch.

Pearl settled the baby on her lap. "Wade mentioned a Fourth of July party. What kin I bring?"

"We have everything pretty well planned, but maybe you could pick up a couple dozen rolls?"

"Sure." Although she seemed like a nice, gentle young woman, Pearl was not pretty, nor did she do anything to improve her appearance. Her lank hair hung with no special style. I imagine the only time she visited a dentist was to have a tooth pulled. Several of her front teeth were crooked. But one thing Pearl had in her favor was beautiful, large hazel eyes. They were kind eyes, eyes full of wisdom.

Leslie crowded so close I could barely move my arm.

Karen began to wiggle and Pearl set her on the floor next to the chair.

"Leslie," I said, "don't you want to play with Karen?"

"I want to stay here," she whispered.

I was a little embarrassed and wondered if I should insist that Leslie entertain Karen. I decided against it. Pearl said nothing, but looked at Leslie with sad eyes.

We chatted about the ranch, and Pearl mentioned how much Randy liked working for John. "His wife had just died, so John wasn't hisself, Randy said, but he was a fair man."

"I can't imagine how difficult this must have been for the family."

Pearl nodded. "I wasn't much help. I'd just had Karen an' I never really kept house before."

I nodded. "It takes experience, especially to step into someone else's home. Wade seems like a nice boy."

Pearl nodded with enthusiasm. "He's great, 'specially with Leslie. Sometimes he'd take her into town. Most boys that age just want to be with their friends, but he'd take his little sister. John just couldn't manage it all. Wade, he tried to be everwhere. Randy says he does a man's job, too."

Visiting with Pearl gave me more understanding of the situation. I was so happy she'd called on me.

I telephoned Abbie Peterson to invite Janelle to our Fourth of July dinner. I had spoken to her a couple of times when we made arrangements for the girls to play together. A sweet girl with curly golden hair, Janelle was Leslie's best friend. Actually her only friend who lived close enough to conveniently get together. They were in the same grade at school.

Her reaction pleased me. "What wonderful news! John is feeling up to having people over."

"Well, sort of half-heartedly, and only the kids' friends and his mother, and of course Randy and Pearl."

"Still, Maureen, I know it's because you're there. You've relieved him of a huge burden."

"He's probably just being polite. I brought the Fourth of July up, wanting to be prepared."

"I don't care why it's happening. I'm just so happy he's joined the living. Barbara Cahill was my best friend and I miss her terribly, but we need to move on. I've been worried about John. It was as though his life ended, too."

I could tell John wasn't enthusiastic about a Fourth of July party, but when the day came he made an effort to warmly greet people. And Wade was right. John's barbecued steaks were delicious. When Wade saw the rolls Pearl brought, he winked at me from across the picnic table.

John's mother Eleanor greeted me politely, but seemed a little standoffish. "I'm glad John has hired some help."

I knew I was just "help," not a part of the family. Unreasonably, I took offense, but tried not to show it. I didn't think of myself as a servant, but rather a helper, someone to make this household run smoothly.

"It's been great having Maureen here, Grandma," Wade said.

"I'm sure it is, dear." She turned to me. "I'd like another cup of coffee, please."

"Of course," I said, but Wade sprung up from the picnic table, swinging his long legs over the bench seat. "I'll get it for you, Grandma."

I felt defended by Wade, and grateful, as though I'd been rescued. I mentally pulled myself away from Eleanor.

The older woman simply stared down at her plate. She must think I am an intruder, or trying to push my way into the family. Maybe she thinks I shouldn't be eating at the same table. Well, I was doing what John wanted and that's all that mattered. I doubted I would ever feel close to this woman.

To everyone's surprise, as darkness approached, John said to Wade, his friend Darrell and their ranch hand Randy, "You guys ready to set off some fireworks?" John oversaw the show. I could see the effort he made to make this a special day.

Although fireworks had never been an attraction to me, I did enjoy the colorful display against the quiet sereneness of the great outdoors. As rockets whistled above our heads, bursting in high arcs against a black star-speckled sky, I felt a thrill for my new life with these good people. Well, except for Eleanor. I sat as far away from her as possible.

After the fireworks John said to Wade and Darrell, "In the morning when it's light, I want you guys to clean up this mess. Be sure to pick up all the wires—I don't want kids or the dog stepping on them and getting punctured feet."

"Yes, sir," they both said. "That was a great show, Mr. Cahill," Darrell added. "Thanks."

"I'm glad you could join us, Darrell."

John took his mother home, tenderly helping her into his truck. I busied myself in the kitchen as they were leaving, relieving myself of having to speak to the older woman, of having to say something fake like "so happy to meet you."

As planned, Wade's friend Darrell and Leslie's friend Janelle spent the night. The day had been wonderful for me, except for the brief incident with John's mother. I think even John had enjoyed himself. For the first time, I felt a real part of things, having fun and not just working.

Unfortunately, Eleanor's remark kept surfacing. I suppose that's what I was, hired help, but at least I felt I served a purpose.

The next morning, Wade was the first one to greet me in the kitchen. Darrell was taking a shower and John tended his morning chores. The little girls, who had giggled late into the night, were still asleep.

Wade sat at the kitchen table. "Maureen?"

I turned from my mixing bowl to see his serious face redden. "I just want you to know... it's great having you here. Things are so much better now." He shrugged. "I just wanted you to know that."

I tingled from head to toe. It wasn't easy for Wade to say that, I know, but it meant the world to me. "Thank you, Wade. I really appreciate your telling me. I'll never replace your mother, but maybe I can help fill in some of the gaps."

He nodded. "This last year's been awful. Leslie just wasn't getting what she needed, none of us were eating good. I've really missed my mother, too." He swallowed. "Dad was in this deep hole and couldn't get out." He looked embarrassed, shrugged his shoulders. "Anyway, that's how it seemed to me."

"Grieving for loved ones is tough, especially when it's someone who's such a big part of your life. And it must have been scary, too. I'm sure John couldn't see how he would manage. You stepped up, Wade, especially with Leslie. I can't imagine how your dad would have managed without you."

Our conversation ended when Darrell joined us. He looked at Wade's and my serious faces and started to back out of the room.

"Good morning, Darrell," I said. "Are you ready for pancakes?"

"You bet!" He sat beside Wade at the table. "Don't we need to pick up that fireworks stuff?"

Wade nodded. "We can eat first."

The girls straggled in, looking half awake.

After breakfast the boys went outside to clean up the yard and the little girls returned to Leslie's room. John remained, apparently wanting to talk to me. "Maureen, I hope my mother didn't offend you."

"Oh, no." I lied, my mind flashing back to my discomfort with his mother.

John ignored my answer. "She took Barbara's death hard and wanted to take care of us. But it was just too much for her. I'm afraid it hurt her feelings when we got Pearl to help. She still came over once in awhile, but one of us would have to go get her. Her eyes are bad and she can't drive any more. I think she feels left out and has sort of a chip on her shoulder." He shrugged. "I dunno...."

"I think people just want to do the right thing, but it isn't always clear what to do."

He nodded, and left the room. It seemed most of his spare time was either in his office, or in his bedroom. Actually, I took that as a good sign. He finally had a chance to mourn without the pressure of trying to keep everything going.

A few days later I heard Wade knock on his dad's bedroom door. "Dad, wanna watch the game with me?" Silence. "Dad?"

"Not tonight, Wade."

The boy watched part of the game alone, then turned off the TV and went to his room.

A few days later, on Saturday night, Wade came into the kitchen with a deck of cards. "Wanna play?"

"Sure. What games do you play?"

"I wanna play, too!" Leslie said.

Wade's face lit up. "I'll see if Dad wants to join us."

He knocked on his dad's bedroom door. "Dad, we're going to play cards. Wanna play?"

"No, thanks, Wade."

The boy returned to the kitchen, his shoulders drooping, but shuffled the cards and dealt a hand of hearts for the three of us.

John strolled into the room. "Whose deal?"

Wade's grin lit up the room. He quickly gathered up the cards and pushed the deck toward his dad. "Yours."

* * *

The rest of the summer rushed by. Once I got the house organized and formed a routine, I began to wander outside. Leslie took me to the barn and another smaller building they called the calving shed. The barn was old, but well maintained and I breathed in the earthy aroma of horses, leather and fresh hay. Saddles and various riding equipment hung in their proper places. In the orderly tack room, equipment for horses lined shelves: brushes, combs, files, cutters, saddle wax. I loved the tack room and enjoyed just browsing.

A horse corral encircled the back and side of the barn surrounded by a sturdy zig-zagged split-rail fence. What a lot of work that must have been, not only splitting those rails, but building the fence.

The calving shed was smaller than the barn and had been more recently built. Inside, small, medium and large stalls were swept clean. An equipment room had a sink with hot and cold water, an older refrigerator, a vinyl-topped counter that ran along one wall, and all sorts of equipment used for calving. I couldn't begin to identify most of it.

Outside, several pastures separated by barbed wire ranged as far as the eye could see. In some of the closer pastures cattle grazed, but I understood most of the cattle were in their summer pastures a distance away.

One late-summer day, while I hung clothes on the outside lines, John made his way toward the house.

"Why don't you have chickens, John?"

He scoffed. "This isn't a farm, Maureen, it's a cattle ranch!"

I thought of a few retorts to that, like, would the chickens care?

School would start soon and both Leslie and Wade needed new clothes. Wade told me his dad had given him money and he would shop for his own clothes.

Uncertain about what to get for Leslie, I called Janelle's mother. "Abbie, what do the kids wear to school?"

"Mostly jeans and sweaters, something warm."

When I mentioned clothes shopping, Leslie couldn't contain her enthusiasm. The men were gathering cattle in the foothills for fall roundup, too far away to return for the noon meal, so I'd packed lunches for them to take.

"After we shop for your clothes, we can eat lunch in town."

The little girl's eyes lit up. My heart filled with gratitude that I could fill this need.

Each trip into town, I traveled around a little bit more. Directionally challenged, I had to work extra hard not to get lost. Before we shopped, I drove past downtown and into a residential area. Leslie pointed to a group of small houses.

"That's where Grandma lives."

"Oh, really?

"Can we stop and see her?"

My heart wasn't into another session with Eleanor, but Leslie would never understand my reluctance. "Okay, I'll bet she would be pleased to see you."

Leslie pointed out the way.

Leslie rang the doorbell and Grandma Cahill answered the door. Surprise registered on her face. "Why, hello!"

"We can only stay for a few minutes," I said. "Leslie and I are shopping for her school clothes today, but we wanted to stop to see how you're doing."

The older woman hugged her granddaughter and gave me a reserved smile. We visited briefly, chatting about what the guys were doing. Although I didn't feel I owed John's mother justification of my worth, I hoped she'd be able to see that I fulfilled an important role to the family and served as more than "hired help."

Leslie's idea of school shopping was a bit different than what Janelle's mother had mentioned. She went straight to the dresses, particularly the fancier ones.

I raised my eyebrows. "I'll tell you what, Leslie. We can get one dress for you for special occasions, but then we need to look at warmer clothes for school." She readily agreed. We picked out the dress first, then fitted her with jeans, a pair of corduroy pants, two sweaters, three tee-shirts and two flannel shirts. In the shoe department we bought new tennis shoes and dressy shoes. This was all new to me—the gifts of clothing I had bought my nieces and nephews were at their mothers' suggestions when asked.

Once home, Leslie couldn't wait to show her dad and brother her new clothes. They both raved about them, Wade even pointed out how great the green and gray flannel shirt would look with the black corduroy pants. Leslie beamed.

Back in the kitchen, John nodded his approval, "Thank you, Maureen. That's really a relief getting that job done. Buying kids clothes—any clothes, really—is way out of my league." He chuckled. "In a hardware store, now, that's a different matter."

"We stopped at your mother's and visited for a few minutes."

"You did? That was nice."

"I'm trying to get familiar with the town, and we happened to drive by and Leslie recognized her grandma's place."

"We get so busy here and I don't see her often enough. She's used to that though. My dad was a rancher, too."

"Was this the family ranch?"

"It was, and my grandfather's before him, but we've added to it. This house is on the new section. The house that Randy and Pearl live in was the original house on this property. The original homestead, my family home, has been torn down and we just use the land for grazing."

That was probably the longest conversation I'd had with John, other than household matters. I was glad he seemed comfortable with me.

He looked at the wall calendar. "We'll be starting fall roundup soon. While I still have Wade here, we'll get some of 'em gathered in the eastern pastures. We'll probably spend a night or two out there. Maybe you could get some cans of stuff for us to take that would be easy to fix. Stew, maybe.

"How about if I make stew and all you would have to do is warm it up?"

He smiled. "That would be great, Maureen." He gave me a long look. "I can't tell you how much I appreciate all you do."

"I'm glad I can help, John." My heart filled with a deep sense of satisfaction.

4

*O*nce school started, I had more time to myself. Wade drove his own truck to school
and, since their school starting times were
different, Leslie took the school bus. John usually took
her down the lane to the school bus stop, but it wasn't
too far for her to walk.

When I had free time, I enjoyed poking around,
discovering my new world. I found a small orchard with
apple, pear and peach trees. As the fruit became ripe, I
tried my hand at canning. I found canning jars and lids
in a laundry room cupboard, and followed directions in
one of Mrs. Cahill's cookbooks.

John's eyes lit up at the counter full of sparkling jars
of canned pears. "This is great, Maureen. It bothered
me to have that fruit go to waste." He started to leave
the room, but stopped and turned to me. "Maureen,
don't feel you have to work every minute. While Leslie's
in school feel free to do stuff on your own, maybe visit
someone. I want you to take time for yourself."

I smiled, relieved that he recognized my needs.
"Okay, John, I will." And I did. Abbie Peterson, Janelle's
mother, and I became friends and she introduced me to
more of the neighboring women. When she learned I
played bridge, I often substituted in her group. Occasionally, I invited one of my new friends over for morning coffee.

One day as I dusted in John's office, I startled when the doorbell rang. Amazingly, no one had come to the front door since I arrived. Everyone seemed to use the back door. I was home alone and peeked out a porch-facing window. *Oh, no!* My younger sister, Diane. My heart sank. *I just won't open the door.*

She rang the doorbell again. I opened the door a couple of inches.

"Hi, Maureen," she said, with artificial brightness.

"Hello, Diane. What do you want?" I could feel my face hardening, my eyes narrowing.

"Is that any way to greet your sister? May I come in?"

"Diane....no. I don't want you here any more than I wanted to see you in Seattle. Good-bye." I started to close the door.

"I need to use the bathroom. I've driven a long way."

I sighed. I could hardly refuse her the use of a bathroom. I silently opened the door and gestured the way.

I literally stood outside the bathroom door. The minute she emerged, I motioned toward the front door.

"Listen, Maureen, this is ridiculous. May I at least have a drink of water?"

"Of course," I darted into the kitchen, grabbed a bottle of water from the refrigerator, turned and bumped into Diane in the kitchen doorway as she started to follow me. We stood, nose to nose.

"Please leave, Diane. You know you are not welcomed here." My heart pounded, I could hardly breathe. I hate to be rude.

"How do you know? This isn't your house!"

"Leave!" I said through clenched teeth.

Diane flinched as my eyes bore into hers, then turned and flounced out the door, me at her heels. She climbed into her fancy red car. I roughly handed her the bottle of water, and shut the car door with a firm clunk.

As timing would have it, John and Randy rode up on horseback. John had apparently seen the car and wondered who it was. The sight of two cowboys on horseback was, of course, too much for Diane. She started to open the door, but without a second's hesitation, I slammed it shut.

The men looked startled. "You have company?" John said. "Maureen, she's welcome to come in."

I stood so close to the car, Diane couldn't open the door. She unrolled the window.

"That's fine. She's just leaving," I answered.

John and Randy glanced at each other and with jangling tack and creaking leather backed their horses and turned toward their original destination.

Diane eyes filled. "Maureen, how many times do I have to say I'm sorry?"

I ignored her question. "Goodbye, Diane. Don't come back."

I stepped back and she started her car, accelerating too high, and sped down the driveway, gravel flying and dust swirling.

My hands shook, my stomach knotted.

Later, as I prepared dinner John came into the kitchen. I felt his eyes on my back as he watched me stir a pot of chili. He quietly asked, "What was that all about?"

I sighed. "That was my younger sister, Diane. We're not...close."

"Apparently. I didn't know you had another sister. I only knew about Sue and your brother Roger."

I didn't respond.

John silently watched me for a few moments, then left to wash for dinner. I imagined he was shocked, but this was my business and I felt no compunction to share with him the sordid details of my relationship with Diane. After what my sister had done, she was dead to me, but I had no intention of talking about this to John, or anyone for that matter.

Later than evening I called Sue from the phone in my room.

"I hear you had company," she said.

"I did. How did she know where I live?" I tried to keep an accusing tone from my voice.

"She apparently called and got the address from Kathie." Kathie, Sue's fifteen-year-old daughter didn't know all the details about Diane's and my relationship. If Diane asked for my address, Kathie would have looked it up in their address book and shared it with her aunt. She later told her mother about the call.

Sue continued. "I thought about warning you, but didn't want you to worry about it. I just hoped she wouldn't go."

I sighed. "I doubt if she'll come back. It was a long drive for nothing."

Sue's silence pretty much said it all. She didn't approve of this kind of family strife, but she understood how I felt.

* * *

Fall roundup, or "pay day" as John called it, was a flurry of activity. For days before the event, John, Randy, and Wade, when he wasn't in school, gathered cattle from the far reaches of the ranch into pastures closer to the house, or "headquarters" as John referred to it. They branded the few calves born after spring roundup. I asked John if I could help and was told to just keep Leslie out of the way.

"When I'm bigger, I'll help," Leslie informed me.

"I'm sure you will. By then you'll really be a big help. You'll probably tell *them* what to do." I winked at her.

She grinned.

We went out to the gathering pens, a distance from the gates, to watch the men sort cattle, separating calves from cows, or culling cows that were no longer productive. In a cow-calf operation such as this, Wade told me, the name of the game is to have as many cows as you can in production.

Cows bellowed for their calves; calves bleated pitifully, panicked to be away from their mothers. I found it heart-rending. Calling out and yelling between the men was sometimes startling, though I think they held it back a bit when Leslie and I were there.

Charlie, the cattle dog, put on an amazing show. With the slightest command, and sometimes even before a command, he'd nip the heels of the cattle, getting them headed in the right direction. He was quick to dart away from a kicking hoof and would often come back and nip the offender in the leg. A loud bellow would follow, but the cow would quickly step in the intended direction. Charlie took no nonsense.

"Charlie won't play with me," Leslie confided.

"Why not?"

"He just won't. Dad says he's not a playing dog. He's a working dog."

"Will he let you pet him?"

"Yes, but I have to be quick."

I chuckled. I guess everyone has their job on a working cattle ranch.

They sorted the heifers from the steers, keeping most of the heifers for future breeding. When I could, I directed my questions to Wade who seemed eager to answer. He couldn't spend much time in explanation though, or he'd get yelled at by his dad. It was an exciting time, full of noise from the cattle, men yelling, hooves pounding, dust swirling. I loved it. My heart swelled to be even a small part of the excitement.

Huge stock trucks came, backing up to exactly meet the chute. One by one, the pens were emptied as the men prodded cattle up the steep ramps and into the mammoth trucks. The cattle were off to market. I shook my head. It wouldn't be long before this beef would appear at grocery stores in little packets. I'd never thought of the process before. Most city people had no idea how burgers or steaks happened to appear on their platters.

For the last two or three days of fall roundup, we had extra help, so I prepared our main meal at noon for everyone. Later, on two occasions, Randy and Wade went to neighboring operations to help them.

During this whole process John only allowed Wade to miss a couple days of school. John was adamant about that and I'd heard some heated arguments a few days before roundup, usually ending with Wade stomping off to his room. Apparently, education was a serious subject with John.

After fall roundup, things settled down to a more relaxed routine. The cattle were now in pastures closer to headquarters. At first they could graze, but with the colder weather, it became necessary for the men to drop flakes of hay to them. Once when Randy was busy elsewhere and Wade was in school, John asked me to drive the flatbed truck so he could toss hay to the cattle. I was thrilled to be asked, though a little nervous that I'd screw up.

"Just follow the tracks," John pointed across the pasture. "If you see a feed rack, I'll use that; otherwise, I'll drop flakes of hay on the ground. Drive slow. You'll be able to hear me as we go along."

I drove the truck along the bumpy tracks, sometimes having to gear down to give John a smoother ride. We finished one pasture and John pointed to a gate. "Drive over there and I'll open the gate." So it went, pasture to pasture. I could see what a help it was for John to have someone drive the truck while he fed the stock. The whole process took about an hour, but with real winter conditions, snow and ice, it could take hours, John told me. At the last pasture, he climbed into the passenger seat and I drove the truck back to headquarters.

"You're a pro, Maureen."

I laughed, but inwardly swelled with satisfaction. "Well, at least I didn't get us in a wreck."

"A lot of women wouldn't know how to shift gears." He'd worked up a sweat and wiped his brow with his handkerchief.

"I learned to drive on a stick shift, but I haven't done it for a long time."

"You did good. I appreciate all you do, Maureen."

After that, both John and Wade asked for my help occasionally. Sometimes, if John and Wade were elsewhere, or Wade was at school, the hand feeding was left to Randy. John knew Randy wouldn't ask me to drive the truck. "Maybe you could watch for him and offer the first time." John laughed. "He's too polite to ask for help."

One fall day, from my kitchen window I watched as Randy brought the flatbed around to load with hay. I quickly put on my jacket and offered to help.

"No, thanks, Maureen, I can do it."

"But it's fun for me. Let me help."

"Well, if you want to. Thanks."

With two to do that job, it went so much quicker. Randy was a gem. The Cahill ranch was lucky to have him.

* * *

Almost before my eyes Wade put on weight and became a muscular, strapping boy, almost as tall as his dad, probably six foot two inches. I asked him soon after school started if he played any sports.'

"Naw. When I was a sophomore, I turned out for football. I liked it, but my mom died that summer, and Dad needed me here, so I didn't turn out last year. The coach asked if I was gonna return this year, but I said no."

"Do you think your dad would object?"

"No, he'd be okay with it, but I've already lost a year." He shrugged, but looked wistful. I imagined he could have been a star on the football field. My heart ached for him. He seemed happy though and generally was quite cheerful.

"Does Darrell play?"

"No, his dad owns the Chewack Hardware in town and Darrell works there after school and during the summer."

On school nights Wade spent most of his evenings in his room doing homework. Once he asked me to go over an essay, due the next day.

"Maybe you can let me know if it makes any sense to you, or if you see mistakes."

It was a paper on a current event, something he'd had to research. He'd chosen a local controversy about cattle grazing on Bureau of Land Management land. Although I pointed out a couple of corrections needed on sentence structure, it was a well-written paper.

"Wade, this is good. After you've made these little corrections, you should show your dad."

He smiled, but shook his head. "It'll just make him get started on me going to college."

* * *

My first holiday season at the ranch approached. I wondered what I should do. Holidays are family times. In the past, I normally spent them either at my sister Sue's or brother Roger's. To be honest, I would go wherever Diane wasn't going to be. When my parents were alive, and when I lived with them, it worked surprisingly well because Diane lived in Wyoming. Her husband was a banker in Cheyenne. She still lived there but visited the family a couple times a year.

But now, what should I do? First, we had decisions to make about Thanksgiving.

I ventured to ask. "John, what do you want to do about Thanksgiving?"

John looked up from his desk as I walked in, and then sat back in his swivel chair. "Would you like to be with your family for Thanksgiving, Maureen?"

"I could, but it's nothing I'm particularly eager to do."

He studied me, obviously pondering about what to say.

"I could fix a Thanksgiving dinner here, maybe invite your mother?"

He smiled. "That sounds good."

"Okay, let's do that." I paused, then blundered on. "What about Christmas? How should we handle that?"

"Same thing as far as I'm concerned. But Maureen, you have a life, too. I don't want us to interfere with your family time."

"Let's just do what seems right as we go along. I'm fine with these plans."

Although Roger invited me to their home for Thanksgiving with the family, I was happy to stay at the ranch. Eleanor Cahill, John's mother, joined us. John occasionally invited her for Sunday dinner and she seemed to warm up to me and not treat me like hired help. She approved that I served Sunday and holiday dinners in the dining room, rather than the kitchen. Eleanor seemed to grudgingly accept me. Still on my guard around her, I could never fully relax when she visited.

The family made a big deal of Thanksgiving dinner. I was glad I'd decided to stay and was not too sure what they would have done otherwise. They raved about the meal and the mincemeat and pumpkin pies, giving me a warm feeling of satisfaction.

Soon Leslie and I were busy mixing and baking Christmas cookies together, storing them in the freezer for closer to the holiday. Once, when we had made cut-out cookies, we invited Janelle to help decorate them. The girls giggled and teased as they tried to outdo each other in "original" Christmas designs. Sprinkles and icing flew everywhere. I smiled at their antics and soon entered into the contest, laughing along with them. At one point John came into the kitchen to see what all the commotion was about. He smiled and shook his head, then returned to his office. We sent a big plate of cookies home with Janelle.

50

The traditional holiday preparations still seemed a strain for John, but he said little about it and tried to show enthusiasm for the kids' sake. My heart went out to him. I knew how hard it was to celebrate after losing someone. At times it was apparently too much for him and he would silently slip away.

John and Wade brought home a nice noble fir Christmas tree. They made a fresh cut in the trunk so the tree would absorb water, and mounted it in the tree stand. John retrieved decorations from the garage. "Maureen, would you like to decorate the tree with the kids?" There was no doubt by the tone of his voice that he needed me to do that.

I smiled. "Sure, I'd be happy to."

He nodded and turned to leave.

"Dad," Wade said, "don't you want to decorate it with us?"

"No, son, you guys go ahead."

Wade stood for a moment looking at his father's retreating back. He glanced at me.

"I think it's still too soon, Wade," I said. "Just give it time."

The boy swallowed hard, then nodded.

"Come on, Wade," Leslie said, "you'll have to reach the high places." She stretched out her arm to hang an ornament.

"Hold on, Les. Let me put up the lights first." He spread a double string of Christmas tree lights across the floor, replaced a couple of burned out bulbs, then worked his way around the tree.

Leslie showed me decorations she and her brother had made over the years. Wade took a couple of well-worn ones out of the box. "I'll just toss these out. They're pretty old. I was probably in third grade when I made them."

We worked together and afterwards stood back in satisfaction at the lovely decorated tree.

"Ohhhh, isn't it pretty?" Leslie cooed.

"Yeah, it's cool," Wade agreed.

I nodded, overwhelmed. Being with this family and experiencing precious moments like this made me realize how much I had missed not having a family of my own.

John had tended to chores outside and when he returned to the house for dinner, Leslie took his hand and led him into the living room to see the tree.

"Wow! You guys did a great job."

Returning to the kitchen, he nodded his thanks to me.

I wasn't too sure what to do about gifts, but bought simple things for everyone, mostly clothes—shirts for the guys, a sweater for Leslie, but also books for her growing reading aptitude. John and the kids gave me a nice blouse which I wore for Christmas dinner.

I hadn't become involved in a church yet, much to my regret. I wanted to check around and find a church where I felt I belonged, but just hadn't taken the time. I especially missed worshiping around the holiday season; not doing so left me with a feeling of longing.

Christmas passed peacefully, the main emphasis being Leslie's excitement. Although the spirit of Santa was in Leslie's heart, she seriously doubted that he was real.

* * *

Winter was colder in Eastern Washington than milder Seattle. Snow was a common occurrence and once fallen, it stayed. One day on my way to town I stopped to have coffee at Abbie's and time got away from me. I still had shopping to do before Leslie returned home from school. As I hurried into town, I turned a curve too fast for those icy conditions and lost control of my car. I panicked as the car fishtailed. I overcorrected, making the car spin in a compete circle. Coming out of the spin, I plunged front first into a ditch.

I turned off the engine and sat in a daze for a couple of minutes. My heart pounded and my breath came in pants. Tears stung my eyes. Finally, I shook my head to clear it and took a deep breath. I forced the door open and managed to scrape away enough snow to open the door wide enough to inch my way out of the car. After much slipping and sliding, I climbed out of the ditch. Snow filled my shoes and even worked its way down my coat collar.

I could see it was hopeless. I could never get the car out on my own.

Limited cell phone coverage had finally come to the area and John, Wade and I had cell phones, though coverage barely reached more than the house and barn. With shaking fingers, I punched in John's number, hoping he would be within range. *Oh, please, please answer,* I whispered as the phone rang and rang.

"Cahill," he answered.

I huffed out a breath of relief. "John, I spun out on the ice and my car's in a ditch."

"Are you okay?"

A car accident was the last thing John needed to deal with.

"Oh, sure, I'm fine. I don't think my car's damaged, but I can't get it out. Should I call someone in town?"

"No, I'll be right there. Where are you?"

"Ah, I don't know."

I could hear him breathing.

"Just a minute. A car is coming. I'll ask them where I am."

The driver of a pickup, seeing my car in the ditch stopped as I stood shivering on the road's shoulder, "Need a lift?"

"Let me talk to him," I heard John yell.

"Would you talk to this fellow?" I handed him my phone.

"Yeah," he said, into my cell phone. "Oh, hi John. We're on Holt, just east of Longanberry."

He handed me the phone. "Would you like to wait in my truck until John gets here?"

My teeth chattered. "That would be lovely. Thank you."

We chatted and before long John drove up in his pickup. My new friend turned to me. "Why don't you just wait here." He climbed out of his truck. His breath formed a cloud in the frosty air.

The men fastened a cable from a winch on John's front bumper to my car. With surprising accuracy, John pulled my car out of the ditch. I held my breath when the car teetered on the road's edge and looked like it would tip over. I reached out, like I could save it. John hit the gas and the car righted itself. The whole process only took minutes, but it felt like hours.

The other fellow drove off and I crossed the street to my rescued car as John removed the towing cable. "That was impressive, John. Thank you. I didn't know what I was going to do." My voice came out shaky.

"No big deal. Take it easy on these icy roads, Maureen. Just take it slow and give yourself plenty of time to make turns and stops."

I nodded. "I will. I'll see you in a bit. I'm going to town to shop."

"Forget it. We've had enough excitement for one day. Let's go home."

John followed me home. I crept along and kept a death-grip on the wheel, afraid I'd do something else stupid. We never spoke of the incident again. I learned to navigate slippery, snowy roads.

* * *

Leslie occasionally plunked out tunes on the piano, finding notes to match a song in her head. I'd never played the piano, so I couldn't help her with that, but I had played flute in school and knew the treble clef. On one of our shopping trips, we stopped at a music store and I bought her an elementary song book. We worked out the fingering for the right hand. I was amazed how quickly she caught on. I wished I knew how to read the bass clef, but she seemed satisfied with being able to play and sing simple children's songs. We heard a lot of "John Jacob Jingleheimer Schmidt," "Mary Had a Little Lamb," "Baa Baa Black Sheep," and "Down by the Station."

The piano stood in the living room, and although they tried to be tolerant, I could see John and Wade would rather have her play some time other than in the evening when they might want to watch TV or read, so I encouraged her to play the piano when she came home from school.

I made a few phone calls and learned that most piano teachers take students once they've reached their eighth birthdays. Leslie had turned eight in September. I called the school and asked for recommendations.

"There's a piano teacher who lives about a block from here," the school secretary said. "Let me give you her contact information."

I talked to the piano teacher, Mrs. Gaylord. She would take a child as young as eight, but first she needed to have a conference with the child and a parent.

I approached John. "I think Leslie has musical talent."

He nodded. "Her mother loved music and played the piano."

I hesitated, never knowing when I might over-step my position. "Leslie is old enough now to take piano lessons."

Surprise registered in his dark eyes. He waited for me to continue.

"I called the school and the secretary gave me a name of a piano teacher who lives close to the school."

"What does Leslie think?"

"I wanted to talk to you first."

"If Leslie wants to take piano lessons, that would be fine. Thank you, Maureen."

"You'll need to go with Leslie the first time to meet the teacher."

He sighed. "Can't you do that?"

"She said 'a parent.'"

"Okay, call her back and make an appointment for us. I hope her lessons are right after school, then one of us can pick her up afterward. That might be you sometimes. Is that okay?"

"Of course!"

I floated into the kitchen. I called Mrs. Gaylord and made an appointment the following Wednesday, right after school, for Leslie and John.

When Leslie came home from school, I asked if she would like to take piano lessons from a "real piano teacher."

She jumped straight up. "Yes!"

Wednesday morning at breakfast I reminded John that he'd have to quit work early, pick up Leslie after school and meet with the piano teacher. He nodded and turned to Leslie.

"If you do this, Leslie, take lessons, it's your deal. I'm not going to remind you to practice, neither is Maureen." He looked pointedly at me. "If you keep up your end by practicing, I'll go along with this. But if you decide you don't want to do it, don't want to practice anymore, that's okay too. Just let me know and we'll stop the lessons."

"Dad, I *want* to practice. I want to play like Mom did."

John nodded.

Leslie sailed off to school, feet barely touching the ground.

Every time I thought about Leslie's big day, it brought a smile to my face. I knew I fulfilled an important role with this family. It was moments like this that made me feel the warmth of satisfaction.

They returned from their meeting, both smiling. "I'm going to do it, Maureen, take piano lessons from Mrs. Gaylord!"

Leslie plowed through her music books. Every day, right after school, she practiced. She took her music seriously, often calling me into the living room so I could hear a piece she'd been working on. I grinned. As though I couldn't hear it from the kitchen.

In the spring, Mrs. Gaylord called to ask if Leslie could participate in an annual student recital. "She is very talented. I've never had a student progress so fast. I'm so glad you took the initiative on this."

The day before the recital, Leslie complained of a stomach ache. She didn't seem at all sick, so I guessed the problem. "Leslie, I'll bet you just have jitters because of the recital. Don't worry about it, honey, you'll do well. You've practiced so much, it's already a part of you. Just have fun with it."

I joined John and Wade for the recital. I felt a little awkward going someplace social with the family, but I wouldn't have missed this special event for anything. Finding empty seats, John gestured for me to go first, then Wade, followed by John.

I felt people's eyes on me. Of course, John was well known in the community. He'd lived here all his life. Three rows up a woman peeked over her shoulder and noticed me, then leaned over to her husband. In a minute, he turned around to look, too. This happened several times with other couples before the recital began. I felt my face heating, sure that I blushed. *Why? Why did I feel this way?* I sighed. *Because I'm a stranger among them. Because they're wondering who I am, what am I to John?* In the meantime, John talked to someone he knew who sat next to him. Although I wouldn't have missed this recital, it reaffirmed my hesitancy to attend social events with John.

Mrs. Gaylord started the recital with the younger children first. Listening to the young players was sort of an ordeal. One little boy forgot the notes and repeatedly replayed the first few measures until it finally came to him, and there were a few chuckles in the audience. Looking around the hall, I could spot the parents of the child currently playing, pride glowing on their faces. People politely clapped at the end of each piece, and each student bowed, as Mrs. Gaylord had apparently taught them.

When Leslie crossed the floor and sat at the piano, perfectly composed, people sat up and listened, nodding. She played her piece perfectly, probably a little faster than was intended. John visibly swelled with pride. When Leslie took her bow, Wade gave a shrill cattleman's whistle. John looked a little embarrassed, but Leslie grinned and waved to her brother. The audience applauded harder. Tears of joy sprung to my eyes. I made this happen. I opened the door for Leslie to enter the world of music. I didn't care what other people thought. *I am doing what I'm supposed to do, helping this family.*

As we emerged from the hall, the local grange, a woman rushed over to me and introduced herself, then waited for me to do the same.

"Hello, I'm Maureen Gardner."

Her eyebrows arched expectantly.

"I'm the Cahills' housekeeper."

"Oh. So nice to meet you." She remained, waiting.

Leslie ran toward us and I gave her all my attention, telling her how well she did and how proud of her I was. I briefly waved to the woman as we turned toward the parking lot. My stomach knotted. *I have to get out of here.*

At home or around the ranch, I felt perfectly at ease. Even with my bridge group and neighboring ranch women I belonged, though admittedly it had taken awhile to feel accepted by some of them. But here in public I felt like an intruder, an outsider. These were unfamiliar feelings for me. In Seattle, around my own territory, I didn't feel this way, even when faced with unfamiliar settings.

In trying to define my feelings, I decided that what bothered me most was what I perceived by others as an expectancy for John and me to become a couple. That isn't why John hired me, and it wasn't why I had come. If there would ever be anything romantic between John and me, I would want the reason to be more than a convenience. But I wasn't expecting anything more from John. I was doing what I was hired to do, and happily content to do that.

I wondered if John felt this strangeness, or was it just me?

Walking toward the car, I put my arm around Leslie's shoulder. She grinned up at me and I smiled at her excited face. A surge of happiness filled my heart. Well, no matter what it took, I would give this little girl my love and attention. *That's why I'm here. It's my job, my purpose.*

I loved watching John's gentleness toward Leslie. I think my being there gave him more time to enjoy his little girl. Although he kept long hours during much of the year, almost every day he took time to spend with Leslie. Of course, when Wade was home from school, John and Wade worked together. Many evenings they also enjoyed watching sports on TV together.

John was slowly coming out of his hole. I often heard Wade and him talking about ranch business. He spoke to Wade man-to-man, which pleased me, and, I'd learned from Abbie, not too common among ranchers and their sons. They occasionally had differences, but they treated one another with respect.

There was one topic, however, that drew heated conversations. During Wade's senior year he and John often argued about Wade attending college. John was a University of Washington graduate and wanted Wade to go to college. Wade adamantly stood his ground.

One day they went at it in the kitchen. They had just come into the house and apparently had been discussing the possibility of Wade's going to college.

"Dad, can we just stop talking about this? I don't want to go to college. I want to be a stockman, like you."

John fought to keep his voice calm. "Son, that's what I want for you, too. But I want you to have a choice. Go to college and see what's out there. You've done well at school—I know you'll do well in college."

"I just want to work on the ranch!"

"How about just taking some agriculture classes, then. I want you to have some college, at least."

They finally compromised and Wade agreed to go to the local community college. Reluctantly, he picked up the registration forms.

Soon after, when it was just the two of us in the kitchen, I said to Wade, "I'm glad you're going to college. You'll find it's quite different from high school."

He looked at me with skepticism, shaking his head. "I think it'll be a waste of time."

* * *

Calving season was soon upon us. I had never really known what was involved, but soon learned that calving is the busiest season on a cattle ranch. And, I would find out, the most exhausting.

For a cow/calf operation, the reason a herd is maintained year round is to produce a crop of calves every year.

Bulls are turned out to breed with the cows sometime in the summer so that the calves will arrive during a two-month period around February and March.

"You mean you bring all those cows to headquarters to have their calves?" I couldn't imagine.

John smiled, accepting his second cup of morning coffee. "No, only the heifers, young cows who have never had calves. They've already been sorted into a separate pasture. Most cows don't need any help from us when they're giving birth. We keep our eyes out for any who look like they're in trouble and bring 'em in, but otherwise, we just tend to the first-timers."

It was beginning to make sense. After fall roundup, the cattle were pastured closer to home, not only for ease in winter feeding, but because of calving. Wade slathered jam on his fourth piece of toast. "We ride out to those pastures and cut out the heavies and bring 'em to that small pasture by the calving shed."

"Heavies?" Like any profession, cattle ranching had a vocabulary of its own.

Wade nodded. "The cows who are about ready to calve. Then we can keep an eye on 'em. We'll bring the first-time heifers into the calving shed so we can help them if we need to."

John glanced at the kitchen clock. "Wade, you'd better get going."

Wade checked his watch. "Right." He climbed the stairs two at a time to his room to finish getting ready for school.

"We'll be keeping awful hours around calving season, Maureen. It keeps the three of us going around the clock. During the school week, Randy and I take turns getting up at night. On weekends, Wade takes his turn. Don't let our coming and going disturb you."

Turn? Doing what, I wondered, but John was already putting on his hat, then pulling on his boots.

Winter feeding went on seven days a week, but, it became apparent, calving is a 24-hour-a-day process. John and Randy set a schedule so that the heavies were checked every couple of hours around the clock.

On a Saturday during calving season, I asked Leslie if she'd like to go out to the pasture near the calving shed with me. It wasn't that I needed her to go with me, but felt a little more comfortable with an excuse. Leslie was always game. "Sure!"

We bundled up and walked out to the small pasture. John rode around the herd, checking each cow. He glanced up at us, but continued his rounds. He stopped and watched as a cow lay down, then in a minute got up and walked around, her tail outstretched behind her. I pointed her out to Leslie.

The cow kept up this behavior for several minutes. The men kept this pasture clean and laid clean straw in places as bedding. She found a spot away from the other cows, and walked in circles. At one point she kicked at her side. I glanced around for John and found him, still astride, motionless, watching.

I spoke softly to Leslie. "I think she's going to have her baby soon. Let's be real quiet."

"Okay," she whispered.

After lying down, then standing, the cow finally sprawled on her side. Within minutes we saw two little hooves, followed by a nose, then the rest of the calf slipped out quickly, covered in slime.

We continued to watch as the cow turned her head and began to lick her baby. Then she stood and licked the entire little body in earnest.

John slowly walked his horse closer to her, then rode to the fence where we stood watching.

"Why does she lick the baby, Dad?"

"To clean it off, and so it won't get cold, but it also stimulates the calf. The calf needs that in order to begin living on its own."

"Is it a boy or girl?"

"It's a nice bull, a boy. About seventy pounds."

"How much do you imagine the cow weighs?" I asked.

"About thirteen-hundred pounds."

I gasped. And, to use their words, they pushed those cattle around all the time.

As we watched, the calf struggled to stand on wobbly legs and make its way to the cow's teats.

"What an amazing sight!" I exclaimed. "Miraculous, really." John smiled and urged his horse on.

At first I heard him get up during the night, but it wasn't long before I slept through the commotion. I did make sure the coffee was always on, day and night, and after the first couple of days, soup simmered in the crock-pot so the men would have some hot nourishment. I made a point of telling Randy to come in to help himself. He was so appreciative, thanking me several times. I put out a stack of throw-away bowls, something they could take to the calving shed with them.

During the school day I often went to the calving shed to watch. John had mentioned that he didn't want Leslie in there, that things often went wrong and he didn't want her exposed to that yet. Calves generally came out feet first as the one we'd watched in the pasture. The first few I watched entered the world without incident.

One afternoon, I watched as Randy struggled with a young heifer, trying to coax her into the calving shed. She was determined to stay with the herd. He managed to get her into the shed, but she was having none of it and turned to leave.

"Maureen, stand in the doorway and wave your arms, keep her from getting out."

"Sure." His directness surprised me. Randy was usually so polite. He was obviously wearing down, too. But it didn't bother me: it made me feel more included. The cow turned toward me and back a couple of times, but finally gave up, and Randy got her into a wide stall to examine her.

"Oh, oh, we got a problem." He sighed, and looked at me. "Better call John."

I reached for my cell phone, always in my pocket.

John had been checking the herd, but luckily still within cell phone range. Within minutes I heard a horse trotting up to the calving shed and the creak of leather as he dismounted. He joined Randy in the stall.

"What's up?"

"We got a heifer in trouble. She's having contractions, but I'm only feeling one foot way back alongside her head."

John hung his hat on a nearby peg and shrugged off his coat before slipping on a shoulder-length plastic obstetrical glove. He slathered the gloved arm with a gel, then reached up far inside the cow to examine the birth canal. "It's a big one." He struggled and grimaced during a contraction.

"There, I got the other foot in position. Get the chains."

Randy dashed into the supply room and came out with chains dripping with disinfectant. John reached into the cow again, this time with the end of the chain. After some grunting on his part and the cow's irritated mooing, he managed to get the chains on both hooves. When the cow strained, they gently pulled and the calf began protruding, then suddenly slipped out along with after-birth and other fluids. Randy took the chain back into the supply room, ran water over it and put it in a pail with fresh disinfectant.

That was the first close-up animal birth I had ever witnessed. What a marvel! Maybe a little gross, quite messy with lots of slime, but still fascinating. To me, the heady smell of blood, after-birth fluids, urine and manure mixed with fresh hay was not an altogether bad smell. I'm sure it was another story if the calf had been inside the cow for too long, if there was trouble.

I followed Randy into the supply room. He glanced at me. "Not every outfit has a calving shed as nice as this one, with hot and cold running water and everything handy."

We returned to the calving area. "Is this barn heated, or is the heat coming from the cows' bodies?" I asked.

John had been helping the cow dry off her baby, using clean straw. "It's heated a bit, as much for our sake as theirs."

The two men watched for a few minutes as the cow and calf bonded.

"Good," Randy said. "That's working." He indicated to the next stall. "Unlike those two. She's a bad mama." While they watched, the cow kicked her calf and it lay stunned, sprawled near the stall wall.

"Okay, let's not fool around any longer." John quickly hobbled the cow's legs. He brought the calf to its feet and, straddling the little bull, half-walked, half-carried him to his mother. John reached down and tugged on the cow teats and put the calf in position. The calf's noisy sucking was reassuring. The first-time heifer stood quietly. John glanced at me. "They're not always that easy."

He turned to Randy. "Okay? Everything under control here? I'm gonna check the east pasture for heavies."

"Got it, boss."

I returned to the house. Leslie was due home from school and I had promised her that after she finished practicing piano we would bake a batch of chocolate chip cookies for dessert.

Later, the final batch of fragrant cookies cooled on racks. "Leslie, let's fix a plate of cookies for Pearl's family. Would you like to take it to their house?"

"No, you can do it."

"Let's go together. All right?" No answer. "Leslie?" She sighed. "Okay."

We wrapped a cooled plate of cookies, put on our coats and walked over to Pearl and Randy's. I tried to hand the cookie plate to Leslie, but she shrank back.

"You give it to her."

Pearl answered the door, holding Karen at her hip. "Hi!" She stepped back. "Come in."

"Just for a minute," I gently pushed Leslie into the house.

As Pearl herself had said, she was no housekeeper. The kitchen counter was cluttered with assorted food, scraggly houseplants, boxes and papers. In the living room, she scooped clean baby clothes to be folded off a chair. "Have a seat." I sat down and Leslie crowded in with me.

I scooted over to make room for Leslie. "We can only stay a minute. I have to get dinner started."

Pearl cleared newspaper sections off another chair and joined us. "Thank you for the cookies. Leslie did you help make 'em?"

Leslie nodded.

Pearl put Karen on the floor and the baby immediately crawled over to Leslie, who made no move toward the little smiling face.

We chatted for a few minutes about the endless calving season, and then left.

Nearing home, I asked, "Leslie, why don't you like to go to Pearl's?"

She shrugged.

"That's a cute baby, don't you think? I'll bet Karen would love to play with you."

She shrugged again. How strange. I decided to let it go. Some day I'd find out what that was all about.

John was obviously bone weary. That evening, Friday, at dinner, he looked at Wade with tired eyes. "How about you and Randy taking over tonight, then you and me Saturday night? Give Randy a break." John wouldn't allow Wade to work school nights, although Wade had offered to do so.

"Sure, Dad. Can I ask Darrell? He's never seen calving."

"Let's hold off. Ask him for spring roundup."

The men rode out to the pastures several times each day, noting new calves and tagging them to identify a link to their mother. They watched for signs of scours, a diarrhea common among calves and treated with antibiotics, usually by injection.

On Saturday morning I watched out the kitchen window as Wade rode horseback to the calving shed with a wet, slippery-looking calf draped across his lap. He laid it across his saddle while he dismounted steadying it with one hand. He reached up for the calf and rushed into the calving shed.

Randy rode in from another direction, apparently seeing Wade, dismounted and hurried into the shed. Wade popped out, swung into the saddle and rode back the way he had come. I was dying to see what was going on, but Leslie was home and John had specifically said that Leslie was to stay out of the calving shed.

Before long, I again watched Wade as he guided a cow toward the calving shed. The cow turned aside a few times, but between Wade and his horse, and at the last minute Randy, they managed to get her inside. The dog must have been with John.

At lunch I learned more about the incident. "Wade, I saw you carrying a calf into the calving shed. Why couldn't you leave it with the mother?"

Wade sat up straighter, apparently proud to be asked. "Sometimes cows won't take care of a new baby right away. After she had her calf, she just wandered away. We can't take a chance that she'll come back and take care of it, so I brought it in to dry it off. Then I went back to get the cow so we could force them together. We put 'em in one of those smaller stalls for a couple of days so they can bond."

"I also watched you bring in the cow. Between you and your horse you certainly managed that well."

Wade smiled shyly, but obviously was pleased that I'd noticed. "I've got a good horse."

John looked up from his bowl of stew. "You do a man's job out there, Wade."

Wade looked at John with open admiration. "Thanks, Dad."

On Sunday Wade came in from outside and plopped down at the kitchen table. I asked if he wanted a cup of coffee.

"Yes, please, and one for Dad. Maureen, he just did a Caesarean section on a heifer. Boy, he's really good."

"Really? I thought vets did that kind of operation."

"They do, but sometimes there's no time to call and then wait for them to come out. This little heifer was in trouble with a big calf and Dad was afraid we'd lose her and maybe the calf, too. He was so calm, gave her a shot in the spine, a local anesthetic, and called out orders to Randy and me. He told us just where to scrub and shave her. Dad made a big incision on the outside, then another one inside."

70

"So then could he just lift it out?"

"No, he pulled out the hind legs, hooked up the chain so we could lift it up and out."

"'What was the cow doing all this time?"

"This one just stood there, but sometimes they're already laying down. She'd been up and down but just couldn't deliver. She happened to be standing when Dad started working on her." He gave me a huge grin.

"I think my dad is the best stockman I've ever known. Well, like I've known so many, but I'll bet he's the best in the county."

"I'll bet he is, too, Wade. Here's your coffee–I've put it in your travel cups."

"Thanks, I'd better get back. I've got a mess to clean up."

Some day I hoped to witness such an event. I really admired John. Not only was he capable of such a thing, but he obviously had all the equipment he needed for this type of emergency.

I felt as though I was fitting in, being a part of things. I couldn't imagine how they would have managed without me, or someone doing my job, especially during calving season. But really, there always seemed to be some season, some major happening on the ranch. *I should call Sue, share with her my satisfaction, my sense of belonging.* This isn't how I'd imagined my life, but I was happy. I wouldn't allow myself to look too far into the future—I'd live for today. I was getting better at that.

* * *

I had always enjoyed going to church and missed worshiping with a congregation, but hadn't taken the time yet to get established in my new surroundings. I'd asked Abbie, Janelle's mother, if they attended church.

"Yes, we go to Calvary Baptist, about five miles from here. It's a nice church with friendly people. The Cahills used to go too, but I haven't seen them there since Barbara died."

I drove around checking out local churches and decided to try Calvary Baptist. It would be nice to know at least one family already.

Calving season was coming to a close. "Only a few left to go—the worst is over," John said. For the first time in weeks we were having a leisurely Sunday breakfast. Wade helped himself to another waffle. I poured a second cup of coffee into John's mug.

"Are you church members?" I asked, not wanting to divulge having talked to Abbie Peterson.

"Not any more," John answered with finality.

"I thought I'd go to the Baptist church this morning. Would anyone like to go with me?"

Leslie perked up. "Can I go, Dad?"

John slowly nodded. "If you want."

Wade looked at his Dad for a couple of seconds, then resumed eating his waffle. I couldn't read his expression.

We hurried through breakfast dishes and I helped Leslie get into her newest dress and cute ruffled socks, then helped comb her hair. I had dressed before breakfast and was almost ready to go.

On the way, Leslie was unusually quiet. Finally, she said, "Dad's mad at God."

"Because your mother died?"

She nodded. "The guy that killed her was drunk."

I prayed for something wise and meaningful to say. "God doesn't stop people from doing wrong things. We all make choices. That man chose to do a bad thing when he drove his car after he'd been drinking. It brought a lot of sadness, didn't it?"

"He died, too."

We arrived at church and Leslie perked up. "Can we sit up front so I can watch the organist?"

"I'd just as soon not sit in the very first row my first time here. How about the second or third row?"

"Okay. Hurry."

I chuckled to myself, so glad I'd invited her along.

We found a seat where Leslie could watch the organist. The first part of the service was for the entire congregation. Leslie craned her neck around until she spotted Janelle's family and grinned at her friend.

When we sang the opening hymn, "Blessed Assurance," Leslie sang with gusto. I was astonished, both that she knew the words and also the tune. "This is my story, this is my song," her voice rang out, "praising the Savior all the day long."

I wish I hadn't waited so long to join a church. This was apparently something Leslie had missed.

The children filed out to their various Sunday school classes, and we adults settled in for worship. After the service, Abbie and I gathered Leslie and Janelle from their classroom.

On the way home I asked Leslie how she happened to know that hymn so well.

"My mom had a book of hymns. She'd play the piano and we'd sing `em together. That was one of her favorites."

From then on, Leslie and I attended church on a regular basis. John never said anything, one way or another. He never encouraged the children to go, but neither did he discourage them.

On Easter Sunday, at breakfast, I placed Easter baskets by the kids' plates. I was a little hesitant with

Wade's, hoping he wouldn't be offended or think it childish. He smiled, and seemed genuinely pleased with his chocolate bars, bags of mixed nuts and a few colored candy eggs. "Thanks, Maureen."

Leslie squealed with delight with her chocolate bunnies and colored Easter eggs.

I invited Wade to join us for Easter Sunday worship. He glanced at his dad, who kept his face absolutely blank. The decision was clearly Wade's.

"Sure. I'll go with you guys. I've gotta change clothes. Be right back."

It was a milestone for me, but after that Wade only joined us occasionally.

* * *

Graduating senior activities approached. To my knowledge, Wade didn't date yet. One morning at breakfast I asked him if he had asked a girl to the prom.

"No, I'm not going."

John glanced up. "Not going to your prom? Why not?"

"I just don't want to. Do you know how much renting a tux costs? Then there are the tickets, flowers, all that stuff."

"Wade, I'll give you extra money for what you need. We should have talked about this before now. Do you have someone in mind you could ask?"

Wade sighed and shook his head.

"How about that Nelson girl, Debbie?"

Wade shrugged. "She's probably already been asked."

"Ask her, son. If she can't go, ask someone else."

I ventured in. "The prom is a big deal, Wade. A girl would be so pleased to be asked."

The next day, when Wade drove up in his truck after school, I thought he had extra spring in his step as he walked toward the house. I didn't ask. I wanted him to bring it up.

At dinner, I could tell he was screwing up his courage to say something. Finally, at the end of the meal—a meal he'd only half-heartedly eaten—he casually said, "I asked Debbie Nelson to the prom."

John's eyes lit up. "What'd she say?"

Wade shrugged. "We're going."

"Good, Wade. Figure out how much money you need. Don't wait for the last minute on this. Get that tux rented. You could use a good pair of shoes, too. Is there other stuff going on? Do kids still do Senior Day?"

Wade could hardly conceal his smile. "Yeah, Debbie mentioned a picnic at Lake Lombard. We're going to that, too."

"Good. You only graduate from high school once," John said. "Make the most of it."

A thought flashed through my mind. "Wade, you're welcome to use my car for the prom." I didn't know if nowadays a pickup would be proper transportation for a dressy event like a prom.

Wade's surprised expression told me he hadn't given it a thought.

John spoke up. "That's a nice offer, Maureen. One of these days we should get another car."

"Mine is always available, John."

* * *

I was continually amazed with how much there was to ranching, and how the seasons ruled our lives. Before I lived on the ranch, I had no idea of the work it took to run a large cattle ranch, to put meat on America's tables. John, Wade and Randy continually checked on the cattle, making sure they had enough feed and water. They routinely moved bunches of cattle from one pasture to another to allow the land to recover from grazing and to grow new grass. Through three generations, the ranch had been expanded, so there was plenty of land, but even so, John occasionally leased more land for his cows to graze.

My wardrobe evolved to jeans and denim shirts, or sweatshirts in the colder weather. I even had a pair of riding boots. I wore slacks and sweaters for a bit dressier occasions.

By this time I had ridden horseback many times. The first time, Wade had saddled Dixie, a gentle, older bay for me, along with Ginger for Leslie, the horse that had formerly been her mother's. After that first time, I could hardly walk the next day, but I knew the remedy for that was to climb right back on as soon as possible.

The second time, after watching him closely, I told Wade I could groom and saddle the horses myself. My body adjusted to riding and I found myself relaxing into it, feeling more and more at ease with each riding session.

In the nice weather Leslie and I rode at least once a weekend, but I rode a couple times a week during the school day. If one of the men was around when I saddled the horse, he always tested the cinch to see that I had it tight enough. It was never quite to their satisfaction and they always adjusted it.

One Wednesday John had errands in town and would pick Leslie up after her piano lesson, so I had extra time. I saddled up and went a little farther than usual, and became absorbed with my outing. I stopped at a stand of Ponderosa pine and gazed up at the huge, older trees. Their rough red bark reminded me of giant jigsaw puzzles. I breathed in deeply their fragrant scent of pine. I relished this opportunity to be with nature. Insects buzzed and clicked. A woodpecker's rapid pecking echoed.

Dixie and I continued through fields of sage. The ranch had a wide range of terrain. We both startled when we flushed out grouse and they squawked with alarm, leaving their shelter with a noisy flapping of wings. In wide-open pasture, I spotted a single prong-horn antelope. We stopped and stared at one another and then it ran like the wind, probably to warn others. I chuckled watching Dixie's ears as they in turn swiveled around to register alarm, curiosity, and contentment.

We wandered through a small grove of Russian olive trees, their leaves evenly cropped by grazing cattle. I deeply inhaled the spicy fragrance. Now in the fall, the silver leaves would soon drop.

When I turned Dixie to go home I realized I was lost. That old, familiar panic set in. When I rode with Leslie she always seemed to know where we were, and I relied on her. The horse and I did several starts and stops and I finally gave Dixie her head. "Let's go home." I had no idea what would happen. My stomach clenched. The horse stood for a long time. When I urged her she would start, then stop, apparently waiting for direction. I think she finally gave up on me and decided that if she was going to get dinner any time that day, she'd better head for home. I urged her to go as fast as I dared, but it was getting dark and I didn't want to push the horse and make her stumble into a gopher hole. My mind was in turmoil. My entire body prickled, afraid for myself, for this horse that wasn't even mine. I worried about being so late and what the family must be thinking. And I was embarrassed, humiliated that I would cause worry. Anger, too, that I had such a terrible sense of direction.

Finally, I recognized the trail in the near dark and I could see the barn's roof. Relief swept through me. Still, I approached with dread and deep guilt.

I could just make out the time on my watch. John and Leslie had been home about an hour. As I approached I could see Wade saddling up and John walking between the house and barn.

Wade glanced up, saw me, and immediately began to unsaddle his big gelding.

Randy came out from the barn and took both Wade's and my reins. "I'll take 'em. You guys go ahead."

"Sorry I'm so late." My stomach churned with guilt.

Wade nodded. "We were getting worried." He walked with me to the house.

Leslie rushed into the kitchen. "Where were you? We were worried!"

"I'm sorry, honey." I'd had dinner lined up, a meaty soup, rolls and a fruit salad. I quickly turned on the burner under the soup. "Leslie, would you set the table?" I glanced at John, standing in the doorway. "Dinner will be in about ten minutes."

After dinner, and after Leslie had left the room, I started to clear the table.

"Maureen," John's voice was stern, "you're free to go horseback riding, but when you do, I expect you to tell someone, or leave a note telling us where you're going and when you'll be back."

I stopped half way to the sink and turned to look at him. "I'm sorry dinner was late, John."

"Being late doesn't have anything to do with it. We were worried and didn't know where you were, where to start looking."

"Neither did I."

"What?"

"I didn't know where I was, either. I got lost. It finally occurred to me to give Dixie her head and let her find the way home."

He couldn't have looked more shocked. "Well, where were you going in the first place?"

"I had no idea. I just wanted to go for a ride."

"Maureen! You can't just go wandering willy-nilly around here. If you get into trouble, or if your horse comes home without you, how will we know where to find you?"

My face heated. I had nothing to say, but I was close to tears.

"If you're going to go riding, figure out ahead of time where you're going. Pay attention how you got there so you can get yourself back home."

I glanced at Wade who sat still as a statue, trying very hard not to smile. His dancing eyes gave him away.

I looked at John's concerned face. "All right."

John glanced at Wade, gave an ever-so-slight shake of his head and left the house, Wade close at his heals.

"Jesus Christ," I heard John mutter.

The next morning John brought a hand-drawn map of the ranch to the kitchen table. "Here, Maureen, I've made this for you. Sit down. Let me explain."

The map showed the house, barn, and calving shed, with pastures outlined. In the distance were the foothills, leading to the mountains. John pointed to the foothills. "Those are to the west, see?

"See that road? That's McClellan Road, the one that runs along the east side of our property. Okay, now look at this. That's the spring that runs along the north end of the ranch. It dries up in the summer, but you can still see what it is. The south end—are you following me?"

"I'm hanging on every word."

He looked incredulous. "Are you making fun of me?"

"No, John. But remember you're talking to someone who can't go around a city block without getting lost."

"That's because you don't pay attention. We don't have blocks here, so you have to always be aware of where you are. Pay attention now."

"John, I am paying attention. This is amazing."

Surprised, he stopped and studied my face. "It's just a crude map, Maureen. Okay, the south end has that big grove of lodgepole pine, then our orchard."

"Okaaaay."

"I want you to carry this map with you when you go riding."

"But what if I can't see any of those things?"

He was dumbfounded. "You'll pretty much always be able to see the mountains. To the west."

I must have still looked unconvinced.

"Wait here. I'll be right back."

He came out carrying a compass, a nice instrument attached to a leather thong. "Do you know how to use one of these, a compass?"

I felt like a total ninny. "Not really."

"Step outside with me."

We stood in the yard, facing the barn. "Okay, look. That red needle always points North. See?" We watched as the needle found north, no matter which way John turned.

John handed it to me. "Practice with this around here, so you're familiar with how it works. Now, take the compass and the map whenever you go anyplace. I, or one of us, will still want to know where you're headed, but hopefully now you won't get lost."

I felt him looking at me for a long minute, but I didn't dare look back. I didn't want to confirm that, yes, sure enough, I was incredibly inept. I studied the compass and it's wobbling all-knowing north-bound needle.

"Okay, thanks." I don't think John could even begin to comprehend how little all of that meant to me.

* * *

In early May, spring roundup dominated our days. When it started, John again cautioned, "If you want to watch, make sure Leslie's out of the way. Cattle get nervous and it can get crazy out there. Just find a safe place a distance away."

We would again have our main meal at noon, with extra hands, so I was busier than usual in the kitchen. I mentioned to Abbie that I would love to do more than cook. I wanted to get in on the excitement.

It was on the second day, Saturday, and they were going to start branding when Abbie called. "Why don't I come over and pick up Leslie? She can stay with us, spend the night. That'll give you a chance to work roundup."

I gasped in pleasure. "What a nice friend you are! I'll ask John, but I'm sure it will be fine with him."

After Leslie left with Abbie, I hurriedly changed into jeans and riding boots and almost skipped to the corrals.

John and Wade were good about answering questions. They loved their life and seemed eager for me to learn about it, too. I tried to ask questions when they weren't busy with a struggling cow..

Men on horseback came between cow and calf, guiding them toward separate holding pens. The air was thick with dust, and the noise deafening with men yelling—I could hear John's voice above the others. Cows bawled for their babies, and the calves cried out fearfully for their mothers.

The cattle and yearlings were herded through chutes to be deloused, vaccinated, and ear-tagged with an insecticide to keep away flies. John set me up to delouse the cows as they made their way through the chute. I used a ladle to pour a smelly solution along their bony spines. I stood on a low bench so I could reach over the chute as each cow passed by.

At one point a cow balked and tried to back up, but Randy slid a board in a slot behind her. Charlie, the cattle dog, nipped at her heel, and in trying to kick at the dog, the cow lost her balance, slipped on the muck, and tumbled onto her side, hooves flying in all directions. She bellowed in outrage. The whole thing happened in seconds, but, above all the noise, I clearly heard John shout, "Maureen, get back!"

There were so many close calls, I was amazed there weren't more disasters. John had given me a list of supplies to update their large first-aid kit. Accidents happen and injuries are not uncommon at roundup. I patched up a few cuts and dispensed some ibuprofen, but this year, at least, no serious accidents.

While some treated the cows and yearlings, others treated the calves. As each little calf was prodded down a chute, Janelle's father, Bob, called out "bull" when it was a male; otherwise, just ushered the little critters through one at a time. Mabel Jackson kept a talley to keep count of the heifers and bulls.

I watched as they vaccinated calves and punched repellent tags onto their ears like giant pierced earrings. The men dehorned and branded them with an electrical device. I had thought they'd have a fire going to heat a branding iron, like in the movies, but Wade said they quit doing that several years earlier. An electric branding iron was less labor-intensive and more efficient. The Cahill ranch brand looked like an up-side-down "U" with a "C" in the middle.

If Bob called out "bull!" the little fellow was ushered into another section where he was put into a squeeze chute and tipped on its side. John castrated him so quickly, the little guy hardly had time to bawl. John tossed the testicles into a bucket.

Wade glanced at his dad. "Can't wait to eat them Rocky Mountain oysters." I heard a few chuckles and realized he said that for my benefit. But from what I understood, we really would be eating them. I couldn't imagine. I doubted I would find a recipe in any of my cookbooks. I shoved the idea to the back of my mind. I'd worry about it later.

The bawling calves were led back to the pasture that held their anxious mothers. I worried that they'd never find one another, but then was amazed how quickly they paired up.

The newly treated cow/calf pairs were herded into more distant pastures, and another bunch brought in.

Spring roundup lasted for several days, but I only participated the one day while Leslie stayed at Janelle's. I so appreciated the opportunity to do more than just cook, though I realized how important that was, too.

Over the next few weeks either Randy, or Wade on weekends, and sometimes Darrell, too, helped other ranchers with their spring roundup.

Soon the men took herds to distant pastures where they would graze until next fall and where the calves grew to become beef cattle, or future mothers.

* * *

The second time for me to go someplace with the family was to attend Wade's graduation. As we did at Leslie's recital, John ushered me in first, then Leslie sat between us. The commencement exercise was a digni-fied affair and an important milestone for the students. This event was better for me, too. The passage of a little time had paved the way for me to feel less con-spicuous. I waved to a couple of friends, mothers or grandmothers of graduating students, which made me feel more a part of the community. No one acted as though my presence was strange. As we filed out of the high school, one of my bridge friends made her way toward me to chat for a moment. She would probably never know how much that meant to me, to be recognized and sought after.

Wade had told me that many of his classmates were going away to college. Since he had to go, he said, he was at least glad to be closer and attend the community college, which would allow him to return to the ranch most weekends.

Before I knew it, I had been with the Cahills a year. I felt deep contentment, much of that due to satisfaction in knowing I filled a void for the family. Although they showed and even expressed their appreciation, I could see for myself that they thrived. The kids were healthy and had positive attitudes. John obviously grew stronger emotionally, though he rarely spoke of his wife. I carried a sense of belonging and even fulfillment. Still, in the night, I often awakened with that familiar sense of hollowness, of dread. At those times my mind often harbored unfulfilled hopes and deep disappointment. I had everything I needed; I felt useful. During these nighttime periods of unrest, I commanded myself to look forward, not back, not to dwell on what might have been.

6

anch seasons and routines began forming a pattern for me and I found myself enjoying ranch life. I continually reminded myself to "live for today" and not dwell on my past, or future. I was never bored. When caught up on my work, I felt free to explore either by walking or riding horseback, reading or visiting friends. John left running the house strictly to me. He never asked for an accounting of my time or money spent. He deposited money in our household account on a regular basis. If I needed more for a special purpose, all I had to do was ask. I'm frugal by nature and I know John appreciated that.

Leslie was a joy, the daughter I would never have. We normally got along well, only occasionally butting heads. Once, John overheard a disagreement. I had asked Leslie to straighten her room so that I could vacuum. When she didn't do it, I reminded her, and she said, "It's my room, Maureen. I don't have to!"

I was taken aback, my feelings hurt, plus I wasn't sure just what I should do. I didn't have to worry for long.

"Leslie!" John strode into the kitchen where we were. "When Maureen asks you to do something, you do it. Now apologize to her."

She fumed, but remained silent.

"Oh—," I started to say, eager to back out of this uncomfortable situation. John held up his hand to silence me.

"Leslie."

She sighed loudly and rolled her eyes. "Sorry."

"That's not much of an apology." One thing about John: he followed through.

She blinked slowly, and took a breath. "I'm sorry I talked back to you, Maureen."

John nodded, and glanced at me.

I smiled at her. "Thank you, Leslie."

She promptly climbed the stairs to straighten her room.

I rarely joined the family in anything social. Sometimes when John and the kids went some place, to his mother's, or to a family event at the local grange, John invited me to join them, but I declined, sure he'd only asked to be polite. I was free to come and go as I pleased and didn't have a need to get away. I was just happy that he was doing something fun with the kids, mostly Leslie, since Wade was gone now so much of the time.

Occasionally, John had to hire an extra man while Wade was away at college. He rarely mentioned that fact to Wade, knowing it would upset him.

As agreed, Wade went to Valley Community College, about a hundred-mile drive. He shared an apartment with three other guys during the week, but usually came home weekends. He took me up on my offer to go over his papers and welcomed my suggestions or corrections.

I asked Wade once if he'd met any girls or ever dated.

"Not much. Debbie Nelson, that girl I took to the prom, goes to Valley, too, and we've gone to some of the school stuff together. But I'm here most weekends and she usually stays there.

Wade fulfilled the promise he'd made to his dad and finished the two-year agriculture program at the college and received an associate degree. At this point, Wade made it clear he had no intention of continuing college.

* * *

One early spring I asked John to prepare a patch of ground for me to plant a vegetable garden. "If you'll rototill it, I'll do the rest."

I'd hoped not to hear that this was a ranch, not a farm. To my amazement, he said, "I'll get Randy to rent a rototiller and do that for you. Get it staked out so he'll know what to do. He should put a fence around it so your garden doesn't get trampled or chomped on."

He looked out the living room window. "I see you've spiffed up those flower beds. They look nice."

The compliment brought warm pleasure. "Thank you. Pretty soon we'll have more flowers coming up."

It became a yearly ritual that John left to me. I loved having my own project, something to contribute to the family. I arranged for Randy to rent the equipment. He initially plowed and made sure the fence and gate were sound, and after that I tended the garden, weeding, planting, and harvesting. It got me outside and put fresh vegetables on the table. The family raved about the produce I served them out of that garden. The men even ate salads. I shared vegetables with Pearl and her family, and Abbie and I traded vegetables, giving us each a nice variety.

Leslie occasionally helped me, particularly with the picking. Sometimes just before dinner I'd ask her to pick something for the table, like tomatoes. She delighted in finding the nicest ones on the vine. As she got older, during the school year her time was taken with school and music, but during the summer, during the real garden season, she often gave me a hand with harvesting and processing. These times gave us a chance to chat, too.

* * *

Pearl gave birth to a little boy, Curtis. When they came home from the hospital, I went over to their house to help. Randy had missed a couple days of work, and I was glad to do it to free him so he could get back to his job. Karen, now four, took my hand and pulled me into her parents' bedroom to see the baby.

"Oh, Karen, you must be so proud of your little brother!"

She beamed. "His name's Curtis. Mom says pretty soon he'll play with me."

Their house was messy as ever and I could barely find a place among the clutter on the kitchen counter to put the casserole I'd brought. I asked Pearl what I could do to help, suggesting I could straighten up the kitchen.

"Thanks, Maureen. That'd be great."

Pearl was doing well, just moving at a slower pace than usual.

It was a school day so Leslie was gone. I'd asked her that morning if she wanted to see the baby, but she declined. She never played with Karen, which I thought a shame. There was no moving Leslie, however. If I insisted she go with me to Pearl's, she sat right by me and wouldn't budge. There was no one for Karen to play with, so it would have been nice for the little girls to get together, even with their age difference. But it apparently was not going to happen.

When Curtis was a little older, I babysat for a couple of hours while Pearl went to a program at Karen's school. He was a cute little fellow, but smelled like pee. Pearl really was not a very good manager. But she was gentle and kind, and a good, conscientious mother.

Shortly before Christmas Pearl received word from her younger sister that their father had died in a house fire. The mother and children had gone to a Christmas program at school and when they returned home they found the house burned to the ground, and their father dead. Pearl's father had apparently fallen asleep on the couch and dropped a cigarette.

Pearl was upset and worried about her mother and the remaining children in the family. I was so amazed when John called Randy to the office and offered to pay for the family to fly to Missouri to see what they could do to help Pearl's mother. I could hear the emotion in Randy's voice when he thanked John.

"Take at least a week, Randy," John said, "more time if you need it. We can manage here."

I'd always thought John a fine man, but this was above and beyond what a hired man might expect from his boss. I realized that Randy and Pearl would probably be a part of the ranch for life. That type of loyalty between employer and employee is to be treasured.

* * *

John was a hard-working man, dedicated to his family and the ranch. As time passed, the intense pain of losing his wife subsided, or so it seemed to me. We often saw humor rise to the surface. I'd hear Wade laugh when his dad said something—I figured it was probably humor intended for male ears only. He was gentle with Leslie but occasionally teased her and I'd hear, "Oh, Dad!" His husky laugh always brought a smile to my lips. With me, he was courteous and often expressed his appreciation. He treated me with respect and thoughtfulness. All in all, I was happy in my position. At times I experienced a sense of longing, but I chided myself. What more did I need?

I made an effort to not think about what might have been. I tried to stay in the here and now. Live each day and let the rest go.

Music helped Leslie through the awkward years that can be so difficult. She gained poise through participation in orchestra and the different musical programs at school, and with her private lessons. She gained much more than musical knowledge. She learned how to cope with frustration, to keep trying when it got hard. She made herself practice even when she didn't feel like it, when she would rather have gone riding. Her music toughened her, gave her direction. I encouraged her whenever I could, often saying to her, "I'm so proud of you."

Leslie was a tall girl, like her father and brother. She complained about being taller than most of the kids in her class. "I'm even taller than the boys!"

"They'll catch up," I comforted her. "As I remember, by the time you reach ninth grade they'll shoot up right past you."

"I hope so," she said. "And I hope I don't stay so skinny. I'd love to have something to put in my bra.

That stupid Bobby Burr said if I stuck out my tongue I'd look like a zipper!"

I laughed and gave her a hug. "I love you just the way you are."

* * *

One day Leslie and I stopped at the Petersons on our way to town. As the girls visited in Janelle's room, Abbie and I sat at her kitchen table having coffee.

"Maureen, have you ever been married?"

I wondered if she would ever ask. Abbie was not a gossip, and, although we chatted about many things, she rarely asked personal questions.

"I came close, was engaged, but it didn't work out." My stomach clenched. I fought against making up some excuse, picking up my purse and leaving.

"You're so good with kids, and such a good homemaker, I'm surprised."

"I love homemaking and enjoyed keeping my own home. Later, as my folks aged, I kept up our family home and took care of them. My dad, especially, was a big eater and appreciated my making new and different dishes. I love children, too, but before coming here the only ones I've really been close to were my brother's and sister's kids."

She nodded, obviously dying to say something more.

"What?"

"I would just think you and John might consider getting...."

"Oh, no, Abbie, John isn't nearly ready for that. And really, I don't think we will ever will."

Abbie obviously had stepped out of her comfort zone. "I'm sorry, I don't...this really isn't any of my business." Her face reddened. She had settled her two-year old son down for his nap and he cried out. "Excuse me," she said, obviously relieved to have an excuse to leave. She hurried out of the kitchen.

My mind was a blur of confusion. This was a topic that for years I'd avoided discussing with anyone.

Abbie returned. "Maureen, I'm so sorry. I..."

"That's fine, Abbie. Don't worry about it. It's only natural that you might wonder."

"I have wondered. It's been five years since Barbara died. But of course, it was a sudden, violent death, which is probably harder to get over than a lingering illness. A lot of John's suffering was, and probably still is, anger. Anger at the drunk who killed her. Still, men seem to remarry after a death or divorce sooner than women. I'd thought John..."

I nodded. "I think that's true of a lot of men. In many ways, women are more self-sufficient than men. When a wife dies, men are left with all the household chores, plus their livelihood responsibilities. Often times they marry too soon, with disastrous results. But I'm doing the household stuff, so it's different with John. To my knowledge, he doesn't even go places where he might meet other women."

"Still, I would think..."

"Abbie, I'm not looking for that type of relationship, nor expecting it. That's not why I came here. I answered John's ad and I'm happy to just do my job. If John needs or wants more, I think he'd say, and he hasn't."

Abbie nodded, but seemed unconvinced.

We chatted about other things, then Leslie and I left to do our shopping.

A few weeks later Abbie called to invite us for dinner the following Sunday. Up to that time, the only meals I'd ever shared with Abbie were our bridge luncheons, and when they came over for our Fourth of July parties. I know the dinner invitation was made in friendship, but it made me uncomfortable. Again, I was faced with making some sort of explanation. My mind spun with possible things to say. I thanked her and told her I would get back to her. I decided the only way to handle the situation was to be honest with her, so I called first, then dropped by when Leslie and Abbie's two older children were in school.

"Abbie, I really appreciate the dinner invitation, but I'm not comfortable doing that sort of thing with John."

"Why ever not? Oh, I'm sorry...." Her face turned red and she squirmed in her chair. My heart went out to her.

"No, Abbie, it's fine. But I need to clarify how I feel." Even though we were friends, I'm sure I was somewhat of a mystery to her. "I've occasionally gone to a special kids program with the family, but I don't do anything that's strictly social. I don't feel it's my place. I've been hired to take care of Leslie and run the household. But that's it. I do not want to put John on the spot and have us thrown together socially. I've given this a lot of thought and I feel a real need to draw a firm line between 'business' and 'social.'"

"Oh, I see. Have you discussed this with John?"

"No, but I think it's always been our understanding. When he hired me, he was quite specific as to why I was hired. I don't want to put him in an awkward position. I love my job and don't want to complicate it with...well, you know."

Abbie nodded, but didn't look convinced. I took a deep breath. She probably needed time to let it soak in.

It was a bit of an unusual situation, but to me it was important to keep those lines clear.

To further convince her, I added, "Abbie, what would happen if I did allow more than a business arrangement and it didn't work out? It could be awkward. I might even have to leave. I feel I have a real obligation to the family. I think my position, especially with Leslie, is really important and I don't want to do anything to jeopardize it."

"But how about if it's what John wants?"

I shook my head. "I'm sure it isn't." Unsaid but uppermost in my mind was that I wouldn't marry for convenience. I fulfilled an important role in the family and I didn't intend to complicate matters by confusing those lines with a fling that might not work out. I would never again set myself up for failure.

I stood to leave. "I'm heading into town. Is there anything I can pick up for you?"

Abbie still sat, looking unsettled. "No, thanks."

"I'll tell John you invited them over."

She sighed. "Okay."

"Bridge at Winnie's on Thursday, right? I'll pick you up. Eleven o'clock."

"Okay."

That afternoon I called a bridge friend who had recently been widowed and invited her to a movie and dinner afterward on Sunday. She accepted the invitation, expressing her gratitude.

That evening as we finished dinner, I mentioned to John, "You and the kids have been invited to Petersons for Sunday dinner."

John looked surprised. "Just us? Aren't you going?"

"No, just you guys. I have other plans. Delores Olson and I are going to a movie and dinner."

John raised his eyebrows, but much to my great relief, Leslie said, "Maureen, tonight will you help me make that nutrition poster for school?"

"Sure, honey. Let's get these dishes cleared up and we'll do it at the kitchen table."

It certainly wasn't that I had never thought of perhaps marrying John, but I always dismissed the idea. Barbara Cahill had been a rancher's daughter and had much more in common with John than I ever would. From the many pictures I saw, she had been a beautiful woman. I very much doubted if he would consider me his type. I did know, and he often said, how much he appreciated all I did. I would be content with that.

* * *

The Cahills were a hearty, healthy bunch, but we put in a difficult month with the flu. Leslie originally brought it home, exposed at school. She was miserable with the usual vomiting, diarrhea and subsequent weakness.

As hard as I tried to keep everything sanitized, I came down with it next. By this time Leslie was well and back in school, but I was totally out of commission. John and the kids managed the meals, and brought me toast and tea once I could tolerate it.

Unrelenting, the flu then struck John. He was outraged. Exasperated with his insistence of carrying on despite having vomited, I said, "John, the flu isn't going to go away because you refuse to acknowledge it. You obviously have a temperature. Go to bed!"

"I don't have time for this shit!"

"Who does? Take care of yourself and you'll get over it sooner."

He glared at me and I glared right back. He stormed off to bed.

Wade had been sitting at the kitchen table, finishing his lunch. I looked at him and said under my breath, "It's been nice knowing you."

He scoffed and rolled his eyes. "Maureen, Dad would fire *me* before he'd fire you."

Pleasure wrapped around me. I hadn't doubted my place, but I appreciated Wade's recognition of my worth. I smiled at him. "Oh, I dunno...."

When the flu attacked Wade, he turned sullen, but he had the easiest time of it.

* * *

Leslie seemed to change to an adolescent almost overnight. Although we were all expecting it, I missed the sweet little girl she had been. We still got along, but she no longer craved my company. Janelle and other friends from school seemed far more important.

In the fourth and fifth grades, she and John often had gone to Saturday night movies together, just the two of them. She had finally outgrown the little kid animated movies and John could tolerate G-rated movies made for family viewing. They occasionally asked me to join them, but I declined, not wanting to interfere with their time together. Later, Leslie wanted to go to the movies with friends, and John and the other parents dropped them off and picked them up afterwards. I occasionally filled that role, too. I thought at times John looked wistful, probably missing his little girl.

When Leslie turned thirteen, John gave her a horse for her birthday, a four-year old registered Appaloosa she named Polly. They had shopped over a period of weeks and finally settled on this one. I thought the mare was an unusual looking horse, dark brown with a freckled nose, and a white and brown patch over her rump that looked like a blanket. Polly was beautiful in Leslie's eyes and the girl doted on her horse, talking to her in low whispers while grooming her. The horse's ears swiveled to Leslie's voice, appearing to listen.

Now Leslie's world consisted of riding Polly, her music, school, and her friends, mostly Janelle, and, of course, her family. She maintained good grades, but often complained about her teachers. John always listened to her complaints, but rarely commented except to say something like, "I guess it's just something you'll have to put up with." I'd never known him to go to school to straighten out a problem.

After Leslie's second year of middle school, I asked her if she would like to redecorate her room. "You have a lovely room, but maybe now you'd like to have more of a teenage girl's room.

Her eyes sparkled. "Yes! I'd love to do that."

I suggested to John that Leslie should have a new bed, and that it should either be a double bed, or twin beds for when she had overnight guests. Leslie opted for a double bed. Leslie and I painted her walls and ceiling a soft yellow. We had the hardwood floor refinished and I gave her a gift of a pretty area rug. With John's permission, she and I shopped together for new curtains and a matching bedspread, and new, colorful sheets. She was thrilled with the transition. After that, she seemed to take pride in her room and kept it tidy.

That next Christmas John and Wade gave her a rich mahogany desk and chair. I think she felt very grown up sitting at her lovely desk in a room decorated for a young woman.

The following summer I asked Wade if he'd like to spiff up his room. "Naw. It's fine like it is." But I did order extra-long twin beds–the one he had was now too short for his tall frame.

In the eighth grade, Leslie started her menstrual periods. I had been expecting it, had intended to discuss it with her. As it happened, she brought it up.

"Maureen, I think I've started my period."

"I wondered when you would. Do you have any questions? Do you know what to do?"

She sighed. "We talked about it at school. A couple of my friends already started. What a drag."

I nodded. "It is, but almost every girl and woman goes through it."

She looked at me with sorrowful eyes.

"We can do a couple of things to make it easier."

"Like what?"

"We'll always have supplies on hand. We can fix up a drawer for you in your bathroom for that. You might want to take a small supply for your school locker, in case you start there. Mark on the calendar when you start, so you can figure out when your next period will be. Being unprepared makes it even worse."

Leslie took a pen from the basket under the calendar. "What should I write? Maybe a big red period." She giggled.

I laughed, too. "That's a little obvious. How about just an "L," something we'll both recognize. Do you have cramps?"

She wrote "L" on that day's date. "No, I just feel kind of full. She frowned. "I hope I'll still be able to ride Polly."

"Sure you will. Maybe on the first or second day you might not want to, but it's okay to ride, do pretty much everything you always do."

"Okay, good."

"Sometimes you might have cramps. A few days before it starts, you may feel cranky or tired. Check the calendar then to see if your period is about to start. It helps to know there's a reason you're feeling down."

She plopped down on a kitchen chair. "It's not fair. How come girls have to have periods and boys don't?"

I nodded. "It doesn't seem fair, does it? But I guess boys have their own problems."

"Like what?"

I shook my head. "I think they worry about proving themselves, about having feelings of insecurity, that sort of thing."

"I'd trade them any day."

I laughed.

One evening after Leslie left the dinner table in a snit, Wade sadly looked at his father. "I guess we're getting into *those* years."

John nodded. "'fraid so."

"I've been dreading it."

John nodded. "Me too. Let's be careful. Not take much shit, but keep in mind she's pretty sensitive, like her mother."

Wade looked surprised, as though he hadn't expected that from his dad. "Right."

I chimed in. "Her periods have started."

John looked surprised. "Already?"

"Right on time," I said. " She's marked it on the calendar. See?"

John nodded thoughtfully. "That doesn't give her license to talk back or have temper tantrums. But now we'll know what's wrong with her, at least."

Surprised, Wade said, "Did Mom do those things?"

"Oh yeah. I just learned to stay clear."

"What would she do?"

"Oh, she'd get her feelings hurt, was quick to cry."

"I never noticed that."

John looked at Wade with fondness. "Kids usually don't notice that kind of stuff."

From time to time both John and Wade checked the calendar. Once Wade made a point of looking at the calendar and muttered, "Well, no wonder."

I couldn't help but laugh to myself. I appreciated that they were aware of Leslie's special needs. She was a lucky girl to have such a thoughtful family.

Later that year, in the spring, Mrs. Gaylord, Leslie's piano teacher, called asking for John. "I'm sorry," I said, "he's not at the house right now."

After polite greetings, Mrs. Gaylord asked if Leslie had mentioned that her piano teacher wanted to talk to Mr. Cahill.

"No. I haven't heard anything about that, but she might have mentioned it to him."

"I don't think so."

"Really? Why would you say that?" We had spoken over the years and had a friendly relationship. After all, I had been the one to call her to arrange Leslie's piano lessons a few years earlier.

"I've actually mentioned it a number of times to Leslie, but nothing's come of it. The thing is, Maureen, I've taken Leslie about as far as I can." She chuckled. "She's outgrown me."

"Oh! I know she loves her lessons and speaks so highly of you. She's thirteen, so she's been with you five years. What will she do now?"

Mary E. Trimble

"That's what I want to talk to her father about. I have a suggestion, a teacher who might take her. I've already spoken to him, Mr. Shaffer."

"Okay. Let me see what I can do."

That afternoon Leslie practiced her piano right after school, as usual. As she put away her music books, I said, "Leslie, you really play well."

She beamed.

"Mrs. Gaylord called." Leslie looked wary. I continued, "She'd like to talk to your dad."

"I know. I want to stay with Mrs. Gaylord, have her teach me."

"She feels you'd get so much more with an advanced teacher."

"But I just want to stay with her."

"Leslie, give it a chance. Do you know Mr. Shaffer?"

"No. I guess he's a music teacher at the high school."

"Honey, why don't you have your dad call her? I'm sure if you really want to, you can stay with Mrs. Gaylord."

Leslie sighed. "I might as well. She'll just keep bugging me."

That night at dinner Leslie told her dad that Mrs. Gaylord wanted to talk to him.

"How come? What about?"

Leslie shrugged.

The next Wednesday, John came in early, took his shower, and left to pick up Leslie from her music lesson. "We'll be a little late. Mrs. Gaylord wants to see me."

Later, while Leslie studied in her room, John told Wade and me that he had gone "to a little recital, just for me. You know, Leslie's really good. I was impressed.

"Mrs. Gaylord thinks she should move on to a more advanced teacher. I think so, too, but on the way home Les was in tears. She really wants to stay with Mrs. Gaylord."

John shook his head. "I've always wanted this to be Leslie's deal. I'm not sure what to do. Mrs. Gaylord gave me this Mr. Shaffer's phone number, but—"

We heard Leslie coming down the stairs. We stopped talking, each taking up our reading.

"Dad," Leslie said, "I guess we can call Mr. Schaffer. I've decided to try him, but if I don't like him, I want to go back to Mrs. Gaylord."

"That sounds reasonable, Les. Do you want me to call him, or do you want to?"

"I will."

John silently handed her the note on which Mrs. Gaylord had written Mr. Shaffer's number.

Leslie went into the office to make the call. She came back to the living room, looking very serious.

John looked up from his paper. "How'd it go?"

"Okay, I guess. He wants to see both of us next Wednesday. He just had a student quit, a senior, so I could still go right after school on Wednesdays, fill that slot. Did you know he lives about two blocks away from my school?"

"That's handy."

"Dad, is this what you want me to do?"

"Your music is your deal, Leslie. It always has been. I want you to do what you think is best."

"Mr. Schaffer costs more."

"That's okay."

"I don't think he's going to be as much fun."

"You won't know until you try it."

"It's going to be harder."

"Probably. But more challenging. I'm sure you'll learn more, get even better."

"But I *like* Mrs. Gaylord!" She plopped down on the couch next to her dad.

"You'll probably like Mr. Shaffer, too, honey."

"But if I don't I can go back to Mrs. Gaylord, right?"

"Sure."

There was never any more talk about Leslie returning to Mrs. Gaylord. Leslie and her dad met Mr. Shaffer at his home studio the next Wednesday. John apparently made it clear to the music teacher Leslie was in charge of her music, and the agreement was that as long as she practiced, he would continue to support it. He would not put himself in a position to nag her to practice. "It's her deal."

Leslie thrived. She was given new music, new ideas, and she gained new confidence. "Mr. Shaffer has actually turned down students, Maureen. He won't mess around with kids who won't practice. He even said he agrees with Dad. It's up to me!"

One Saturday afternoon Leslie and I were in town and happened to pass by Mrs. Gaylord's house.

"Maureen, can we stop and say hello?"

"Sure, let's." I parked the car and we went to Mrs. Gaylord's door. We had a lovely, though brief, visit. "Mrs. Gaylord," Leslie said, "I loved taking lessons from you and hated to leave. But I like Mr. Shaffer, and it's okay now. Thank you for all you did for me."

"I knew you'd like him, Leslie. And I knew he'd like *you.*"

As we left, Mrs. Gaylord gave my arm a friendly squeeze. "Thank you," she whispered.

Maureen

* * *

That late spring on a Saturday morning at break-fast, Leslie, fourteen, announced that she and Janelle were going to ride horseback in the foothills. Although she had a lot of freedom concerning where she rode, John always wanted to know her destination. Unspoken was the fact that John, Wade or sometimes Randy often rode in that direction to make sure she was safe.

"No," John said, "there'll still be ice on the trails. Wait for summer, at least until June, before going there."

Indignant, Leslie retorted, "Dad! I can handle it." She turned to me. "Maureen, we're gonna take a–"

"Leslie!" John's stony face and voice made me cringe. "Did you hear me? I said no, you're not going there this time of year."

"But Janelle and I have already made plans! We're taking our lunch and—"

"Listen to me! You are NOT going to the foothills this time of year. Is that clear?"

Leslie's face turned red. My face heated too. Oh, boy. I wanted to rush out of the room.

"Is that understood?"

No answer.

John stood, his chair scraping the floor behind him.

Leslie glared at her father. Wade stopped eating and stared at them.

"Answer me!"

She swallowed. "Yes, I understand."

John continued glaring at his daughter, obviously not satisfied.

Wade took the last couple of bites of scrambled egg and stood. "You want me to ride fence at the north pasture?"

The uncomfortable spell was broken. John nodded. "Better take the fence stretcher, everything you need. I know it needs fixing."

After the men left the house, Leslie began packing a lunch.

I felt duty-bound to say, "Leslie, your dad—"

"I know, Maureen," she snapped.

Later, at lunch, Wade said to his dad, "I just noticed that Leslie took Ginger today. Polly's out in the coral. Did you know that?"

John put down his sandwich. "No."

The two stared at each other. John pushed back his chair and started to stand. Wade put his hand out. "I'll go, Dad." He left the table, grabbing his sandwich to eat on the way.

Ginger had been Barbara Cahill's horse. She was quite old now, not up to working with cattle, but still used for riding.

Seeing John's and Wade's alarm, I felt a shock of worry.

John abruptly rose, went into his office and came out carrying a rifle. Just as Wade reached the back door, John handed him the gun. Without a word Wade took it.

With dread, I watched as Wade rode out, rifle in its leather saddle scabbard.

Actually, I was surprised that John didn't go. Maybe he couldn't force himself to face what might have happened, simply couldn't go through it again. Of course, he had total confidence in Wade.

John might as well have gone. He spent the whole time pacing the floor. Once he came into the kitchen and watched me stir a tapioca pudding as it came to a boil.

"I wished to hell I'd gone."

"Wade can handle it. One of you needs to be here."
He abruptly turned and strode into his office.

Wade and Leslie returned almost three hours later, both on Wade's horse. Leslie slid off the horse's rump and ran into the house, rushing by me in tears.

I followed John out the door.

"What happened?" John asked.

Wade handed his father the rifle. "They went to the foothills. I found two scared kids and an almost-dead horse. I had to shoot Ginger, Dad."

John nodded. He looked at Wade, waiting for the rest of the story.

Wade dismounted and continued. "Leslie was in the lead, Ginger slipped, couldn't get her footing, and slipped backwards into a deep gully. Leslie jumped off about halfway down. She's okay, scratched up some.

When it happened, Janelle stopped where she was on the trail and tied her horse to a branch. She tried to help Les. Leslie had gone to the bottom and wouldn't leave Ginger. When I came along, I met Janelle on the trail. She was on her way to get help.

"So Janelle and I went back to where Leslie was. I told Janelle to stay on the trail, and I climbed, mostly slid, down to Les. When she saw me coming, she...." Wade shook his head.

"What, Wade?"

He swallowed. "She begged me to help Ginger. The mare's leg was obviously broken, but I think it was more than that. She was done, Dad."

John nodded.

Tears came to Wade's eyes. He tried to blink them back. Tears of sympathy filled my eyes. I ached for everyone, for John's loss, for Wade having to put down the horse, for Leslie's disobedience and the guilt she must have.

"Wade, you did what you had to do." John rested his hand on Wade's arm.

"I had to drag Leslie off her, but she went back. I finally had to get rough with her and told her I'd tie her to a tree if I had to, but I had to end Ginger's suffering."

Wade roughly brushed his tears with the back of his hand. "When I shot the horse, I thought Leslie was going to pass out. I just held her for a few minutes then said we had to get home, that you were worried. She came without a struggle. Well, we had a struggle climbing out of that gully...."

John shook his head. "She must have known she might have trouble. She took Ginger rather than Polly."

Wade nodded. "She thought Ginger would be more sure-footed, that Polly might panic if she slipped. We'll have to go back for Les's saddle."

John turned to me. "Tell Leslie I want to see her."

I climbed the stairs to Leslie's room, my heart full of dread. I couldn't imagine how she must feel. I knocked on the door.

Her voice was almost a whisper. "Come in."

"Leslie, your dad wants to see you." I stepped into the room.

She flew into my arms. "Oh, Maureen, I killed my mother's horse!"

I felt the dampness of her tears on my cheek, felt the moisture of the mud still on her clothes seep into mine.

"Maureen, Ginger screamed when we slipped down that gully. It was so awful. I can still hear it." She shuddered.

"Oh, honey, that must have been terrible."

I felt Leslie gather herself, work up the courage to talk to her dad, to face whatever it was that she had coming. She stood back. "Should I wash up?"

"No, I think he wants to see you now."

Leslie seemed to know she would see him in his office. She slowly descended the stairs and went to the office door, hesitated and entered.

Without closing the door, she said, "Dad, I'm sorry! I killed Ginger." She sobbed. "I'm so sorry!"

"I know, Leslie."

I softly closed the office door.

Leslie came out some time later, climbed the stairs to her room, and I soon heard the shower running.

Later, she strode into the kitchen with a determined air about her. "Where's Wade?"

"I don't know, probably in the barn." I hadn't seen him since they'd returned. I did know and had seen for myself, that when Wade was upset, he'd keep to himself, often working with leather, maybe cleaning and oiling his saddle.

She left the house, heading toward the barn.

In a few moments I saw them slowly walking toward the house, chatting. Wade had his hand on her shoulder, and she had her hands in her front pockets, nodding at what her brother said.

That night at dinner, Leslie's eyes were swollen, but she seemed at peace. I felt myself relaxing for the first time all day.

After dinner as I had my last cup of coffee for the day and everyone else was leaving the table, John pointed to Leslie's denim shirt, clean after she took her shower. Blood had stained the sleeve at the elbow. "Let's take a look at your arm."

They went into the bathroom to get the first aid supplies, leaving the door open. Leslie slipped her arm out of the sleeve.

"Does it hurt?" her dad asked.

"Not so much now, but it sure stung when I showered."

"There's still dirt in it, Les." He ran water into the sink. "It won't heal as long as it's dirty."

As he treated the wound, I heard Leslie sniffing.

"Am I hurting you?"

"Not really." A sob chocked her voice. "I feel so awful about what I did," she wailed.

I heard his voice, strong and steady. "Leslie, we all have regrets. What you have to do is learn from it, forgive yourself, and move on."

"Can *you* forgive me?"

"Of course I forgive you. But I want you to trust me to know what's safe and what isn't, and to listen to me."

"I will, Dad."

My admiration for John grew. He had to be upset about his wife's horse dying such a terrible death. I marveled at his inner strength, of his ability to help Leslie through the tragedy. I felt lucky to know him, to be apart of this family. Well, not really a part of it, but near them at least.

I learned how different a ranching family is compared to a family living in a city. Most city kids leave home by the time they're eighteen or so. Roger's two oldest kids and Sue's oldest daughter had already moved, either to attend college or to live in an apartment near where they worked. City offspring begin lives and occupations separate from their families. Even if kids follow their parents' profession, they usually live on their own.

On a ranch, if kids chose to carry on the family tradition, their livelihood is right there. Their lives are entwined with their work; there is no separation. Wade was old enough to live on his own, but theirs wasn't a nine to five job, it was around the clock, seven days a week. It wouldn't make sense for Wade to live separately, to try to cook and manage alone. The men often worked before breakfast, getting things ready for the day. Then, last thing at night one of them checked the horses in the barn or coral, and checked the calving shed if any stock was in there. And they always had one ear cocked to listen for the dog's warning barks.

John's grandfather founded the Cahill ranch, seeking a milder climate than the extremes of eastern Montana. Years later, his son, John's father, ran the ranch, buying neighboring property to expand it. John was the third generation Cahill stockman, and he had also expanded the ranch, making it one of the largest cattle ranches in Washington. I gave John a lot of credit, insisting that Wade go to college to make sure this is what he wanted to do. Since I'd lived here, I knew of strife in families when the next generation didn't want to continue ranching. But I doubt Wade ever considered doing anything else. It was obviously his vocation.

* * *

"Dad," Wade said as they stood in the laundry room pulling on their boots. "Charlie's getting old. He's slowing down and I'm afraid he's going to get kicked."

John nodded. "I know. Bergs have a new litter of blue heelers. He called me the other night and said they're ten weeks old, almost ready. Let's go out this afternoon and look at 'em."

"Have you already seen them?"

"I saw the pups at six weeks. A couple of them look promising."

"Yeah, let's go today."

"Wade, this one is going to be your dog. The choice will be yours."

Wade straightened and looked at his dad with wonder. "My dog?"

"Yep. This one is yours."

Wade was a man now, twenty-five years old, tall and muscular. But at that moment he had the expression of an eight-year-old with a grin spread across his face. It warmed my heart. Wade drew a good wage and could have bought the dog himself, but getting another dog was his dad's decision. Obviously, the fact that his father had given him the responsibility of a cattle dog meant the world to Wade.

Blue heelers, or Australian Cattle Dogs, I'd learned, are invaluable to a rancher and can make their lives so much easier. With good training, they can do the work of another person. A pup costs several hundred dollars, so it's a real investment.

Leslie heard the tail end of the conversation. "Can I go see the puppies?"

John shook his head. "No, Les, just Wade and I'll go this time."

John followed Wade out the door.

Leslie turned to me, indignant. "They think I'd want to pick out the cutest."

I laughed. "That's probably true. Wouldn't you?"

She nodded, glum. "I guess."

"That big yellow barn cat is about to have a litter of kittens. When they're weaned, why don't you claim one for your own, bring it into the house. Would your dad let you do that?"

"I think so. But it would probably just go back out to the barn with the others. They always do. Those cats are almost wild."

Leslie was right. She did claim a cute kitten, but as soon as it was old enough it joined its family in the barn. Apparently chasing barn mice is more fun that eating cat food out of a bowl.

When the pup reached twelve weeks, they brought her home. Wade named her Duchess, plus a couple of names tacked on for her purebred registration—VanCamp Valentine—after her mother and father. But they always called her Dutch.

I suppose I've never seen a puppy who wasn't cute, but Dutch was truly darling. Her little face was perfectly symmetrical with white, black and grey markings. Both eyes had black patches and beween them and down her little face was a pure white strip that fanned out from her nose. Her body was several shades of gray with a narrow white stripe across her chest. Her tail ended with a white spot. She was still roly-poly and had tiny razor-sharp teeth. Wade let Leslie bring her to the house once. She sniffed my shoes and immediately made her way under the kitchen table to pee. "Oh, no!" Still, I thought she was darling. I loved holding her, knowing I probably wouldn't have another opportunity. Wade took training very seriously.

Although Wade worked tirelessly with her, much of Dutch's training was Charlie's job. The older dog would take no nonsense when they were working. I watched them together sometimes and found it amazing that Charlie realized that training was his responsibility. They gradually increased her training time and Dutch thrived.

The dogs slept together and at that time Charlie tolerated the pup's playfulness, sometimes softly growling when Dutch bit his ears. She grew to be a well-trained dog, one that could be relied on. Occasionally Dutch let Leslie pet her, but if there was work to be done, she was off to do her job. The dog was constantly at Wade's heels, or doing his bidding. At the end of the day, when the dogs were fed their dinner, she knew to hang around the barn.

Charlie would live another three years, but the last year he mostly just stayed around the barn. I went out there occasionally, kept him company and gave him treats. It's always sad losing a beloved pet and the family grieved when he passed on. John and Wade buried him along the edge of the orchard. I shed tears right along with the rest of them.

Maureen

* * *

Occasionally, when the mountain passes were clear of snow, normally during the summer, I took a few days off to visit my siblings, Roger and Sue, in Seattle. John encouraged me to do this and even complained that I didn't take enough time off. "We can handle things for a few days, Maureen. You need to take time for yourself." I usually went to the Seattle area three or four times a year, but only for two or three days each time.

I did enjoy visiting my family. Two of Roger's oldest of four kids were now on their own, so I had the privacy of a spare bedroom. On one visit, Roger mentioned that our sister Diane wanted to stop by and visit with me.

"How did she know I was here?"

"She called, just to say hi. They're visiting David's folks, and I told her you were here."

"Roger, you know I don't want to see her. This is your home and if you want to have her over, you have every right to do that. I'll just go someplace, visit someone, while she's here."

"Maureen," he said, exasperated, "you can't keep doing this. It's not right."

"Don't tell me about right."

He threw up his hands and left the room.

I followed him. "When is she coming?"

"I don't know. In a day or so."

Luckily, when she did come, I happened to see her car pull up. As Diane entered the front door, I quietly slipped out the back door. A friend of the family lived about a block away, and I made a surprise visit to her. She never knew why I just happened by. I stayed a couple of hours and when I returned to Roger's, Diane was gone.

My brother glared at me when I returned. "You're a Christian, Maureen. Christians forgive."

"Some things aren't forgivable."

He didn't say another word about it. We carried on as though it never happened. Roger's wife Ellen understood the situation and never commented. I liked Ellen and had always thought Roger's family was the epitome of ideal family life. I suppose that's what bothered him. My situation with Diane was far from ideal. I don't like strife either and I knew my relationship with Diane was upsetting to the family, which I regretted. But the blame fell to Diane.

The next visit I spent a few days with my sister Sue. We went to the movies like old times, sat and gossiped for hours. My brother was really no fun in that regard. He wouldn't gossip. Sue occasionally brought up Diane's name, but never with the idea of our getting together.

"Diane and David aren't doing that well," Sue said. "I think he gets tired of her always wanting more. She's never satisfied. She's gotten them into quite a lot of debt, I think. I won't be surprised if they get a divorce."

"I wonder where she'll live?"

"She'll probably come back to Seattle. It doesn't sound like she's ever warmed up to the people in Cheyenne."

I shrugged. "They probably don't have anything she wants."

* * *

Over the years, Roger and Sue's families occasionally visited the ranch. John was always cordial, offering to sleep in Wade's room so they could use his bedroom. Mostly when they came they didn't spend the night, but had a couple of meals with us and stayed at Chewack's only hotel.

Once Roger planned the trip during spring roundup, something he'd read about but had never seen. When I mentioned it to John, I could tell he wasn't wild about the timing. "We're pretty busy then, Maureen."

"I know. They won't be staying at the house, he made that clear. Ellen can help me in the kitchen with the noon meal. They'll only be here for one day. Roger just wants to see it. He'd love it if you could put him to work."

John nodded vaguely.

Roger and Ellen, without their kids, came on the second day of roundup. Roger immediately went out, shook John's hand, and chatted for a minute, until John's attention was taken with roundup business. We watched as John assigned Roger a spot by a chute and ordered one of the guys to give him a pole to prod the cattle when they balked.

"That's nice of John to give Roger a job," Ellen said. "I'm sure he's in heaven." We watched and laughed as Roger played the part of a real cowboy.

As he had done with Wade, John allowed Leslie to miss a school day or two during spring roundup. In her first year of high school, she was such a conscientious student, she only took one day off that year. Because John had insisted she take honors classes–those designed for more capable students–she had a lot of homework that kept her even busier week nights and on the weekends. "I can't miss more than one day of orchestra Dad, we're getting ready for the spring concert."

"That's fine, Les. We can use your help, but you do what you need to do for school."

The following Saturday at breakfast—the men had already worked a couple of hours—Wade turned to Leslie. "You plan on helping us today?" He had an edge to his voice that we all noticed.

Leslie glared at her brother. "What's it to you?"

Wade took the bait. "It's time you did a little something around here. Everyone else is—"

"Okay, you guys, knock it off," John interrupted.

"Well Wade seems to think—"

"Okay, Les, leave it," her dad said. "We have a couple of bum calves that need to be hand fed. I'd like you to take over that job."

Leslie still glared at her brother.

John remained calm. "Les?"

"Okay. I can do it on the weekends but I won't have time during the week."

"That'll be fine."

Leslie finished her breakfast and left the table to get ready to help outside.

"Dad," Wade fumed, "why can't she get up early during the week to feed those calves, and then do it after school? She's not pulling—"

"Wade, stop. I don't know why you can't under-stand that Leslie's work is different than ours. Right now her work is school and her music. When she can, I'd like her to help, but she's busy enough."

"Busy! She doesn't do a damn thing!"

"She does, Wade. She's a good student, gets good grades. Her music is a huge part of her life and she puts a hundred-ten percent into it. I won't ask more of her."

"What does that have—"

"Wade! You're a rancher, I'm a rancher. She isn't. Her work is different than ours. That's not wrong, it's just different."

Wade took a couple of deep breaths and shook his head.

John noticed, but said nothing.

The two calves that needed hand-feeding had been abandoned by their mothers. One, a little bull, was the calf of a first-time heifer who wouldn't accept her baby. They'd try again with her next year and if she again abandoned her calf, she'd be sold for beef. The other was a twin who's mother apparently couldn't handle two babies. The men had started the hand-feeding, so by now the little calves had pretty much caught on.

Leslie walked through the kitchen in her oldest clothes. "I'm going out to feed those calves, Dad." She avoided looking at her brother.

"Fine, Les. The bald-face bull is the hardest. Make him wait while you feed the other one. He'll cooperate more if he thinks he's losing out."

"Okay."

After I finished the breakfast dishes, I went to the calving shed to watch Leslie. As I approached, I could hear her talking to the little calf. "Come on, now, don't you want your breakfast? There! Oops. Let's try again."

I entered the shed. Leslie was a mess with slobber on her shoulder, mud, or maybe worse, on her jeans. "I can see why you wear your old clothes for this job."

"Yeah, they're messy at first. But it won't take long now." The bottle she held looked like a regular baby bottle, but much larger, about two quarts, and had a huge reddish-brown nipple.

"Maureen, Wade makes me so mad. I'm really busy during the school week. He just doesn't understand."

"No, you're right, he doesn't understand. Ranching is his whole life. Although he wasn't a bad student, he didn't work nearly as hard as you do. And he was never involved in music, which takes so much of your time. Your dad understands, Leslie."

"Oh, no! Now look what you've done!" The calf had pulled the nipple out of the bottle and the formula spilled all over Leslie's leg. She sighed, pushed the calf aside and stomped into the equipment room to prepare a partial bottle. "I love calves, but I don't like this job."

"I can see why. What a mess!"

With a newly prepared partial bottle, Leslie wrestled the stubborn little calf into place and began again. "Okay, you squirt, let's do this." She grasped the bottle at the top, gripping the nipple so tight her knuckles turned white.

That morning all of them, about eight people, worked feverishly, hoping to finish everything by the end of Sunday. I heard Wade call out to Leslie. "Les, get Dutch out of the tack room and bring her out here." Still a pup, Wade locked her up during roundup when so many cattle were crowded together and there was a greater risk of her getting kicked or stepped on. "Give all the dogs water. Keep your eye on Dutch–don't let her get underfoot."

Leslie waved that she'd heard. She carried out the pup, trying to cuddle him as she carried the squirming little thing to the trough. She rinsed out an oval galvanized tub, filled it with water, and called the other stock dogs who had come with their people to help. She held Dutch up to the tub so she could drink, too.

I took the opportunity to call out, "Lunch is ready when you are." They put their work on hold while they came into the house to eat and rest. I would have served the meal on the picnic table, but it was in the direct sun. I thought it would be cooler and more restful inside.

I heard Wade say to Leslie, "Thanks, Les. The dogs really needed that drink. I forgot to fill that tub for them. Did you put Dutch back inside?"

"Yep. She cried, but that's better than getting stomped on."

Wade nodded. Their tiff seemed to be over.

*A*s John's mother's health failed, they visited her more frequently. I often sent with them small, frozen containers of casseroles, soup or stew that I thought she would enjoy. She also had attentive friends who lived in the retirement village, some of whom still drove. One day a friend picked Eleanor up to shop for groceries and later dropped her off with her few purchases. She apparently went into her living room, sat on a chair, and died. The next day, Sunday, John and Leslie stopped by to visit, and they found her.

Leslie talked about it later. "Maureen, I don't think she suffered at all. Her shopping bag and purse were on the floor next to her chair. I think it was really quick. Dad talked to her friend who had dropped her off. She felt bad about not going in with her, that maybe she could have helped her. But Dad said Grandma died like she wanted to—quick and easy." Tears filled Leslie's eyes. "Dad cried though. Not out loud, but he had tears in his eyes."

I nodded. "Still, it's better than suffering through a long agonizing death. My mother had several strokes before she died and that was really hard on her and everyone else. My dad died in his sleep a couple of years later, and that was so much easier. For everyone."

For the next few days John and the kids, subdued and saddened, spent time remembering Eleanor. John talked about how hard she'd worked on the ranch by his dad's side. Wade and Leslie remembered stories she'd told them about the old days. From what I gathered, Eleanor hadn't been a lot of fun, but she was a dedicated mother and grandmother. John again spent time in his room grieving, but a death of an aging parent is an expected loss and, in my opinion, the family had a healthy attitude about Eleanor's passing.

Through the years Eleanor and I had become a little closer, but never what I would call friends. She seemed to recognize and appreciate my contribution to the family.

After the funeral, the four of us cleaned out her small bungalow and gave away some of her things to friends. John kept a few picture albums, a nice chest of drawers from her bedroom, and a necklace he had given her. We gave everything else to the local thrift shop.

That winter John added an office on to the house. I thought the floor plan ideal. The new office could be approached from the kitchen or from outside. What had been the office was now a guest room, the spare room they lost when I came on the scene. John bought a new king-size bed for himself and put his old bed in the guest room, along with what had been his mother's chest of drawers.

John seemed pleased with his new, spacious office. Although we were welcome to go in there, it was his domain. After I thought about it, I realized that building a new office was an indication that he was finally becoming comfortable with himself and moving on. At least that was my interpretation.

John gradually turned more of the ranch management over to Wade. John still did the accounting, ordered supplies, dealt with the veterinarian, ran errands in town, and rode horseback when necessary to get a job done. He had been having trouble with his knees, his left knee in particular, the knee that was most affected when he mounted a horse. His doctor had told him to curtail riding, or mount from a stool, which he refused to do.

To me, he still seemed strong and vigorous. Sometimes I indulged myself and wondered what it would be like to be married to John. Those thoughts usually made me sad though and I forced myself to stop thinking about it. I was here with this family to take care of Leslie and to keep their home running smoothly. *That* I could do.

I was more physically active now that I could ride more frequently and work outside in the garden. John asked, "Maureen, are you losing weight?" He sat at the kitchen table while I stood at the counter making sandwiches for lunch.

A thrill made its way down my spine. "Oh, a little, I suppose. I'm more active outside, and am trying to watch my diet."

"I think you're fine like you are." I glanced his way. He looked embarrassed, opened his mouth to say something more, but thought better of it. He frowned.

"I'm fine John." Actually, I was more than fine, but couldn't think how to express my feelings to him. I had an inner contentment. Sometimes a longing to be more a part of things cropped up, but I always tried to dismiss the ache, to shove it aside. This was my life and I was determined to enjoy the now and not relive the past.

Maureen

* * *

A few months before Leslie turned sixteen, John asked Wade to teach her to drive. She would take driver's education as well, but he wanted her to have road experience before taking the class.

Wade looked surprised. "Why don't you do it, Dad? You're a good teacher; you taught me."

"There wasn't much teaching to do. You'd been driving equipment for years before you got your license. Leslie hasn't. You're calmer and more patient. I want you to do it. I'll see that she gets her permit."

"Okay," Wade said. I think he understood that in his father's eyes, Leslie's driving opened up the possibility of danger. John didn't want Leslie to feel his nervousness.

For some time John had allowed Leslie to take his truck down the long driveway, and then back up in reverse, and finally parallel park by a piece of equipment. She eventually managed that very well. I secretly hoped he would never ask me to do that. Backing up was definitely not my strong suit.

What wonderful opportunities the Cahill kids had, growing up on a successful ranch with a father who recognized their potential.

Wade took his job seriously. He even read Leslie's driver's manual. He apparently kept his cool—they always came home in good spirits. "She's doing good, Dad," Wade said when they came home after a driving session. "I know she has to take the classes, but I think she'd be able to get her license right now."

Leslie's smile lit up the room.

About the time Leslie got her driver's license, John bought a nice little dark green SUV. It was intended to be a family car, but it gave Leslie something to drive besides a truck. My car was getting old. John had paid for repairs the last time, saying I drove it more for the family than I did for my personal use. He didn't want Leslie to drive every day to school; he just wasn't ready for that. They compromised and she took the car on Wednesdays so she could get herself to her music lesson and home without one of us having to pick her up.

Leslie was a busy girl. A good student, she had mounds of homework. Sometimes she complained. "I have more homework than most of my friends, more than Janelle, because of those stupid honors classes."

John chuckled. "Those classes aren't stupid, Leslie. They'll help you get into the college of your choice. You're too smart to just take the minimum."

"Well, it would be nice to have some free time, to not always have all this homework. Janelle even has time to watch TV in the evenings!"

I did notice though that Leslie took pride in her school work and showed us papers with good grades on them. Her music was still uppermost in her interests. Rarely did she miss practicing at least an hour. Once in awhile, if she had Friday night plans, she didn't practice, but made up for it over the weekend. She usually helped me set the table, perhaps make a salad, and she cleared the table after dinner, but right after that she headed upstairs to her room to study.

Sometimes her dad called up the stairs to her room: "Okay, Leslie, call it a night and turn in." They had a nighttime ritual. Once Leslie was ready for bed, her dad would climb the stairs and tuck her in. Even as a teenager. When his knees were particularly bad, she'd come downstairs and kiss him on the cheek. "Goodnight, Dad."

"Goodnight, honey. Can you tuck yourself in?"

Maureen

John and Leslie's nighttime ritual always warmed my heart. I thought theirs was one of the nicest father/daughter relationships I'd ever known. John was a tough man. I heard him with the men, working, and giving orders. But with Leslie he was nothing but gentle, though he could be firm. I inwardly sighed. *I'll bet he was a good husband.*

I still maintained my rigid line between business and social. It rarely came up between us anymore. In any event, John only occasionally did anything away from the ranch. Once in awhile he played poker with a group of men, and sometimes Wade joined him. He only went to grange meetings when he thought the meeting might be important, never for the social aspects. He hadn't gone to church, other than for a funeral or two, since I'd been there. Once in awhile a woman called, I think it was someone he knew from the grange. If I answered the phone and he wasn't in, I'd take her name and number, but I don't think he returned the calls.

On one of those occasions the woman called back a couple of days later, indignant, saying that he never returned her calls. I mentioned it to John.

"If she calls again, just tell her you gave me the message. Blame it on me."

She called back when he was home in the evening and I called him to the phone. I was amazed, even stunned, when I overheard him say, "Judy, thank you, but I'm really not interested."

There was a long silence on his end, and I heard him say, "Good-bye."

Once at dinner, Leslie mentioned that Janelle asked her to go to a movie that Friday night. "We're going to see that new Brad Pitt movie, *Legends of the Fall.* I hear it's really good."

127

"It *is* good," I said.

Everyone's head jerked up to look at me. "I saw it Thursday."

Leslie was the first to speak. "You've seen it? Who did you go with?"

"Les," her father sputtered.

"Oh," she said, looking down at her place, her face red.

"That's fine," I said. "Delores Olson and I were going to go, but her daughter came with her baby unexpectedly, so I just went alone."

"Alone?" I'm sure Leslie couldn't imagine going to a movie alone.

"Sure, I do that every once in awhile if there's something I want to see."

After dinner John lingered at the table. Leslie went to her room to do her homework and Wade turned on the TV in the living room to watch the news.

"Maureen," John said, "I would be happy to take you to a movie."

"Thank you, John, but I don't need anyone to take me. I don't mind going alone." I simply could not picture myself asking John to take me to a movie.

He stared at me.

"Have you ever gone to a movie by yourself?" I asked.

"Never."

"Well, people do. I enjoy taking in a movie once in awhile. I normally go to a matinee because it's so much cheaper."

Without another word, he left the table.

* * *

Trouble started toward the end of Leslie's sophomore year. On a sunny Saturday morning, Leslie announced that she and Janelle were going to go horseback riding.

"Before you go, Leslie, I want to talk to you."

"Okay, about what?"

"Let's go into the office; I have something I want to show you."

Before long, I overheard Leslie's voice behind the closed office door. "Dad! I don't want to go there! I want to stay here!"

All I could hear from John was a murmur—he was apparently trying to stay calm. Soon Leslie burst from the office, put on her riding boots and slammed the back door.

John came out grim-faced. "Well, that went well."

I shook my head. "It didn't sound like it."

"I want Leslie to go to Rosemount, a private girls' school in Spokane."

"No wonder it didn't go well."

John's eyes flashed. "Rosemount is one of the finest schools in the country! It's rated very high academically, has an outstanding music program. The percentage of graduates going to college is almost one hundred percent."

"I take it Leslie wasn't impressed?"

He sighed. "No. She wants to stay here, go to Chewack, be with her friends, ride Polly. She can come up with a hundred reasons."

"She'd have to board there. Only come home some weekends."

"Of course."

I looked at him and recognized that stubborn look he could get. He strode into his office and came out with the packet, a large envelope from Rosemount. "This is what I showed Leslie. You can see what a beautiful campus it is."

I took the packet from him. *Stay out of this.*

Secretly, it frightened me. I couldn't imagine life here without Leslie. Would they even still need me? The question made my head spin.

From then on, it was rounds of arguments. Wade and I grew weary of listening to it. When they got into it, we would leave the room. Wade would generally head outside, I'd get busy elsewhere in the house. Still, I could hear them.

"Dad! Why are you doing this to me? Why don't you want me here anymore?"

"Leslie," John kept his voice slow and deliberate, "it isn't that I don't want you here, it's that I want you to have the advantage of a better education than you can get at Chewack."

"I'm doing fine at Chewack. I'm taking the honor classes, just like you wanted, and I'm getting good grades..."

"Honey, I know you're doing well. It's the school."

"What's wrong with the school? I think it's a great school!"

"The percentage of graduates that go to college isn't that good."

"But I *am* going to college."

"Some kids are using drugs."

"I'm not! I won't!"

"Les, I know that. I just don't want you around that sort of thing."

* * *

Toward the end of her sophomore year, a boy from school, Kip, asked Leslie to go to a school dance. She asked and received permission to go. John insisted that Kip come to the house to pick her up. "I don't want any of that honking and you running out business, and I don't want you meeting him somewhere. I want to talk to the boy who's taking out my daughter."

Leslie sighed. "He will, Dad."

When Kip came to pick Leslie up for their first date I answered the front door and invited him in. Kip introduced himself and I was impressed with his politeness. He was a nice looking boy, tall and well-groomed. I called Leslie and stopped at John's office to tell him Kip was here. I left the living room, but from the kitchen I could hear enough of the conversation to know that John was sizing the young man up, and was apparently satisfied.

From the kitchen door I watched as Leslie strode into the living room wearing a lovely spring dress, one we had shopped for together. It was rare for her to wear a dress nowadays and when she entered the living room Kip's mouth actually dropped open. Both Kip and John spontaneously stood.

Leslie looked mildly surprised, but I could see her pleasure by her rosy cheeks.

John and Leslie had already agreed on a midnight curfew. "You'll be home by twelve?" he asked.

"Yes, sir," the young man answered, ushering Leslie out the door. John, satisfied, closed the door.

Leslie's dad didn't really relax all evening. He constantly looked at his watch, picked up a cattlemen's magazine, put it down, turned on the television, turned it off. I finally couldn't stand it anymore and went to my room to read in peace and quiet.

Leslie and Kip arrived home promptly at midnight. From then on John seemed more relaxed when Leslie dated, but never went to bed before she arrived home.

The arguments about Rosemount continued through the remaining school year. Then a dreadful thing happened that, for John, was the final straw. Tracy, a classmate of Leslie's, was raped after a school dance.

"I don't want you exposed to that kind of thing. You attended that dance—it could have happened to you."

"Dad! When I go to a dance I stay with my date. Kip and I went in together and we left together. Tracy was raped after she left the dance, alone. That has nothing to do—"

"Leslie! I'm tired of arguing about this. At Rosemount you'll be safe, you'll have a good education—"

"What about Mr. Schaffer and my music? I won't have that there!"

"Rosemount has an excellent music program; I've told you that."

Leslie stormed out of the room.

Leslie's sophomore year ended. As usual she received excellent grades. She brought her report cards to the dinner table. "See, Dad. I took that full load, two of them honors classes, and I got good grades."

"I'm proud of you Leslie. You work really hard and your efforts are recognized."

Leslie opened her mouth to say something, apparently thought better of it. Maybe she didn't want to ruin the moment with an argument.

After she finished dinner and left the table, Wade said, "You know Dad, Leslie really works hard. It seems to me she's doing great."

John glared at his son. "Don't you get started on me. She's going to Rosemount. That's it!" He strode into his office.

Wade and I stared at each other. Wade shook his head and left the table.

The first two days of her summer vacation, Leslie just had fun. She rode Polly to Janelle's one day. The next day a group of friends met at Lake Lombard and spent the day.

On the third morning Wade joined us at the breakfast table for a cup of coffee. He had been up for hours, but Leslie was just having her breakfast.

"Sis, I need your help today."

She stopped, toast half way to her mouth. "Doing what?"

"We got some signs of pinkeye and need to treat it right away."

"Where's Randy?"

"He and Dad have some other stuff to do. Look, Les, you have time now. I need your help."

"But I was going to practice piano! And then Janelle—"

Wade stood. "Practice tonight. I need you now."

"You're probably just going to yell at me all day."

"Not if you do what you're told."

"Oh, right—"

John stepped out of his office and into the kitchen. "Leslie, Wade's the boss out there. If you follow his orders, give it a hundred-ten percent, he won't yell at you." He glanced at Wade and got a tiny, barely perceptible nod of acknowledgment in return.

Leslie sighed. "Okay."

Wade said, "Wear something old. Gentian violet will make a mess of your clothes."

She nodded.

John stepped into the laundry room, put on his hat, and left.

Wade turned to leave. "I'll get Polly saddled."

Leslie hurriedly finished her breakfast. "Maybe if I help out this summer, work hard, Dad will see that I'm trying to....fit in, and he won't send me away."

It broke my heart. For the life of me, I couldn't think of anything comforting to say. In her mind, Leslie was being sent away. In John's mind he was giving his daughter a wonderful opportunity. The two were on different planets.

* * *

Wade went out most Friday nights. Since the high school prom and then college and afterward, he and Debbie Nelson dated. One Sunday she came for dinner, at my suggestion. She seemed like a nice girl, but, in my view at least, Wade didn't seem terribly in love.

One Saturday morning, we discussed our day's plans. "I'm going to a tea at church," I said. "In fact, I'm on the committee and have to go early to help set up."

John nodded. "Okay, don't worry about lunch; we'll manage. I'm sticking around the house until the vet gets here, hopefully around nine."

"Why, what's wrong?" Leslie asked.

"We've got two heifers limping. I can't figure out why."

We were just leaving the breakfast table when I asked, 'Where's Wade?"

John shrugged. "I guess he hasn't come in yet; must be outside getting—"

Leslie shook her head. "I don't think he's up yet. His door was still closed when I got up. Maybe he had a late night."

Just then we heard Wade clomping down the stairs, but he seemed to have a different gait. It really didn't sound like Wade.

My back was to the door, but when I saw John's face, I knew something was wrong.

John stood. "What in the hell happened to you?"

"I'm okay, Dad."

"You don't look okay! What happened?"

Leslie looked at her brother and gasped. "Wha—" John held up his hand to silence her.

Wade gingerly sat in his chair at the table. He looked terrible. One eye was purple and black and almost swollen shut, his lip split open. He held himself in, like his ribs hurt. Seeing him in this kind of pain, made my stomach hurt.

"I just got in a fight. Don't worry about it."

"A fight! With who?"

"You don't know him. Dirk something. Some wannabe cowboy jerk who was coming on to Debbie."

"Where were you?"

"Jake's."

"Jake's Road House?"

"Yeah. We met up with Darrell and Sally there."

I poured him a cup of coffee.

John went over to Wade's chair. "Turn around here. Let's see that eye."

"It's okay, Dad. Just let me have my coffee."

"Wade, turn around."

Very carefully, Wade turned.

"Your ribs sore, too?"

"Yeah. The asshole kicked me."

John took Wade's bruised right hand in his. "Can you move your fingers okay?"

"Yeah."

"Look up at me." John examined Wade's swollen eye, turned his head from side to side. "You need to see a doctor about this."

"No, I don't. Just let me be."

"Wade, don't argue with me. You're going to the doctor to have that eye looked at. He should look at your ribs, too. Your lip could have used a stitch or two, but it's probably too late for that. Eat your breakfast, get ready to go."

He stood for a moment, thinking. "Leslie, get ready to take your brother to the doctor."

Her eyes widened in surprise.

Wade sighed. "Dad! I can drive myself. How do you think I got home?"

"God only knows! You can hardly move, can barely see."

"Well, I don't need Leslie to drive me to the damn doctor."

John had his "don't give me any crap" look. "I can't do it. I'm waiting for the vet to look at those heifers. Maureen has plans at church. I need Randy here. Leslie will take you."

Wade fumed, but ate part of his breakfast. He tried to sip his coffee but apparently couldn't stand the cup against his lip. He left the table and gingerly climbed the stairs to get ready.

"Leslie," John said when Wade was out of hearing range, "try to go into the examining room with him. Learn what you can about his eye, his ribs. I'm more worried about his eye and how active he should be."

"Okay, Dad. But I can't imagine Wade going along with that."

"Don't ask. Just tag along."

She nodded.

The two of them left, Wade grim and silent, Leslie quiet and gentle, even holding the door open for her brother.

John shook his head as he watched them climb into the SUV. "I've never seen him so banged up. That eye looks terrible."

As Leslie smoothly drove off I said, "I'd love to be a fly on that windshield."

John nodded. "I wonder what the other guy looks like."

I found the tea at church interminable. When I got home, Wade and Leslie had long since returned from seeing the doctor. She had just finished practicing her piano and was heading out the door. "I'm going to Janelle's, Maureen. Dad said I could take the car."

"Before you go—how did it go at the doctor's? Where's Wade?"

She sat at the kitchen table. "Once he calmed down, Wade told me about it. It happened around midnight. They had just finished the last dance of the set and Wade told Debbie he was beat and needed to get home. They'd been there about three hours, anyway. She said she wasn't ready to go. I guess that guy Dirk had come on to her and she was sort of encouraging him. You know Wade: if he takes a girl out, he expects to take her home. But Debbie said she was staying and sat down at Dirk's table. Wade wasn't sure what to do, so he went over to the table and said, something like, 'Come on, Deb, let's go.'

"Dirk shot out of his chair and punched Wade. That's the cut lip. I guess he said something like, 'Looks like she wants to stay with me.' Wade told him he didn't want to fight, but he had brought Debbie and he intended to take her home. And the guy hit him again. That's the eye. Wade stumbled on a chair and fell to the floor. That's when that jerk kicked him. The guy must not be very bright. Wade got to his feet and creamed him with one punch, knocked him out. I guess when Wade hit him, he lifted the guy off the floor a couple of inches and he slammed down hard, cracking his head. The aid car was called and they took him to the hospital."

"Oh, my gosh," I gasped. "So what did the doctor say about Wade?"

"That was funny. When Wade's name was called, I just sort of followed him in. He can only see out of the one eye, but when he noticed me he said to just wait in the waiting room." She giggled. "But the doctor said, 'Oh, she's fine. Here Leslie, sit over here,' and he pulled out a stool for me to sit on.

"After looking him over, Doctor Brown said Wade was in better shape than the other guy. The doctor treated that Dirk guy at the hospital. He has a broken jaw and a concussion. Then the doctor said, 'I hope you have a good attorney.'"

"Uh-oh." I could see this situation exploding into something even more serious.

"Well, the other guy started the fight, got in three punches before Wade's one and only. Wade said before he left the bar Darrell was getting names of witnesses claiming that Dirk started it."

"So who did Debbie go home with?"

"Darrell said he and Sally would take her home. But, Maureen, Wade's done with her. She really caused the whole thing and even seemed to get off having two guys fight over her. He said if she calls, he doesn't want to talk to her."

I nodded. "Okay."

"What a slut!" Leslie looked at my shocked expression, shrugged one slim shoulder and left for Janelle's.

I added a straw to a glass of lemonade, fixed a plate of cookies, and climbed the stairs to Wade's room. I softly knocked on the door. He was such a sound sleeper that if asleep, he wouldn't have heard me.

"Come in." He lay in bed, stretched out, with an ice pack on his eye.

I put the lemonade and cookies on his night stand. "How are you feeling?"

"Better. My eye's not really damaged, just sore and swollen. I have to put ice on it a few times a day for the next couple of days."

"I thought they put beef steak on black eyes."

He chuckled. "Ouch, it hurts to laugh."

"What about your ribs?"

"Just bruised. Doc taped 'em so I'd be more comfortable. No riding for the next few days. He gave me some pills for pain."

"Your lip?"

"Too late for stitches, but he thinks it'll heal okay. He gave me some ointment and I need to ice it, too. The doc wants me to just rest today, then take it easy for a couple more days."

"Okay, I'll let you rest. Leslie says if Debbie calls you don't want to talk to her."

"Right." His voice turned steely.

"I can't imagine what she was thinking." I closed his curtains against the afternoon sunshine and left the room.

"Thanks, Maureen."

Later, Debbie did call. I happened to answer the phone.

"Hi, Maureen," she said cheerfully. "Is Wade around?"

"He is, but he's not available."

"Oh. Will you have him call me?"

"I'll give him the message."

She tried to work up a conversation. "How have you been?"

"Fine, thank you. I'll tell Wade that you called." I hung up.

She called later and Leslie answered the phone. I'd told her about my earlier conversation, and we decided politeness wouldn't work. "He doesn't want to talk to you, Debbie," Leslie said.

I could hear Debbie's voice, but Leslie hung up.

When she called the third time, Wade took the phone from me. "Hello." Then, "Debbie, stop this. You've made your choice. We're done. Stop calling here and bothering my family." And he hung up.

That pretty much settled that.

There were no legal repercussions. Dirk never pressed charges. Apparently Darrell's long list of witnesses claiming that Dirk started it and Wade simply defended himself convinced Dirk it was prêtty hopeless. No damage was done to the bar, so no problem there. Wade healed quickly, though John had his hands full trying to keep him off his horse for three days.

9

Wade had a pretty new girlfriend, Teresa Campbell, a teacher at the elementary school. He met her through Darrell's girlfriend Sally who also taught at the school. It didn't take Wade and Teresa long to become "a couple," and we all liked her. Tall and athletic-looking, she and Wade made a handsome couple. He seemed different, as though his spirits had lifted. That episode with Debbie had wounded his pride and affected his confidence, or so it seemed to me. Now he was back in stride, laughed easily and seemed comfortable with himself.

At the end of a work day, John and Wade sat in the office, discussing their July schedules. John sat at his desk, Wade sprawled on a chair facing him. Leslie joined them, leaving the door open, and plopped down on the other chair. "Are we going to have a Fourth of July party? The Fourth is just a couple of weeks away!"

"Sounds good to me," I heard John say.

"Who should we ask?" Without waiting for an answer, she said, "Janelle and her family, Randy and Pearl, the Jacksons, Kip..."

"Teresa," Wade said, "and Darrell and Sally."

"Great!"

John cleared his throat. "I'd like to invite a friend and her daughter."

I froze. I stood at the stove stirring a spaghetti sauce and craned my neck to listen. He's seeing a woman?

"Who?" Leslie asked.

"Her name is Lilith MacIntrye; her daughter is Roxanne."

"How old is Roxanne?"

"Thirteen."

"Oh."

My heart thumped like a flat tire. What is the matter with me? Cool. Keep cool, I chastised myself. I resumed my stirring.

John continued. "Let's count on about twenty-five people, Les. You invite your friends and the neighbors, Wade and I will take care of the others. I'll barbecue steaks. You and Maureen work out the rest. Okay?"

There was a long period of silence.

"Okay, Les? Wade and I need to get back to what we were talking about here."

"Yes, okay."

Leslie closed the office door and joined me in the kitchen. She lowered her head to mine as I stood at the stove. "Maureen, did you know that Dad is *seeing* someone?"

"No, I didn't, but it's been a long time since your mother died, Leslie." I tried to keep my voice normal.

"Well, I didn't know about her. I'd always hoped you and Dad...."

My heart skidded to a stop. "Oh, honey, your dad's and my relationship—"

"When does he see her? He's almost always here, even Saturday nights."

"I suppose when he goes into town." I put on a bright smile and a cheerful tone. "What did I hear about a party?"

We discussed the menu and the guests to be invited. I forced myself to concentrate on the party and what I needed to do.

The Fourth of July dawned clear and perfect for a party. Ranch work was minimal for the holiday so we could concentrate on the event. The neighbors had all offered to bring dishes; I made a huge potato salad and a garden salad. In the early morning I baked two pies and Abbie brought a large sheet cake. Pearl brought a big bowl of chips and store-bought dip.

John came into the kitchen looking self-conscious in his dressy clothes. My heart pounded. I thought him very handsome, still strong and energetic looking. John and Wade had similar, muscular builds although John's waistline had thickened, and his hair receded a bit. He looked grand in a shirt I had never seen. Basically white, the western-cut shirt had shiny trim at the yoke and pockets. The belt on his western-style twill pants bore an oval silver buckle.

Guests began arriving in the late afternoon. We planned to eat around six. The first to arrive were Darrell and Sally. Wade had gone to pick up Teresa and they arrived about five minutes later. The four of them set up chairs in the shade, cracked open beers, and settled into the afternoon.

Leslie was in and out of the house, helping me take out pitchers of lemonade and keeping ice in tubs containing beer and soft drinks. "I've put the tubs in the shade, Maureen, so they'll keep cold longer."

"Good idea. Where's Kip?"

"He had to go to Oregon with his family for a re-union. He said he'd rather come to our party, but his folks wouldn't let him. They'll be gone for the four-day weekend."

"That's too bad."

"I don't really care. Janelle is coming. And her boyfriend Wally."

"What's he like?"

"Okay, I guess. He's not much of a mixer. He'll probably spend most of his time with the men." She brightened. "But that's good; Janelle and I can spend more time together!"

I smiled. Those girls never seemed to tire of one another's company.

Leslie stood by her dad as he cleaned the barbecue grill. A car I'd never seen made its way toward the house and parked with the other cars by the barn. A woman I recognized from the bank walked toward John. He took Leslie's arm and they met her part way. She was a nice-looking woman; I could see how John could be attracted to her. I wished my heart would stop pounding.

John made the introductions. Leslie shook the woman's hand. The three walked back to the car and the woman stood by the open car door talking to someone. A young girl flounced out.

I gulped. Oh, my. The girl had spiky crimson hair and the sides of her head were shaved. A plump girl, her baggy tee shirt did nothing to improve her appearance, and her jeans looked uncomfortably tight. The girl's head and the rest of her body looked as though they belonged to two different people.

John said something to Leslie and the two girls walked toward the barn. One of the mares had just had a little filly that I imagined Leslie was going to show their guest. I couldn't read much from Leslie's posture.

It wasn't long before Leslie came out of the barn with Roxanne dragging along behind. Leslie looked uncomfortably stiff.

I could almost feel her relief when Janelle's family arrived. Janelle and Wally in his truck were close behind. Good natured commotion followed. Wally immediately headed over to join a group of men. Leslie, Janelle and her mother came into the kitchen and Janelle carefully put a sheet cake, decorated with a big American flag, on the table.

"Maureen," Abbie asked, "what can I do to help?"

Leslie and Janelle slipped away to Leslie's room. I glanced out the window where the picnic table was in full view. Roxanne hovered by the potato chip bowl, happily dipping chips into Pearl's store-bought dip.

John had introduced me to Lilith and now I saw the two of them chatting to our neighbors, the Jacksons. Lilith looked very professional, and seemed a little out of place on a ranch. Her being there made me sad as though I were losing something precious. But then I felt selfish. I had said all along that a relationship between John and me wouldn't work, and I still felt that way. What if it didn't work out, if we weren't compatible? I couldn't remain here under those circumstances. It would be awkward. How many times did I have to go over this? *God, please help me find peace with this.*

Standing by the barbecue, John glanced up to Leslie's window two or three times. I called upstairs: "Girls, I need you to shuck the corn."

They clomped down the stairs and Leslie took the bags of corn on the cob and Janelle grabbed the large boiling pot. They sought out a place in the shade under the magnolia.

John walked over to them. Leslie emerged and talked with Roxanne, and the girl reluctantly joined them, looking around for her mother as she did so.

Within a few moments, Roxanne stomped over to her mother. Even from this distance, I could read her pouting body's expression. I frowned. *What on earth?*

John whirled around and stared at Leslie and Janelle, then resumed brushing sauce onto the steaks at the barbecue pit.

Leslie sat with Janelle's family and Wally during dinner. John, sitting with Lilith and Roxanne at the other table, noticed, but apparently didn't want to make a scene. I sat at the end of the second table so I could easily get in and out, if need be. People raved about the meal, but I could barely eat. I couldn't shake the uneasy feeling I had in the pit of my stomach.

After the meal, Leslie, Janelle and Abbie helped clear the table, leaving snacks for our guests to enjoy. Abbie loaded the dishwasher while I cleaned the counters. We excused the girls and they disappeared outside.

When we finished, I stepped into the yard and sat in the shade to chat with Abbie and a few of the other neighbors. John looked around, glanced up at Leslie's bedroom window, and glanced at me. Looking around, I couldn't see the girls. I briefly shrugged and shook my head. John said something to Lilith, then walked over to where Wade sat with his friends.

I watched as Wade made his way to the barn. Soon he and the girls emerged. John walked toward them, determination in every step.

Janelle split off, seeking out Wally. Abbie and her family had to leave; their baby was getting fussy. Wally left, too, saying he had planned to help his older brother with fireworks at another party. Janelle would go with him.

John and Leslie looked as though they were having a heated conversation. John returned to Lilith and

Roxanne. Leslie, her face flushed, rushed into the house. I excused myself and followed, as casually as I could. My gosh, this was like a soap opera.

Leslie emerged from the bathroom.

"What's wrong, honey?"

"Oh, Maureen! Dad's mad at me for ignoring Roxanne. I've tried to do things with her, but she's, she's... I just can't stand the little snot! Dad said if I don't pay more attention to her, I would be spending the rest of the day in my room!"

"Why don't you ask her if she wants to play croquet? Maybe your dad and Lilith would like to play, too."

"Oh, *goody.*"

"We do have responsibilities to our guests, Leslie."

"*I* didn't invite her."

"She's still our guest."

I filled a pitcher with fruit punch and sliced oranges and lemons to add to it. My hands shook so much I had to be careful not to slice my fingers. I watched as Leslie, putting up a brave front, walked over to Roxanne and said something. She pointed to the croquet set. I saw Roxanne shrug her shoulders and look away.

Leslie almost ran back to the house, bursting into the kitchen. "You know what? I'd *rather* be in my room!" She stormed upstairs and slammed her bedroom door.

Oh, boy. I simply avoided John and busied myself with our other guests. Some time later I saw John go into the house. He was gone quite a long time, but then emerged with Leslie in tow. They both looked relaxed.

We had dessert with coffee, and later John and the men set up the fireworks. Leslie stayed with Teresa and Sally. Lilith and Roxanne sat somewhat apart from the others.

After everyone left and Leslie and I finished cleaning up the kitchen, she said, "Did you know Lilith and Roxanne went through the house this afternoon?"

"No! Really?"

"I was in my room, reading, and they opened my bedroom door. That stupid Roxanne said, "What are you doing?"

"I said, 'Reading.' Lilith was all over herself apologizing. She said Dad had told them to feel free to look around, but they didn't know I was in there." Leslie shook her head.

I groped for a logical excuse. "Maybe they've never seen a ranch house."

"I don't know. But I guess Lilith thought Dad had sent me to my room. She told him she knew I had tried with Roxanne, but that she wasn't very sociable. Dad told me this. He asked me to join the party and not to worry about entertaining Roxanne."

"That was nice of Lilith to stick up for you."

She sighed. "I guess. She seems okay, but I really can't stand Roxanne."

John and Wade returned to the house after cleaning up the yard. John turned to me. "Thank you for making this such a nice party."

"Yeah, Maureen," Wade said, "it was great."

I flushed with pleasure. "You're welcome, but you guys did as much as I did."

John seemed cheerful and it appeared he and Leslie were fine. Things seemed to be back to normal and I felt my stomach relax.

The next morning after breakfast John and Wade left the house. After the screen door slammed behind them, Leslie said in a voice loaded with emotion, "I woke up about two hours after I went to bed, and I knew, Maureen. I know why Dad is sending me away."

Shocked, I could hardly respond. "Leslie, you dad isn't 'sending you away.'"

"Of course he is! What do you think he's doing when he talks about Rosemount? And now I know why."

"Why?"

"Because of Lilith and Roxanne! He's going to marry Lilith and they'll live here. He knows I could never get along with Roxanne, so he's getting rid of me!" Tears filled her eyes, and she turned to leave the room.

"Leslie, wait. Sit down."

"No. I'm going to my room."

"Leslie, please."

She reluctantly turned. "There's nothing you can say, Maureen."

"Honey, talk to your dad. Tell him how you feel. Tell him just what you told me. I know this isn't the reason he's sending...he wants you to go to Rosemount. He wants—"

"You said it yourself, Maureen. He's been alone, or at least without a wife, for a long time."

"Leslie, talk to him. Tell him how you feel."

"I have talked to him. You know that! He shuts me off the minute I bring up the subject!" With slumped shoulders, she wearily climbed the stairs to her room.

I stood where she left me, stunned and with a heavy heart. My ears rang. My girl was suffering and I could do nothing to help. My vision blurred as my eyes filled with tears.

* * *

Leslie had worked along side her dad and brother almost every weekday since summer vacation began.

She didn't keep the long hours that they did, but worked several hours most days. Apparently, it had gone well. Although I heard there had been some yelling, I also heard both her dad and Wade praise her, tell her she'd done a good job. She still managed to practice piano at least an hour a day, and visit with her friends some evenings.

One day she worked with Randy while John and Wade tended to another project. "It's so different working with Randy, Maureen. For one thing, he never yells."

I laughed. "I suppose he's hesitant to yell at the boss's daughter."

"I guess. When he wants me to do something, he'll say something like, 'You want to flank them cows on the other side?' Wade would yell "Why aren't you flanking them! Fill up that hole!"" She laughed. "Actually, I'd rather work with Dad or Wade."

That evening at dinner, Leslie said to her dad, "Janelle and I want to camp in the foothills, just the two of us."

John looked at her, concern lining his face. "I don't know if that's a good idea, Leslie."

"Just for one night? Please? The weather—"

"The weather has nothing to do with it." But I could see him softening.

"Could we, Dad?" Leslie could see it, too.

"Okay, one night."

After Leslie left the room, John said, "I just couldn't turn her down. She's so upset over this Rosemount thing, I felt I should let her do this."

I nodded. "I think it's a good idea, John. They won't really be that far away. They're reasonable girls with good judgment."

He nodded vaguely.

That evening, I heard Leslie talking to Kip on the phone. John, Wade and I were watching the news when she stormed into the living room.

"That stupid Kip!"

"Why, what did he do?" Wade asked.

"He called and wanted me to go out Saturday night, the night Janelle and I plan to go camping."

John turned the volume down on the TV. "I hope you didn't tell him your plans."

"No, Dad, I didn't. I don't even want him to know. I just said Janelle and I had plans."

John nodded. "That's good. Don't tell anyone about those plans."

"Kip got all bent out of shape, but then said he'd call Wally, Janelle's boyfriend, and we could go on a double date! I said, no, just Janelle and I had plans and it was going to just be the two of us.

"And do you know what that jerk said? He actually said, 'You mean you'd rather do something with just Janelle than me?'"

Wade smirked. "What'd you say?"

Leslie whirled on Wade. "I said, 'As a matter of fact, I would.' What makes boys think they're so special and that *anyone* would rather be with them than with another person?"

Wade shook his head. "I don't know, Les, but it sounds like you handled that just right."

After she left the room, Wade said, "Leslie has a good head on her shoulders, Dad. She's not like a lot of boy-crazy girls. I think she's doing fine at Chewack."

John and Wade regarded each other for a few seconds. John finally said, "Leslie's going to Rosemount, Wade. I know she's fighting it, but I'm convinced that as soon as she allows herself to, she'll be as enthusiastic about Rosemount as she is about Chewack."

Wade shook his head. "I'm not so sure."

John turned the TV volume back up.

Leslie and I packed her share of the food they'd take. Her little-girl excitement brought joy to my heart. They planned to leave first thing in the morning and return home by dinner the next night. That time of year there was plenty of grazing for the horses. They could get water from the lake, which now in summer was really a big pond.

I asked if she'd heard back from Kip.

"No, I think he's really pissed off. But you know what? I don't care. There's another boy from school, Jordan, that I sort of like, but I don't think he'll ask me out if he thinks I'm still going with Kip."

She was silent for a long minute. "But if I'm not going back to Chewack, it won't matter anyway." She gave me a sorrowful look. Her excitement about the campout temporarily forgotten. "Maureen," she almost whispered, "I don't think I can talk Dad out of sending me to Rosemount."

"I don't know, either, honey." I tried not to show it, but dread pooled in the pit of my stomach and in the back of my mind I heard warning bells.

The girls returned from their camping trip as planned, Leslie enthusiastic about their good time.

A couple of days later, John asked Leslie if she'd completed the application forms for Rosemount.

"No."

"We have an appointment to see the school on July 25th and they need that paperwork no later than July 10th. I've told you that."

Leslie shrugged.

"Go to your room and get those forms filled out. I want them by tonight, Leslie."

She stood absolutely still, stared at her father, and then silently turned to go to her room. About an hour later she walked into his office and set the forms on his desk.

"Okay, thanks, Leslie." She didn't respond, simply left his office and returned to her room.

I happened to go by his office and could see through the open door. John shook his head as he read the completed forms, and sat back in his chair. I didn't want to hear about it, so kept myself scarce.

10

*L*eslie sat on the edge of her chair at the kitchen table. "Maureen, did you know that students have to wear *uniforms* at Rosemount?" Her tearful voice tore at my heart. "Isn't that stupid? I decide what I'm going to wear. They probably look like a bunch of penguins." Her voice caught and she swiped at tears.

Leslie and John were scheduled to leave in a few minutes for Leslie's interview at Rosemount and to tour the campus. At John's request, Leslie wore a skirt and blouse. She leaned over to tuck in her blouse, then shook her head. "I feel like a dork." John joined us in the kitchen. "Okay, ready to go?"

"I'll never be ready to go there, not ever."

John's voice softened. "Leslie, give it a chance. Try to keep an open mind."

Leslie simply looked at him. Her eyes again filled with tears. My heart ached for her. How could he keep this up? I knew John loved his daughter. Beyond words. How could he not see the pain he caused?

It was a distance to Spokane. They would leave early and return late the same day. I had thought perhaps they'd stay in a hotel, have a mini vacation, but I think John could see that it wouldn't be fun for either one of them.

The day slogged along. I kept myself busy processing garden vegetables for the freezer, but my mind was never far from wondering how it was going at Rosemount. I don't know how many times I glanced at the kitchen clock. I prayed Leslie would rise above her anticipated dislike and view the school in a positive light. Surely some students liked it there. In the literature I read, many families had second, even third, generations attending.

At nine that evening Wade and I heard tires crunch on gravel. The door burst open and Leslie, her face red and contorted, arms full of shopping bags, climbed the stairs and slammed her bedroom door. John hadn't even walked in the house yet.

"Oh, boy," Wade said softly. "I was afraid of that."

John joined us in the living room, sighed and sat in his chair. He took off his Stetson and rubbed his eyes.

"How'd it go?" Wade asked, eyes riveted on his dad.

"Not good. She already had her mind made up." His shoulders drooped.

"So did you, Dad."

John gave his son a long, hard look, stood and went to his room.

Wade slowly shook his head.

"I think it's going to happen, Wade." I said softly.

He merely looked at me and went up to his room.

I sat for a long time, trying to imagine this home without Leslie. Of course, one day she would be leaving anyway, but it shouldn't be happening for at least two years. What would I do without my girl? A weight bore down on my shoulders.

Would they still need me? Caring for Leslie was one of the main reasons I was hired in the first place.

Surely by now I'd shown my worth in other ways. But now with Lilith in the picture... My stomach ached.

The next morning, I delivered folded clean laundry to Wade's and Leslie's rooms. Leslie sat on her bed, reading. I pointed to the bags that she had brought back from Spokane. "What are those?"

"School uniforms."

"May I see them?"

"Sure. Go ahead."

I brought out two navy blue pleated skirts with pin-stripes of burgundy and four plain but nice white blouses. In the other bag was a navy blue cardigan made with soft wool. The price tags were still on the clothing. The clothes looked expensive and of good quality.

"These are really quite nice, Leslie."

She shrugged. "Did you know that the first time first-year kids can go home is for Thanksgiving? That's supposed to give them time *to adjust.*"

"No," I said, fighting panic. "I didn't know that." Every response that came to mind was wrong. Nothing could help this situation. I quietly left the room.

* * *

Abbie called me first thing the next morning. Janelle had heard that Tracy, the girl who had been raped after a school dance, had taken her own life, had hung her-self in her bedroom.

"No!" Bile rose in my throat. My breakfast threat-ened to come back up.

John had gone into town that day and came home grim-faced. Leslie and I were in the kitchen putting dinner on the table. "Leslie, did you hear about that girl, Tracy, that she committed suicide?"

"Yes." Her voice held no emotion. She kept her face absolutely blank.

He stood still, looking at his daughter, but said nothing. He didn't have to; we all knew what he thought.

About a week later I heard Leslie and John talking in his office. John normally kept the door open, claiming the room got too stuffy when it was closed. "Dad, could I use the car to drive to Rosemount with Janelle?"

"Why? That's a long drive, Leslie."

"She wants to see it so she can picture me there. We could leave real early so we won't be getting home late. I can show her the buildings, the dorm, show her around Spokane a bit. Please?"

I could imagine John's dilemma. Spokane was a long way for Leslie to drive, but on the other hand, maybe she was warming to the idea of Rosemount.

"Okay. Don't go on a Friday because traffic is always bad then. Keep track of the time so you're home at least by 9:00."

"Thanks, Dad."

"And stop every once in awhile, take a break, stretch your legs."

"We will."

The date was set and early Thursday morning the girls took off. It was a long drive. I personally wasn't very comfortable with the idea. But maybe it was a good sign. Maybe she was finally accepting the idea and wanted to show the school to her best friend.

Leslie was home in the early evening. She didn't have much to say about her day, just that she and Janelle had fun and that Janelle thought Rosemount looked like a nice school. "I wish she could go, but her folks could never afford it."

But within a day or two, Leslie's attitude about the school returned to the negative. With me, she was loud and vocal about it. She knew she could express herself without recrimination from me. The visit with Janelle apparently had no affect on her resistance to attend Rosemount.

I tried once more when John came in for a cup of coffee. "John, I'm afraid this Rosemount business is—"

"Maureen, I don't want to hear about it. What I *do* want is for everyone to give it a chance!"

I clamped my mouth shut. That ended the conversation.

A few days after Leslie and Janelle's trip to Rosemount, Leslie brought in a big ugly suitcase, like a small trunk. It looked old, with dents and deep scratches. "Where in the world did you get that?" I asked.

"I bought it when we were in Spokane. It's been in the trunk of the car."

"What will you do with it?"

"Put stuff in it to take to school."

"You have a nice suitcase and you could put the extra stuff in boxes. That thing looks awful."

"I don't care how it looks, Maureen. Personally, I think Rosemount looks awful!"

She struggled with the ugly thing up the stairs to her room.

* * *

John's friendship with Lilith seemed to take place mostly in town. He occasionally mentioned he wouldn't be home for lunch. Once he mentioned to Leslie that the two of them had been invited to Lilith's for dinner, but Leslie declined, claiming that she'd already promised Janelle to do something with her. "My time with Janelle is really limited, Dad. She's feeling sad about my leaving."

Leslie wasn't about to pass up an opportunity to make her point.

John accepted the invitation for only himself. With just the three of us, the cheerful atmosphere at the dinner table was a relief.

After dinner Leslie went to Janelle's. Their "plans" had been to babysit Janelle's two younger brothers while Petersons went out to dinner and a movie to celebrate their anniversary.

* * *

The first Wednesday of August, Leslie went to her music lesson as usual. She seemed awfully quiet when she returned home. She joined me in the kitchen and set the table for dinner.

At dinner, John looked at his daughter and smiled. "How was your music lesson today?"

"Fine. It was my last one."

John's head jerked up. "What? What do you mean? You have almost a month before school starts."

Leslie shrugged. "There was no reason to put it off. I've quit piano."

We all stopped eating to stare at her. I could barely swallow my last bite.

"We've signed you up to take lessons at Rosemount. They have a great—"

"I've quit piano, Dad. My music has always been my business. I'm no longer studying music."

She was stony, untouchable...unreachable. She took one more bite, looked directly at me and said, "Excuse me," and left the table.

Not a word was spoken. For what I imagined to be the first time in his life, Wade turned down dessert. The meal was pretty much over. Leslie never came down from her room that evening. John went up to say goodnight, but he returned right away. They apparently didn't exchange more than a couple of words.

* * *

Leslie had worked with Wade all morning. They returned to the house in good spirits, Wade teasing Leslie about her inability to lasso, she giving him a line that she was really, really good, but just didn't want to show him up.

We sat at the table for lunch.

John smiled at their banter. "Leslie, how about if we throw you a farewell party next weekend. I thought you could invite some friends, we'd have the family, some of the neighbors...."

"No, thank you."

"You don't want a party? Honey, it would be nice for people to wish you well, to—"

"I don't *want* a party," she snapped, glaring at her father. She leaned forward. "Tell you what. After I'm gone you guys can have a great party to celebrate. You can invite *your* friends."

The hurt on John's face was unbearable. Tears filled Leslie's eyes, but she continued to glare at him. I didn't know who I felt sorrier for.

Without a word, John left the table, went into his office and closed the door.

* * *

Although Leslie seemed preoccupied, she rarely brought up the name Rosemount again. I think she could see it was hopeless. With Wade and me, she chatted, even laughed. I heard her offer help to Wade and he eagerly accepted. She turned down another invitation to go to Lilith's, this time she had a date with Kip. The month of August dragged on.

Leslie occasionally still played the piano, but never when her father was in the house. However, without a lesson plan, she didn't have the dedication as before. Plus, I think it made her sad. For the first time in eight years she had no assignment, no weekly goal.

Over the next week or so, Leslie made several trips into town. Her reasons were vague. One day she brought home several cardboard boxes and started carrying them to her room.

"What are you going to do with those?" I asked.

"I'm just sorting stuff. I'll probably have some things for Goodwill and for your missionary church group."

"Honey, you don't have to do that now. We can do it together any time."

"That's okay, Maureen. I'll just sort out stuff while I'm packing."

One day after she came back from town, I glanced at her coming toward the house from the car. At first I didn't even recognize her, though I recognized her walk.

She strolled into the kitchen.

"Leslie! What in the world!" She had had her hair cut, very short. Gone was the long ponytail that she always kept so tidy.

She smiled. "Do you like it?"

"Well...yes! I do! But it makes you look so much older! I hardly recognized you." My stomach clenched. I was losing her already.

"My hair always has been long. I needed a change. Do you really think it makes me look older?"

"Definitely."

When Wade came in for dinner, he took a double take at Leslie. "Les, what the hell...?"

"What? Don't you like it?"

"You don't look like my little sister! But yeah, it's a nice style."

The strongest reaction was John's. He came in for dinner, washed his hands and face in the laundry room and stepped into the kitchen.

Leslie had just turned from putting a salad on the table. He grabbed both her arms and stared at her. "What have you done?"

The shock in his voice startled all of us.

"I had my hair cut."

He gave her a little shake. I actually thought he might slap her, but to my knowledge it would have been the first time. He never raised his hand to Leslie. He released her and sat down at the table. We all did. He never spoke another word about Leslie's new look.

* * *

The morning I'd dreaded finally arrived. I fixed breakfast with a heavy heart. My chest ached. I heard Leslie stirring around her room. John and Wade were already at the breakfast table, John dressed in his good clothes for the trip to Spokane. Not a word was spoken.

Leslie joined us, looking pale and grim. As I dished up scrambled eggs, I burst into tears and rushed out of the kitchen. *I really have to stop this, for Leslie's sake.* I quickly washed my face and returned to the kitchen, promising myself that after they left I'd have a good cry. John had taken over for me and filled everyone's plate. He glanced at me and dished up mine, too.

He buttered a piece of toast for Leslie. "Do you want jam, honey?

"No, thank you." She kept her eyes downcast to her plate.

In fact, she only ate half her egg and a couple bites of toast. Leslie's appetite was the first thing to go when she was upset. She left the table, heading toward her room.

John glanced at her. "We need to leave in just a few minutes, Leslie."

"I'm almost ready," she said.

Soon, we heard her struggling in her bedroom doorway.

Wade left the table and headed up the stairs. "Geez, Leslie, what all are you taking? What's in this big thing? I thought you were going to use my pack to go back and forth."

"I am. The pack's in here, and just stuff I'll need. If you'll carry this, I'll get my suitcase."

Wade carried the big, ugly trunk into the kitchen. Leslie followed with her suitcase.

"When did you get that old thing?" John said with alarm. "I would have gotten you a large suitcase to match that one." He pointed to the nice suitcase she carried, a Christmas present from him last year.

"I bought it in Spokane the day Janelle and I visited Rosemount. I thought it would be good to hold a lot of stuff."

John said no more, apparently not wanting to make a bad day worse.

He and Wade carried out her luggage. She melted into my arms. "Oh, Maureen."

"There now, honey. Some day we'll laugh about how sad we all are today, but you'll see. You'll love it there." It sounded lame, even to me.

She stepped back and looked directly into my eyes. "Good-bye, Maureen. Thank you for everything."

I watched as she walked to the car, my heart pounding. Her gait was stiff, not her perky purposeful walk. She said something to her dad then went into the barn. I imagine Wade was there, and Polly, of course.

In a few moments, she emerged and climbed into the car.

After the car disappeared down the long driveway, I went into the living room and just sat. My mind was a jumble of sadness. Numbness paralyzed me. I couldn't even cry. Although Leslie had become more independent and not so needy of me, we still had a strong connection. She'd become like my own daughter. I was still important in her life. But now what? She was going to a whole new world, only coming home to visit. Was my time here ending?

Wade wandered in, looked around and joined me in the living room. He stared at me. "It's rare for you not to be doing something."

"I don't have the oomph to do anything. I'm drained."

"I know what you mean." He sighed. "Hell of a deal."

"Yes."

"I wish I felt as sure as Dad that this was the right thing to do."

"Me, too."

"I tried two or three times to talk to him, but he was so damned sure."

"I tried, too."

"How do you think she'll do, Maureen?"

"I honestly don't know. She's one of the brightest girls I've ever known. She's very sensitive; it's what makes her the way she is, so special."

"She can be tough though, and stubborn."

"Yes, that too, as she's shown us these past weeks, months. If she puts her mind to it, she'll probably make a good adjustment, but otherwise..."

Wade sat forward, elbows on his knees, his big hands folded between them. My heart lurched. John often sat that way when he was seriously concentrating. Wade sighed again. "I should have fought harder. I feel like I let her down."

"I don't think it would have done any good, Wade. It was going to happen, no matter what we did."

We sat in silence for a few minutes. Wade suddenly slapped his leg. "Well, I've got work to do. I'll be in the barn." He tromped out.

I continued to sit, not moving, my mind whirling. Finally, I got up from my chair to clear the breakfast remains and think about dinner. Dinner without Leslie.

Mid-afternoon the phone rang. "Cahill residence."

"Is Mr. Cahill in?"

"No, this is Maureen, Cahill's housekeeper. Mr. Cahill is out right now—"

"Maureen, this is Mrs. Holmes from Rosemount. I'm afraid I have some bad news."

My knees went weak. "Bad news? Haven't John, Mr. Cahill, and Leslie arrived yet? What—"

"Yes, Mr. Cahill and Leslie arrived, they took her things to her room, and he left. Her roommate and her parents arrived and told me that Leslie said she had the wrong suitcase and that she'd be right back, that she had to catch her dad...." She paused, then almost whispered. "That's the last anyone saw of her."

"Maybe John, Mr. Cahill, changed his mind and she's with him?" *Please, please let it be that.*

"No. Mr. Cahill would have let us know."

"Maybe she's just on campus someplace and—"

"No. I'm sure she's not. She didn't come to the orientation. That's when I learned she wasn't here. Her roommate's parents looked for her, and then told me they were worried about her, that she seemed distracted. We've looked everywhere."

"Oh, my goodness." My knees went weak, I sank onto a kitchen chair. "I don't know what to say."

"Should we call the police?"

"I'll talk to Wade, her brother. We'll decide what to do."

"Please stay in touch. I feel so awful about this, and I'm afraid she's got a few hours start."

Mrs. Holmes seemed like a decent person and sounded genuinely concerned.

"She was pretty determined she didn't want to go to Rosemount," I said.

"Yes, I know, but her father and I thought she'd come around once she got here."

As soon as I got off the phone I called Wade on his cell. "Wade, come to the house right away."

"Why, what's up Maureen?"

"Just come."

I'd barely hung up when he stormed through the door, concern written all over his face. "What is it, Maureen?"

"It looks like Leslie has run away from Rosemount."

"Goddamnit! How could that happen?"

"I don't know. What should we do? Mrs. Holmes from the school asked if we wanted her to call the police, but I said we'd take care of it. Should we do that?"

I could see that his mind was spinning. His eyes darted back and forth. He hung his head. "No. I'll find her."

"But she's all the way to Spokane, Wade. By now she's probably even left there!"

"I've gotta get going. Maureen, get me a recent picture, maybe her school picture, the one on Dad's desk. I'll get my sleeping bag and toss in some clothes."

I rushed into the office to get the picture. A sinking sensation came over me. Since she had her hair cut she looked so different from that picture taken only a few months ago.

Wade came in from the laundry room where he'd picked up his sleeping bag from a deep cedar-lined storage closet. "Damn that kid! She has her sleeping bag, too. That's what was in that big suitcase. Maureen, she'd planned this all along."

I nodded. "This is the best picture we have, but it really doesn't look like her now."

"She thought of everything. See if you can find some clues in her bedroom."

I climbed the stairs to her room, opened the door and almost fainted. "Wade, look," I croaked. My heart pounded.

He'd picked up a duffle bag from the laundry room closet, and climbed the stairs. "What? I've gotta get some clothes..." He looked into Leslie's room. "Oh, my god."

The room was devoid of anything Leslie, except for a blue vase that had always been on her windowsill.

The mattress and pillows were stripped of linens. I opened dresser drawers. Empty. The walls were bare of all decorations, no pictures, posters, not even her calendar remained. We looked into the closet. There were several boxes, all neatly marked. "Goodwill" or "Maureen/Church." Stuffed animals were jumbled together in a box labeled "Janelle/brothers."

The desk was empty of the usual books, pictures and papers, except for three envelopes. Wade picked up an envelope with his name, and handed me one with my name neatly printed on it.

Dear Maureen,
Thank you for all you've done for me. I've thought of you as a mother and I love you very much.
I would like you to have the vase on the windowsill. When I was little I gave it to my mom for Mother's Day. After she died, I kept it in my room to remember her. I'd like you to have it now.
In the closet are boxes of clothes and things I'd like you to give away.
Love,
Leslie

Wade's eyes looked haunted. He stepped over to the window and looked out. "I can't believe this is happening."

Without a word, we exchanged letters. His read:

Dear Wade,
   Thank you for being such a great
brother. Sometimes I thought you were
sort of mean, but you were always there
for me. Have a good life. With Teresa?
Hope so.
   Would you see that Polly is taken care of?
Thanks.

Love,
Leslie

We hated to do it, but if it would give us any clues, we had to read the letter to her dad. Wade tore open the envelope.

Dear Dad,
   I'm sorry I've been such a pain lately
It's just that I don't want to leave you
and my home. I know you think it's
the best thing for me, but I don't agree.
   You've given me a wonderful life.
I've loved my home, and I love you.
Thank you for everything.
           Your loving daughter,
           Leslie

"Oh, shit." Wade wiped his eyes. "Explain to Dad why we had to open it."

Besides the letters and the vase on the windowsill, the only hint of Leslie was her laundry hamper where her sheets and last-worn clothes were, including her pajamas. Wade reached down and took the pajama bottoms.

"I'm taking Dutch with me."

He started to leave the room then turned to me. His face was a picture of fury. "Show Dad this room. Don't touch a thing. He needs to see this."

"Okaaay." I wasn't looking forward to that.

"She didn't run away, Maureen. She's *gone* away. In her mind it's for good."

Back in the kitchen, he stuffed the pajama bottoms into a plastic bag. "I'll go load up my truck."

"I'll put together some food for you." I threw together sandwiches, tossed apples and the remaining two oranges in a bag. I'd just made a batch of cookies the other day and I emptied the cookie jar into another bag. I filled a thermos bottle with coffee. I put water and sliced lemon in a couple of jars, iced tea in another, and stuffed the whole mess in a cardboard box.

Wade had loaded a large wooden box on the truck's bed. Randy was there, helping Wade pack it with the stuff he was taking. He'd brought out a large bag of dog food from the barn and loaded that, together with Dutch's food and water dishes. The two men shook hands.

I had some money in my wallet, plus there was about $60 in a cashbox, my household money. I went out with the food box and the cash and handed it to Wade. "There's probably only about $150 there. Do you have a charge card with you?"

Wade looked in his wallet. "Yep, and I have a couple of twenties." He turned to look at me, nodded, climbed into his truck and whistled for Dutch. She scampered over his lap and into the passenger seat. Wade closed the door and rolled down the window.

"Maureen, don't let Dad leave. If he should call, don't tell him over the phone. He'd never make it home. Make him stay here. Tell him I said he needs to take care of things here, be here to make decisions. And call that damn Rosemount, tell them I'm on my way. Who should I see?"

"Mrs. Holmes."

"Okay."

He climbed back out of the truck. He bent down to hug me, to pat my back. "I'll find her, Maureen."

My voice, against his chest, came out muffled. "Wade, now you be careful. I know how you feel, but it won't help if you're in an accident. You drive carefully. Try to calm yourself once you get on the road. Eat regular meals."

"Yes, ma'am."

He gently stepped away from me and again climbed into his truck, started the engine, and drove off. I watched until his truck disappeared down the drive, just as I had done when John and Leslie left only a few hours before.

Randy, never wanting to intrude, had stepped back and stood at the barn door staring down at his boots.

I trudged back to the house and sat at the kitchen table, numb. I roused when I remembered I was supposed to call Mrs. Holmes at Rosemount. My conversation with her was brief, just that Wade was on his way and that he needed to talk to her.

I didn't think I should take it upon myself to call neighbors, not even Abbie. I'd wait until I talked to John.

I did call my sister Sue, told her the situation, and asked her to pray. I'm afraid my own prayers were a desperate jumbled string of words. Well, God would know.

And then I waited for John.

I watched John park the car, climb out, then head for the barn. He turned to say something to Randy as he came out. John's body stiffened, and I saw him look at the house. My stomach quivered. I dreaded the next few minutes. He was a strong man physically and over the years I believed he had grown tougher emotionally, not as vulnerable as when I first came to the family nine years before. But this was news that could break the strongest of characters. I prayed that I could tell him in a way that would spare him of....of what? How could I possibly say this in a kind way?

He came into the house pointing his thumb back over his shoulder. "What's Randy talking about? He said something about my going right to the house, that you wanted to talk to me."

Of course. Randy knew; Wade had told him.

"Yes, I do. Why don't you sit down?"

"Just tell me, Maureen. What is it?"

"Leslie has run away from Rosemount."

"What? I just left her there!" He fumbled for a kitchen chair and sat down hard.

"Apparently after you left, she did, too. Mrs. Holmes called. You and Leslie were seen coming in, then you left. Her roommate and her parents came to her room and they visited for a minute or two. Then Leslie left with that big suitcase, saying you had brought up the wrong one and that she had to catch you before you left. No one saw her after that. She wasn't at the orientation. That's when her roommate's parents told Mrs. Holmes, at the orientation."

John's eyes grew bigger with each word. His mouth dropped open. I could see his struggle, his anguish. His eyes darted around the room. "Where's—?"

"Wade left for Spokane," I glanced at the clock, "about three hours ago."

John stood and grabbed the car keys he'd tossed on the table.

"No, John. Wade said for you to stay here, that someone needed to be here to make decisions."

He hesitated. "No way. I've gotta find—"

"No. Absolutely not." I couldn't believe I spoke to John in this manner. "Wade's right. Things will come up and you'll need to talk to him. You need to stay right here. He needs you here."

He plopped back down. "Oh, my god. How could this happen?"

I tried to keep my voice soft. "I don't know, John. But if anyone can find her, Wade can. And will."

I continued. "Okay, this is what's happened so far. Wade got his sleeping bag out and saw that Leslie had taken hers, too. That's probably what was in that big suitcase. He took the picture of her that was on your desk."

"She doesn't even look like that anymore."

"I know, but when Wade shows it to people, they can imagine her with shorter hair. He's taken Dutch."

"Dutch is a cattle dog. I don't know how useful she'll be."

"He's taken Leslie's pajama bottoms to use as scent."

John put his head in his hands.

"Mrs. Holmes asked if we wanted the school to call the police, but Wade said to hold off. He's on his way to Rosemount. He's going to talk to Mrs. Holmes and then decide about calling the police. He'll call here and will want to talk to you.

"Leslie left us each a note; we found them on her desk. We opened yours, John, to see if we could learn something more." I handed him all three notes, his on top.

He quickly read his, Wade's, then mine. "I can't believe this is happening."

"I know."

He leaned toward me. "Did you find any clues in her room?"

"Ah, not really."

But he was already at the door leading upstairs. I let it happen. He raced up the stairs, flung open the door and stepped in.

I waited a couple of minutes, then followed him up the stairs and stepped into the stark, empty room.

John sat on her bed, on the stripped-bare mattress. Tears streamed down his face. He looked up at me with haunted eyes. "My god, Maureen, what have I done?"

I sat next to him. "John, you did what you thought was best. There's no doubt how much you love your daughter. It's just that you both have different opinions about what's best for her."

"And now, because of me, she's in terrible danger." He breathed heavily.

"We have to have faith, John. Faith that Wade will find her." I hesitated, "Faith that God will help Wade find her."

John turned his head, angry eyes bore into mine. He said nothing.

I steeled myself. "Let's just wait for Wade to call, see what he finds out. He said it would be late by the time he got to Rosemount. Mrs. Holmes told me she would wait for him. She seems nice."

John nodded absently, and glanced at his watch. He rushed down the stairs and into his office, rummaged in his desk drawers and pulled out a Washington map. He returned to the kitchen and spread it out on the kitchen table.

"Would you eat if I fixed us a simple dinner?"

"No, you go ahead." His finger rested on the space Spokane took on the map.

I fixed two sandwiches and a few celery sticks with peanut butter and put the plate next to him as he studied the map. He absently reached for and bit into a half sandwich. "I hope to hell she doesn't head for Seattle." He looked up at me.

I realized then how important my role here would be. It was my job to keep John calm, to keep him focused on Wade's efforts. Help make decisions. I prayed I could do that, not show my panic.

"Do you think she's apt to do that?" I asked. "Do you know anyone in the Seattle area?"

"Not anyone she would go to. I have a cousin in Seattle, but...no."

"Would she take a train, I wonder? The bus?"

He shook his head. "Hard to tell. I wish Wade would call. This waiting is killing me."

"It could be awhile." And it was. The phone didn't ring until almost ten o'clock.

"Cahill." Then, "My god, Wade, why did you wait so long to call? Where are you? What have you found out?"

We learned that Wade arrived at the school, and met Mrs. Holmes. She had brought to her office the smaller suitcase Leslie left behind. Together they opened it and found the school uniforms, still with price tags on. Nothing more was in that suitcase.

They went to Leslie's dorm room and Wade took Dutch with them. Dutch performed like Wade hoped she would. Wade used the pajamas to give Dutch the scent and said, "Dutch, where's Leslie?" The dog sniffed all around and wagged her tail at a particular spot on the floor. Her roommate said the dog sniffed where that big old suitcase had been.

Mrs. Holmes and Wade talked about how she might get out of town, if she was out of town, and decided that Greyhound was the most practical way because it was the closest to the school, a short city bus ride away.

They went to the bus depot, and once there learned that given the schedules, the logical bus to take would be either to Seattle or Pendleton. They asked if anyone had seen Leslie—Wade showed them her picture—but the people working then were on a different shift. They said to contact the man who had worked the day shift. They wouldn't give Wade his name, but one of the clerks tried calling him. No answer. They waited awhile, then he called again, but still no answer. The fellow suggested Wade return in the morning and talk to the man who probably had sold Leslie the ticket.

"So now what, Wade?" John paced as far as the phone cord would let him.

From what I gathered from the conversation and what John told me later, Wade had to know if she left for Seattle or Pendleton. He'd lose even more time if he went in the wrong direction. He'd have to wait until morning to find out, when the fellow would be back on the job.

John looked deflated. Wade asked his dad about calling the police. "I don't know. What do you think?"

Wade was for holding off, saying he was afraid it would cause Leslie more trouble.

"I think I can find her as well as they can, and this way she won't have a record. Another thing, if she suspects someone is after her, she'll be even harder to find."

"Okay, let's hold off, then."

When they hung up, I was delighted to hear John say, "I need to have a positive attitude when I talk to Wade. He has a tough job and doesn't need to hear me moaning and groaning."

"You're right. He'll need your encouragement. And that means that you'll have to take care of yourself, John."

He nodded and picked a couple of grapes from a bowl in the center of the table. "I guess Mrs. Holmes was a real help, even gave Wade a legal pad to keep track of things." He shook his head. "I'll bet she feels awful."

I don't know how much sleep John got, but I tossed and turned all night. I realized that Leslie couldn't imagine our anguish. She had troubles of her own.

The next morning Wade called saying the man at Greyhound recognized Leslie from her picture, said he'd seen her before when she picked up a schedule. Probably that was when she'd gone to Spokane with Janelle. He noticed that her hair was shorter now. Yesterday she bought a ticket to Pendleton.

"It looks like she's been planning this for some time," John said. "So you're on your way to Pendleton? Wade, let's set up a schedule. I need to hear from you on a regular basis."

They decided that each day Wade would call at six o'clock at night, and before that if there was a reason.

They would depend on the regular phones. Many of the places Wade would be had no cell phone coverage.

"Okay," John said. "In the meantime, I'll go talk to Janelle, see if she can shed any light on this."

John no sooner hung up when the phone rang. It was Lilith. I continued to sit at the table while John spoke to her. I couldn't move. He briefly told her what was going on. He listened to what she said and shook his head. It was a short conversation. When he hung up, he said Lilith had seen Leslie at the bank that Friday before she left and that Leslie had withdrawn all her savings, a little more than $4,000. Leslie had told Lilith that she needed cash, that she would put most of it in a Spokane bank, but that she had some supplies to buy for school.

I was alarmed with Leslie's thoroughness. "Well, at least she'll be able to buy food."

John brought out an Oregon map and spread it out on the table over the Washington map.

I busied myself around the house while John went to Petersons to talk to Janelle. That night, during the six o'clock call, John told Wade that Janelle had been shocked to hear Leslie had run away. After Janelle's mother had instructed her daughter to tell John anything she could think of that might help, Janelle mentioned the old suitcase, but she thought Leslie would use it for school. Also, she verified that they had stopped at the bus terminal, that Leslie said she wanted to pick up a schedule because she would use Greyhound to go home for the holidays.

Once John had told Petersons, I felt free to discuss it with Abbie. It was a relief to talk to someone not so directly involved. "I can't believe Leslie didn't tell Janelle her plans. Those two are so close."

"I'm not surprised. I would have known right away that something was wrong. Leslie knew I'd be able to get it out of Janelle. My daughter couldn't keep a secret like that from me."

Abbie asked my permission to call some of the church members and start a prayer chain. I readily agreed, but chose not to tell John. I didn't want to take a chance on upsetting him even more.

At the next call Wade said he checked motels close to the Pendleton terminal and found the one where she stayed. She had ditched the old suitcase at the motel.

"Why would she leave it there?" John asked. Then, "Pack? What pack?"

Leslie had asked Wade if she could have his old gray pack, saying she'd use it to go back and forth from school to home. The pack must have been inside the suitcase, ready to go, along with her sleeping bag.

John rubbed his eyes. "She thought of everything, didn't she?"

Wade had checked out Pendleton, but was pretty sure she wasn't there. He was on his way to LaGrande, with a hunch she would continue heading south.

Wade's call the next day was much more en-couraging. She had gone to LaGrande, and was looking for work.

"Work? John's tone was incredulous. "She has $4,000! Why would she be looking for work?" John drew a line on the map from Pendleton to LaGrande.

Wade seemed to think she must be trying to find a place to live. At least she was smart enough to know she had to work to survive. I thought that was a good sign.

But John looked downcast. "I drove her to this, Wade." Then, after Wade's response, John said, "Well, I was apparently the only one. There's no one else to blame." John's voice was thick. "So what happened after LaGrande?" He rested his head on one hand.

"Nothing? Okay, Wade, take care of yourself. She'll probably stop at night. You do the same. You're within hours of her, that's really encouraging."

Wade asked about fall roundup.

"We've started, but I'm pretty useless. Actually, Randy has taken over and between him and Bob Peterson, they scrounged up a few neighbors to help. I worked a few hours today, but I just couldn't keep my mind on it."

Wade's closing words were, "Dad, don't worry. I'll find her."

The next day Mrs. Holmes from the school called and I talked to her. She had thought the world of Wade and said that if anyone could find Leslie, Wade could.

At the next night's call Wade told his dad that he had good news and bad news.

"Go ahead."

The good news was that Wade was in Baker City, Oregon, and that Leslie had been there, too, just yesterday. She had changed clothes at a gas station and had looked for work.

The bad news was that his truck broke down.

"How bad?"

It was the timing belt and it could be fixed. He'd had a tow truck take it to a garage and they could fix it, but they had to send for the part and his truck wouldn't be ready until noon the next day. It happened to be the same station where Leslie had changed clothes. Dutch had picked up her scent.

"Hang in there, son. You've made good progress." His face softened. "You've found exactly where she's been. Several times. I think that's remarkable."

Wade said something that made John chuckle.

John asked Wade if he thought they should call the sheriff, but they decided to hold off, since he was so close.

After John hung up, I praised him for his encouraging words.

He nodded. "He's really discouraged, feeling bad that he can't go anywhere until his truck is fixed; berating himself that he hadn't had that timing belt looked at. What lousy timing."

"What did he say that made you laugh?"

John smiled. "When I told him that his progress had been remarkable, he said 'not as remarkable as it will be when I put my hands around that kid's scrawny neck.'"

About an hour later, Wade called again. John filled me in after the call. Because his truck was in the garage, Wade was staying in a motel, one that would take dogs. He had dinner at the motel's restaurant, and, as usual, asked around if anyone had seen Leslie. A guy came forward who had met Leslie, had spent time with her a couple of days earlier. His name was Cyrus, a Tacoma teacher who was on vacation and hiking in the Wallawas, a mountain range in Eastern Oregon.

Cyrus had said that Leslie told him that her father was replacing her with a woman and her daughter, a girl she couldn't stand.

As John listened to Wade, his eyes grew huge, his face flushed. "She told him that? That's ridiculous!"

John and Wade bantered back and forth on that issue, then John said, "Well, she's wrong. Lilith had nothing to do with my decision. I barely knew Lilith when the subject of Rosemount first came up!" He sighed, then, with a ragged voice said, "I've come to the realization that there was another reason though. I was afraid, Wade. Afraid of her growing up, afraid of being the father of a teenage girl." He brushed at his eyes. "I worried about her all the time. It scared me to think of what could happen to her. That girl getting raped didn't help my peace of mind."

He nodded. "But I understood you. I didn't always understand Leslie. At Rosemount she could get what I couldn't give her."

After they hung up, John looked at me. "Wade told me that what I can give Leslie—my love— is all that she needs and wants." He took out his handkerchief and blew his nose.

"John, she knows you love her. It's just that she somehow got the idea...."

"I know. I should have been more sensitive about that."

I really had nothing to say. I changed the subject. "John, do you mind if I sit here and listen when you're talking to Wade?"

"No, I want you to, Maureen. It's going to take all of us to get her back. Wade and this fellow, Cyrus, are going to join forces for a couple of days and look for her. I guess Cyrus knows the area pretty well. He's on foot though, so they have to wait for Wade's truck to get fixed."

"Still, that's encouraging to hear from someone who has talked to her, spent time with her. Maybe Wade's truck breaking down was a blessing."

John looked at me with skepticism, shook his head and shrugged. "Wade did say that Cyrus told him he only stays in motels once or twice during the three-week period. This happened to be one of the times, and they met in the motel restaurant."

"Well, that's more than a coincidence, don't you think?" To me it meant God was watching out for her. Our prayers were being answered.

The next day Wade called earlier than usual. John had been in and out of the house, but happened to be in when the phone rang.

The news was not good. Leslie had bought a car, an old junker from a vacant lot that people used to sell their own cars. Dutch had repeatedly circled the place where the car had been. Cyrus had guessed that the dog smelled Leslie at that spot. The lot was right across the street from the repair shop where Wade's truck was. The repairman looked across the street and remembered the missing car. He had serviced that car over the years and could give Wade the former owner's name and the car's license number.

Wade called the fellow and asked about Leslie. Although she fit the description, she was going by another name, Linda Carpenter.

"I thought you had to be eighteen to buy a car," John said. "Oh, no."

Leslie now had a fake driver's license with the name Linda Carpenter that showed she was eighteen. Cyrus verified that was the name she told him, too, but he had never believed it. Being a school teacher, he was pretty wise about kids.

John and Wade agreed that it was time to call in the law. "I hate to do it, Wade, but we've got to get this stopped."

Right after they hung up, John called the Baker City area sheriff, gave them all the information he had, the car's description, her description, and the places she'd been so far. He took a lot of heat from the sheriff about waiting so long to call, but tried to explain his reasons.

When he hung up he shook his head. "We might have made a mistake, waiting to call."

"John, you did what we all thought best at the time."

At the six o'clock call that night Wade reported no progress. Now that she had a car, Leslie could get around a lot faster.

I asked John if I could speak with Wade.

"Here, Maureen wants to talk to you."

"Hello, Wade."

"Hi, Maureen, how's it going?"

"We're fine. Are you taking care of yourself? Are you eating well and getting enough rest?"

"Yeah, Maureen, I'm fine." His voice turned hoarse.

"Well I just wanted you to know that I'm praying for you out there."

"Thanks, Maureen. Pray for Les too."

"Oh, I am! I am! Good luck, Wade."

John couldn't stand it any longer and reached out for the phone.

"Here's your father."

"Wade, where are you? What's next?" They continued talking about locations and strategy.

At the next night's six o'clock call, John learned that Wade and Cyrus had gone into Idaho, made a brief circle of small towns, then returned to a place called Rome in Oregon, then made their way to Burns so that Cyrus could make arrangements to get to Portland, where he had left his car. School would be starting soon and he had to get home. Wade appreciated the time spent with Cyrus and the moral support and ideas he'd had.

"What did you find out in Burns?"

Wade said he talked to a woman who had seen her. The woman said Leslie looked tired and miserable. She asked the woman how far it was to Frenchglen.

John slumped in his chair. "Why doesn't she call us? Okay, what's next, Wade?"

"According to the woman at the grocery store, there isn't much in Frenchglen, but since Les asked about it, I think I should go check it out."

A couple of hours later, the Sheriff's Department called. They had found Leslie's car. It had been hot-wired, apparently stolen. There was no evidence of a struggle. The car was probably abandoned when it ran out of gas. They found $200 under the driver's seat.

John paced around the house after hearing the news. "I don't know if this is good news or bad news. I know she'll be more desperate, but on the other hand maybe easier for Wade to find."

The next night, Sunday, Wade called, discouraged. By now he'd been searching for Leslie a whole week. He'd checked out Frenchglen, which was a tiny little berg. He'd continued south, into high desert country, and had wound around Hart Mountain. He'd stopped in Plush and dropped down to Adel. Nothing. The town of Lakeview had looked promising; it was an industrial town with lots of stores. On Sunday most of the stores were closed though and no one he talked to had seen Leslie "It was all pretty much a waste of time," Wade said. "I guess she could have been here, but just drove through.

"I don't think so, son. The Baker County Sheriff's office called." John repeated what they had told him, concluding with, "She must be getting low on money after buying that damn car, then having it stolen with that $200 in it."

There was silence between the two. John finally said, "Well, at least she might be easier for you to track now that she's afoot again. What's next, son?"

Wade's plan was to check out Klamath Falls, then head north to Bend.

It helped my peace of mind to do my routine work, but Leslie was always on my mind. I prayed constantly, even mentally talked to Leslie, giving her encouragement, telling her how much she was loved. I pretended we chatted.

John tried to help with fall roundup and managed to be there when the big stock trucks rolled in. When about half the cattle had been loaded he rushed to the house to ask if there was any news, then hurried back to finish loading. Randy was a life saver, quietly going about his job. John had always said that Randy was a good hand, would do anything asked of him, but that he didn't have much initiative. But when this crises came, he certainly stepped up to do the job.

Pearl either stopped by daily, or made brief phone calls, asking for any news. Abbie did the same. Early on John had called Leslie's piano teacher, Mr. Schaffer, to ask for any information Leslie might have shared. She had said nothing to him, but now Mr. Schaffer also called asking for news. Everyone we knew was praying. I didn't know if John prayed or not. For sure, he carried a terrible burden of guilt.

At the six o'clock call, Wade sounded weary, his voice thick when he asked for his dad. Klamath Falls had looked promising, but he came up with nothing. She apparently had not been there. He'd stopped at some little towns along Ninety-seven. He was on his way to Bend, but it would be too late to ask around about Leslie at stores. He planned to camp at Tumalo State Park for the night. He mentioned that he'd been using the yellow tablet Mrs. Holmes had given him. "You should see all the entries I've made with places, dates and times."

The next day, mid-afternoon, Wade called. I could hear his excited voice as he talked to John. "Dad, I found her!"

"Oh, thank God. Where? She okay? When did— Okay, son, go ahead."

I could hear some of it, but after the call John filled me in. Wade had stopped at a grocery store in Pritchard. The grocery clerk recognized Leslie's picture and mentioned how much alike she and Wade looked. The clerk saw Leslie and a customer talking in the parking lot, and saw Leslie get into the woman's car. The clerk knew the customer and gave Wade her name, Ellie Mae VanAlmkerk, and directions to their ranch.

Wade said that Leslie was working there and helping gather cattle for their fall roundup, but that he hadn't seen her yet.

John glanced at the clock. "Okay, call me back as soon as you actually see her and talk to her."

Wade's excited voice boomed from the receiver. I'd never heard him so animated. I could easily hear him from across the table. "I will. Take it easy now, Dad."

"All right, son. Call me back as soon as you can." After hanging up, John slumped in his chair, clearly relieved. When he looked up at me, his dark eyes sparkled with tears. Time dragged. About an hour later, the phone barely rang when John answered. "Cahill."

It was Wade. "Guess who I've got here."

I heard his voice and held my breath.

John leaned forward, his shoulders hunched. He frowned. "What's wrong? What's—?"

Wade had hung up, saying that Leslie wasn't quite ready to talk to her dad. Wade had assured John that she was fine, but he thought Leslie needed time.

John looked at me and shook his head. "Will our lives ever be normal again?"

I tried to conceal my anxiety. "John, this must be a shock to Leslie, seeing Wade, then having him talk to you. Let's just give it time."

John didn't leave the phone. He studied his map, looked out the window, stood, then sat back down. "Why isn't he calling back?"

In a few minutes the phone rang again, but it was Mr. Schaffer. "Wade's found her, but I can't talk, I'm waiting for him to call back. Thanks," and John hung up.

Finally, Wade's call came. John held the phone out a bit so I could hear.

"Dad? Tell you what we're going to do. Leslie has been staying at an outfit near Prichard, working on fall roundup and I'm going to give them a hand tomorrow, along with Les here—"

John's eyes widened and he started to sputter an objection.

"Hold on, Dad, let me finish. Then we'll head out first thing Thursday morning."

By this time John was standing. "What? Why—? Yes, of course, put her on."

He sat down. The anxiety in his face melted into a smile. "Oh, Leslie, honey. Are you all right?"

He clutched the phone as he leaned forward. I couldn't hear her response. But then he said, "I'm better now that I know you're safe." His voice caught. "I'll be even better when you get home."

Leslie apparently asked him if she would have to go back to Rosemount.

"No, honey. I want you here with us." There was a pause while Leslie spoke. Then, "I'm sorry, too, honey. Leslie, everything will be fine. We'll see you Thursday?"

I don't know when my heart ever felt lighter. John's face glowed.

"Okay," he said after hanging up and glancing at the calendar. "We have the rest of today and all day tomorrow. They should be home sometime late Thursday." He rubbed his eyes, then turned to look at me. "Wade did it. By god, he did it."

Tears filled my eyes and I had a huge lump in my throat. All I could do was nod.

The rest of that day we simply recovered. John asked me to telephone all those who had called and tell them our good news. He and Randy drove cattle into pastures closer to headquarters. John came in early. "I'm going to get my first night's real rest in over a week."

I was beyond tired, too. Without Leslie and Wade the house seemed quiet, especially now that we knew everything was okay. I actually prepared a complete dinner and found we had appetites.

The next day, Wednesday, dragged on. We both just put in time, so anxious for Thursday. I asked John if he thought I should at least make up Leslie's bed, thinking her room looked so stark.

He thought a minute. "Yes. Why don't you make up her bed—she'll be tired when she gets here—but leave everything else. Let her work through that."

Thursday I shopped for groceries with great anticipation of dinner plans, although I wasn't sure just when they would arrive.

At six o'clock Wade's truck popped into view at my kitchen window. Wade opened his door and Dutch bounded over his lap and onto the ground, and briskly walked to the barn, stopping at the door to take a quick pee then dashed inside, probably for a drink of water.

Two weary passengers emerged. They perked up when John rushed from the barn and I clambered down the back steps of the house. Leslie hesitated, then ran to her dad's outstretched arms. They stood for a long time. John finally stood back and cradled her face in his rough hands. I couldn't hear what he said, his voice was soft, but Leslie nodded, tears streaming down her face. Wade stood by me, his arm across my shoulders.

I looked up at this wonderful man, this boy who was now twenty-six years old. "Thank you, Wade. I can't imagine how you did it, but you saved this family, and me, from unbelievable grief."

He shrugged. "I knew I had your support. I don't think I could have done it without that."

Wade reached for Leslie's pack, but John took it from him, and Wade brought in the few things he'd taken, including the wrinkled and creased yellow tablet Mrs. Holmes had given him.

I'd fixed a pot roast in the oven, surrounded by potatoes and carrots, something that would hold until they got home. I quickly put rolls in the oven and set the table while Leslie and Wade took showers. Dinner seemed fairly quiet. I had so many unspoken questions, but I knew they would get answered in time. Total contentment reigned. I saw John look at Leslie and she looked back and smiled. Wade, as usual, shoveled in food so fast he didn't take time to look around, but when finished he sat back and grinned. "Great dinner, Maureen."

I smiled back. All was well.

Leslie called Janelle and they made plans to meet the next day. School had already started and Leslie asked how that was going. Her dad would take her to school the following day, Friday, and get her registered. She'd have a week of work to make up.

I had made up Leslie's bed, as agreed, found a pair of pajamas in one of the boxes, and laid them out for her. I went to her room and asked if she wanted me to wash her clothes. She yawned and said that would be great and would I tell her dad that she was ready to say goodnight.

Wade sidled up to me when I returned to the kitchen after talking with Leslie and starting her laundry. "I want to talk to you guys once Leslie is asleep. I'm going out to the barn to check on a couple of things. I'll be right back. Will you let Dad know?"

"Sure. He's outside someplace. I'm sure Leslie's dead to the world. She's exhausted."

When John and Wade came in we sat at the kitchen table. We were all tired. From relief, this time, not anxiety. Everyone was home. And safe. I poured cups of coffee.

Wade looked at us both. "I have so much on my mind, I hardly know where to start."

He shook his head. "Well, to begin with, we should be proud of Leslie. She did what a lot of people, most people, I expect, could never do. I've told her this, too. She struck out on her own, even camped in the wilderness. When things got bad, really bad, she mustered her courage and went on. I think she showed real bravery. I know what she did was wrong, and there were times I could have cheerfully wrung her neck if I could have gotten my hands on her, but she did what she felt she had to do. She took an honorable path and didn't do what a lot of kids would have done. She looked for, and found, honest work.

"Then, I think we owe a huge debt of gratitude to those folks who took her in, Ellie Mae and Buck Van-Almkerk. They stuck their necks out and gave her a safe place to stay. I don't know how much longer Les could have lasted on her own. She was broke after those kids stole her car, her food, and her stashed money. She was hungry, exhausted, and really getting desperate.

"Ellie Mae and I had quite a while to talk before Leslie returned with Buck and them. They were in the middle of fall roundup. I'll get back to that. Anyway, Ellie Mae told me that Leslie had over-heard her talking to a grocery store clerk—just a little mom-and-pop place. It's where I later learned where Les was. Anyway, Ellie Mae was telling the clerk about her bad back and how behind on her work she was, that her house was a mess, that she couldn't even pick the ripe vegetables from her garden. Leslie followed her out to the parking lot. She went up to the lady and told her she could help her, could clean her house, help in the garden—she listed all the things Ellie Mae had said needed doing. Leslie told her, 'Ma'am, I really need a job.' Ellie Mae noticed how thin Les was and offered to buy her breakfast. Ellie Mae said she could tell Les was really hungry."

"Oh, my god," John said. "Why—"

"Dad, let me finish."

"Okay, son." John glanced at me. My eyes were riveted on Wade, enthralled hearing this side of the story.

"Anyway, after breakfast Ellie Mae took her home, mostly, she said, to keep her safe until she could figure out what to do. But, in all honesty she could use the help. She said Leslie set right out cleaning up the kitchen." Wade chuckled. "But when Buck came in and learned she could handle stock, Ellie Mae said she 'lost her girl to him.'"

Wade looked at me. "But what I wanted to tell you was what Ellie Mae said." He imitated how Ellie Mae talked. "'I knew right off what a fine girl she is. That kitchen hadn't looked so good since the day we moved into this old house. She fixed an elegant salad from my garden vegetables, and she set a proper table. Her room—the room she stayed in—was neat as a pin. That girl knows how a house should be run.'"

Wade looked steadily at me. "That's because of you, Maureen."

Tears sprang to my eyes, but they were tears of joy. I *had* made a difference. Leslie knew how a house should be run because of me. I nodded my thanks to Wade, not trusting my voice.

"Then the next two days she worked for Buck. She paired up with Clem, a hired hand, an old guy that was on the ranch when they bought the place." Wade looked at John. "Buck told me, and I know he meant it, he said 'that girl's a top hand. She follows orders, and she gives it her all. A hundred-ten percent.'"

John's face lit up. "He said that?"

"Yep, that's what he said, Dad, A hundred-ten percent.

"I watched as they came in, herding the last bunch of the day. From a distance I didn't even recognize Leslie. She wasn't wearing her own clothes and had on someone else's old hat, but then I recognized her by how she sits in a saddle. That kid is a pro. Somebody left a back gate open and a bull was racing toward it. Les noticed and took off after that bull. You would have had a heart attack watching that, Dad. I've never seen her ride like that."

Wade laughed and we did, too, delighted with his story. "That's when Dutch got away from me and raced across the pasture and just flew at that bull, nipping his flank, turning him away. Les jumped off her horse and shut the gate and swung back on her horse. But then she stopped, turned and looked at Dutch. But Dutch was running back to me. Right then the old guy called

Les's name—well, the name she was using, Linda—and she caught up to them, opened a gate and helped push the cattle into a holding pen. It was really amazing to see. I was so proud of her. You should be proud of her Dad. She was giving it everything she had. A hundred-ten percent."

"I am proud of her," John said, his voice thick. "And you, Wade, you found her and brought her back to us."

Wade nodded, and smiled. "But I've got a story of my own."

John and I leaned forward, eager to hear more. "When Les and I were talking about working for Buck, she said at first she was really scared that she would screw up. She'd be working on land she didn't know, on a horse she'd never ridden. She didn't even know the people. Then, she said to herself, 'Think of Wade. Imitate him. Do what he'd do.'" He smiled as he blinked away tears.

I sighed. "That's a wonderful story, Wade."

"Another thing. That evening, the day I found her, I noticed VanAlmkerks had an old piano. Almost kidding, I asked Leslie if she'd played. She looked sort of sheepish and said yes, then looked at Ellie Mae and said she'd played it the night before when Buck and Ellie Mae were in town visiting Buck's sister at the hospital. Ellie Mae asked her to play and we had a little concert. It was beautiful. It was like hearing her for the first time." Wade shook his head.

"Son, thanks for telling us all this. You did a remarkable thing, finding her."

Wade nodded and sighed. "Boy, it wasn't easy. It's the toughest and scariest thing I've ever done. I was so scared for her, and for me if I couldn't find her. I don't think I could have handled not finding her.

"Anyway, let's do something for VanAlmkerks in appreciation for all they did for us. Just as Les and I were leaving, Leslie and Buck were out by my truck. Ellie Mae and I were still in the house and I was thanking her. She said, 'Leslie is a very special girl. It has been our pleasure to have her.' We can never repay them for what they did, but maybe you could call 'em Dad, to thank them. And let's be thinking of what else we can do."

John nodded. "I'll do that, Wade. But one thing you already did was to put in a full day's work. And Leslie did, too. I'm sure they appreciated that. But of course, that's nothing compared to what they did for us."

Wade smiled at his dad. "I'll bet you couldn't believe it when I told you we were going to stay another day to work for them. But they were in a bad fix. Their son had broken his leg when a green horse rolled on him. It was a bad break; he was in a huge cast." Wade chucked. "It was killing him, not being a part of things. Another guy and I went to his house and loaded him on the back of my truck. We propped him up on a couple bales of hay and he worked the tally from there. Leslie felt an obligation to stay to help, because they had been so good to her, and because they were short-handed. I'm proud of her for that, too. She was thinking of someone else, of what they needed."

Wade hesitated. "But there's one more thing, this one not so good. Dad, one of the first things Leslie said to me was, 'Are Lilith and Roxanne living at the house now?'"

John's head jerked up. "That's ridiculous! Why would she even think that?"

"Dad, I told you this before, after I talked to Cyrus. That's what she thinks. Early on, way last summer, she told me the reason you were sending her away was because of Lilith and Roxanne. I told her at the time that wasn't true and that she should talk to you about it, but apparently she didn't."

I spoke up, guilt making my voice quiver. "She told me that, too, the day after our Fourth of July party. She said it dawned on her during the night. She said you knew that she wouldn't get along with Roxanne, so you were sending her away. I told her that she should tell you that, exactly what she told me." My voice came out weak and thin.

John, barely able to control his anger, said, "Why didn't *you* tell me?"

"Well, I...."

"Dad, it's sort of a touchy subject. I didn't feel like I could tell you, either. And I guess Leslie couldn't bring herself to do it. What we've got to do now is to make sure she knows it isn't true. Right now she's happy to be home, but we've got to make sure she knows just where she stands."

"Well, for god's sake, she's my daughter! I love her beyond reason!"

"Don't tell us, Dad, tell her!"

"Wade, I've told her. I've told her I love her. I've given her every advantage I could. I've—"

"But with Lilith and Roxanne in the picture, she somehow doubted her place. Right or wrong, it's what she thought." Wade thought a moment. "You know, when she told me why she thought she was being sent away—"

"Goddamn it! She wasn't being *sent* away! She was being given an opportunity to go to one of the finest—"

Wade leaned toward his father, his eyes blazing. "Dad! It doesn't matter what you think, it's what *she* thinks. Now let me finish. When we had...that talk, I told her I thought it would be good for you to remarry some day, so you wouldn't be alone after I got married and she left for college. In thinking about that now, I think she thought leaving was the thing to do." Wade shook his head. "It doesn't really make sense why she would leave Rosemount, but I guess that was anger, a feeling of rejection."

I spoke up. "I'm so sorry, John, I wish I could have told you...."

He held up his hand. "No, Maureen. I can see where that would be awkward. And both of you did tell her to talk to me about it. It's my own fault."

"Dad, I don't think it's anybody's fault. It was a misunderstanding, but a misunderstanding that has to be cleared up before it gets blown out of proportion again. That's all I'm saying."

John nodded. The poor man was drained. "I will. I'll talk to her first thing in the morning, maybe on our way to get her registered for school." He looked at me. "Maureen, we've got to get some meat on her bones. She's really lost weight."

"We will, John. When her life calms down, her appetite will come back."

John looked at us both in turn. "Thank you both. This has been an awful week. I know I've been tough to live with."

"Dad, one more thing. Don't give up on Lilith because of this. If you do, Leslie will feel guilty about that. She just needs to know that nothing will replace your love for her."

John chuckled and looked at Wade with great fondness. "How did you get to be so wise?"

"I'm not wise, Dad. It's just easier for someone else to see from another perspective. I think you're a great dad. I've always thought so, and I know Leslie has, too."

"I hope so. Now I'll make sure of that. I'm going to encourage her to talk to me about her feelings, and I need to be a better listener."

Wade slapped the table. "Boy, I'm beat."

"Sleep in if you can, son."

"Oh, yeah. Like you will."

John shrugged. "I'd better. I'm about ready to drop in my tracks."

12

*L*eslie and I sat at the breakfast table. It surprised me that she would go to school on her first day home. "I just want to get it over with, Maureen. I know all the kids will be talking about me and wondering what happened. I'm really dreading it." She giggled. "You know what Wade said?"

I smiled, surprised that she could find any humor at all in something she was dreading. "What?"

"He said to just keep my explanation simple. Say something like I didn't like the school so I took off and found a job on a big ranch working fall round-up. He said they'd be jealous as hell."

I laughed. "That's a really good idea."

"I think so, too. I won't tell 'em I walked my legs off, then bought and lost a car within about twenty-four hours, nearly starved to death...." She sobered. "That was a really long week. I sure missed you, Maureen. I wanted to just sit and talk to you."

I reached for her hand and gave it a squeeze. "I can't tell you how much I missed you, too. I'm so glad you're home. I hope you and your dad will be able to talk about anything that's bothering you."

"I'm going to really try."

"I'll bet Janelle will be glad to see you."

She hesitated. "When I called her last night she seemed...distant. I dunno."

"Honey, I think she felt bad that she didn't know your plans. It's probably the first secret you've had between the two of you."

"I couldn't tell her! Her mother would have known something was wrong and my plan would have ended before it started."

"I know. Maybe if you tell her just that, she'll understand."

Leslie shrugged. "I sure hope so. She's my best friend."

John walked into the kitchen from outside. "Are you ready to go?"

"Almost, Dad. Give me two minutes." She sprang up from the table and headed toward her room.

"This is going to be a hard day for her," I said. "But I agree. Get it over with and then Monday she can start fresh."

John nodded. "She has courage. I admire that."

"Yes, she does. I wonder if she'll still be in the honors program."

"I'm sure she will. She also needs to talk to Mr. Schaffer about getting reinstated with her piano lessons. I don't think there will be any trouble there, either"

"I'll bet things will be back to normal in no time."

John nodded. "Normal sounds good."

As they climbed into the car, I saw Wade walk out of the horse corral and give them a wave and a "thumbs up" to Leslie. She waved back. I prayed for her, that she'd have the stamina to take the kids questions and teasing. Kids can be mean, especially to anyone who attempts to do anything different. In my opinion, Leslie was a cut above the normal kid, on many levels. I prayed her transition back to Chewack would go smoothly.

When John returned from school almost two hours later, I appreciated his sitting down at the kitchen table and telling me about his morning at Leslie's school.

John said Mr. Green, the vice-principal, at first was a little huffy. "He said her records were already transferred to Rosemount, and this all takes time. Blaa blaa. He sort of rambled on. But then Bob Erickson, the principal, came in, shook my hand, patted me on the shoulder, looked at Leslie and said, 'Welcome back, Leslie. It's good to see you. I'm sure Mr. Green will get your reinstated right away and into your classes.'"

My heart soared. "Oh, how wonderful of him."

John shook his head. "I have no idea how, but they seemed to know she was back. For Pete's sake! She just got home last night!"

"People knew. On the day Wade first called that he'd found her, I made those phone calls to people who had been concerned. Mr. Schaffer was one of them and he probably told the principal and some of the other teachers. I think that probably helped pave the way. I hope her day goes well."

We laughed about what Wade had told her to say. "It's not a bad idea," John said.

Leslie took the school bus home. When John saw her, he came to the house to see how it went. She looked tired, but happy enough. "You wouldn't believe how much homework I have. I did get the honors classes and I have almost a whole week of work to catch up. There goes my weekend."

"How about Mr. Schaffer and your piano lessons?" I asked.

"Oh, yeah. We're back to Wednesdays after school."

John nodded and smiled.

She reached into the fruit basket in the center of the table and selected a bright red apple from the Cahill orchard. I poured her a glass of milk. She took a bite of the crisp apple. "I'm glad you guys called people. The teachers all seemed to know I was back. The kids didn't though. I did what Wade suggested. Just kept it simple. A few rolled their eyes, but my friends were good with it.

"When I went to orchestra, Bobby Burr was first-chair piano, since he was the only piano player at the first of the school year. Mr. Schaffer said that I'll have to challenge up if I want to have first chair. That's how it works for all the instruments. You challenge up to get a better spot.

"How does the challenge work?" I asked.

"Mr. Schaffer has you play something that the orchestra has rehearsed, then he has you play something unfamiliar, to test your sight-reading. The kids vote. Mr. Schaffer always makes it clear that the vote has to be for the skill, not friendship or popularity."

"So are you going to do it?" John asked.

Leslie shrugged. "Really, I am a better player. But I kind of hate to ruin Bobby's hopes. I've decided to just let it go. I'll be second chair."

She turned to her dad. "Is it okay if I go over to Janelle's tonight? We really need to talk and didn't have a chance at school. I'm going to be doing homework the entire weekend. When I go back Monday I want to be all caught up."

"Sure. Don't be late though. You need to catch up on your rest, too."

Our days returned to normal. None of us will ever forget Leslie's leaving, but we survived. And, a few lessons were learned, too. Hopefully John and Leslie would talk things over more freely and really listen to each other. Wade firmly established himself as a hero. I heard him on the phone making Saturday night plans with Teresa, modestly telling her how he'd found Leslie. And I confirmed how powerful faith is, how other people joining in prayer keep a positive momentum going. I personally believed the prayer chain among church members had a powerful effect. Some day I hoped to tell John about it.

It wasn't long before Leslie was talking about Jordan, a boy at school, and the following Friday they had a date.

Wade smiled. "What happened to Kip?"

"He's history. Unless he's the center of my life, he can't stand it. You'll like Jordan. He seems so much more mature than Kip."

John put down his paper to listen to their conversation. "Is he a junior, like you?"

"Yes, but he's a year older. He missed a year of school when he was little. Some health problem, I guess. You'd never know it now. He's a few inches taller than me. *Really* cool looking."

"Do the kids talk much about your being gone?" John asked.

"Some do. I just shrug and say I'm glad to be back at Chewack."

John nodded. "Good for you, Les."

The next day when Leslie came home from school she announced that she was again first chair piano. She smiled. "Mr. Schaffer told me to challenge. He said he needs me in first chair to keep things moving. Bobby Burr isn't a bad player, but he can't read music and follow Mr. Schaffer's baton at the same time. I really hated to do it, but I challenged him and was voted first chair. Bobby was a good sport and even said he was relieved. We take turns playing anyway, but I'll be the main player."

The following Friday when Jordan came to pick Leslie up for their first date, I was impressed. He was a strong healthy-looking boy. He and John talked about ranching. Jordan's father was in real estate, but it was apparent Jordan had knowledge about different kinds of livelihoods. Their first date was a house party.

"The parents will be home?" John asked.

"Yes, sir. My folks won't let me go to a party without the parents there, either."

John nodded. "Good. You guys be home by midnight."

"Yes, sir. I'll have her home by then."

Our fall and winter were good. I continued to be impressed with the smooth working relationship between John and Wade. Leslie, as usual, was consumed with school, her music, and Jordan. Her good grades made her dad proud.

John and Lilith's relationship sort of rambled on. Lilith invited John and Leslie for dinner, but Leslie had other plans. On another occasion it was obvious John was talking to Lilith on his office phone. I say obvious because he seemed to use a different tone of voice when talking to her. Not a fakey voice by any means, just different. His office door was open and both Leslie and I could hear the gist of the conversation. When she heard her dad say, "Saturday? I'll ask her. Thank you." Leslie immediately turned to me and said, "Maureen, tell Dad I'm at Janelle's. I'll be back in a couple of hours. I'll take Polly."

I was amazed when I saw her tear out of the barn, riding Polly bareback, which was rare for her.

John came out of the office and asked where Leslie was.

"She asked me to tell you she was riding to Janelle's and that she'd be back in a couple of hours."

He nodded and returned to his office.

Leslie returned about dinner time. Soon after we sat down John said, "Leslie, Lilith has invited us for dinner Saturday evening."

"Oh, I'm sorry, Dad. Janelle's mother invited me for dinner and to spend the night."

"You know, Leslie, Lilith has invited us two or three times."

"Ummm. Well, you go ahead."

John didn't say anything, but I could see she hadn't fooled him.

After dinner and when John was out of the house, I asked Leslie to sit down, that I wanted to talk to her. She looked leery at my tone. We sat at our usual talking places.

"Leslie, Lilith is making an effort to be friendly to you. It's obvious you're avoiding her offers. You're putting your dad on the spot, trying to cover for you." Unreasonably I felt I betrayed myself, but this was my job, teaching Leslie to think of others, to let go of self, to be a better person.

"Maureen! I don't want to go there. Put up with that weird girl for a whole evening in a dinky little apartment? No thanks!"

"Leslie, you need to think of your dad, of what it would mean to him."

She sighed and slumped in her chair.

I continued, "It's awkward for him to keep making excuses, but he's trying to be patient. I think you need to do your part and at least give it a try."

She shook her head. "I can't imagine how boring it will be."

"Sometimes we need to put others' needs before our own."

"I didn't realize it's been so obvious."

I nodded.

"Okay." A moment of silence. "Maybe I'll take a book to read."

My head jerked up and I opened my mouth in objection.

"Maureen, I'm kidding. Still..."

"That really would be rude!" I laughed.

Wade's girlfriend Teresa often joined us for Sunday dinners. They were obviously very much in love. We all liked Teresa. She grew up in Yakima, the daughter of two teachers. She loved the outdoors and horses, was an experienced rider, and easily fit into Wade's lifestyle.

One Sunday when Teresa had joined us I noticed Wade hardly ate his dinner, just pushed food around his plate, rare for him. Leslie noticed, too. Finally, she couldn't stand it any longer.

"So, are you two going to make some sort of announcement?"

Wade narrowed his eyes at his sister. Teresa giggled.

We all stopped eating. Wade cleared his throat and looked at his dad. "I've asked Teresa to marry me."

Leslie grinned. "What did you say, Teresa?"

"I said yes!"

John rose from his chair and went around the table to shake Wade's hand and to hug Teresa. "That's wonderful news. Congratulations!"

I clasped my hands in joy. "I am so happy for both of you. Two terrific people, made for each other!"

"All right!" Leslie said. "When?"

Teresa's radiant smile lit up the room. "Probably not for awhile, maybe a year."

"Maybe sooner," Wade added. He gave Leslie a long look, smiling.

She smiled back and nodded, then pointed at Teresa's left hand. "Where's your engagement ring?"

"We'll shop for it in Yakima. We couldn't find anything we liked in Chewack."

Leslie folded her hands together. Her eyes sparkled. "I can't wait to see it."

Teresa laughed. "Me neither."

My heart swelled in happiness. Wade and Teresa were so perfect together.

The next morning at breakfast Wade asked his dad, "Remember awhile ago you said when I married I could build a place by the orchard?"

"Yep. Is that what you plan to do?"

"If it's still okay."

"Of course it's okay."

"Maybe Randy and I can start clearing it, getting it ready."

"Have at it."

"I thought we'd put a double-wide in there."

"I'm not that crazy about those things. Why not a real house?"

"A mobile home is about all we can afford."

"Well, let's talk about that later. You guys start clearing. I'll give you a hand when I can."

Leslie invited Jordan to dinner the next Sunday. During dinner Wade mentioned something about clearing the land for their house and Jordan offered to help the following Saturday.

"You bet!" Wade answered. "I'm not going to pass up a good offer like that."

Jordan arrived early the next Saturday and he, Wade, Randy and Leslie made a lot of progress. They cut down several ponderosa pines. Randy used a chain saw to cut them into rounds and Wade split them for firewood. Leslie and Jordan loaded the pieces into Wade's truck and stacked them in the woodshed near the house. They stopped for lunch, then returned to work the rest of the day.

Jordan stayed for dinner, but their evening was short, both too tired to stay awake to even watch a movie.

The following week Lilith again invited John and Leslie to dinner. We were just finishing our meal when Lilith called. John took the call in his office.

"It's her," Leslie said.

John returned to the table as Leslie carried plates to the sink. "Leslie, Lilith has invited us to dinner next Saturday."

I raised my eyebrows to Leslie. She glanced at me and took a breath. "Okay. Should we take something?"

John looked pleasantly surprised. "I usually pick up a bottle of wine."

When they returned Saturday night, Leslie and I didn't have a chance to talk, but on our way to church the next morning, Leslie told me all about it.

"Their apartment is pretty nice. Actually, it's the first apartment I've ever been in. It's bigger than I thought it would be."

"What did you have for dinner?"

"Some chicken dish. You're a LOT better cook. I liked her fruit salad though—it had coconut."

"Does Roxanne still have spiky red hair?"

"No, it's tamer than it was, and her normal color, brown. But Maureen, you wouldn't believe her bedroom. Roxanne's an artist, a really good one. I've never seen anything like it." She spread her arms wide. "One whole wall is a mural. It's kids playing on yard toys at a park, like a swing and teeter-totter, stuff like that. And guess what? She has three kids playing horse shoes. She said she'd never seen that game until she came to our house that Fourth of July. So she went home from our place, painted over whatever was there, and added that scene!"

"My word! It sounds like she's really good."

"She is. She told me about her dad. He's a gambler and got their family in a big mess. They lost their home and everything. Maureen, she told me how mean the kids at school are. She cried telling me about it. She feels fat and ugly and says no one likes her." Leslie looked at me, her lips pressed together in sympathy for Roxanne.

"Oh, how sad." We pulled into the church parking lot.

Later that day Janelle rode over to meet Leslie and to ride horseback to another friend's. The girls sat at the kitchen table to have a couple of cookies before they left.

"Janelle," Leslie said. "I want us to be friends with Roxanne."

"You're kidding."

"No, we really have to." She went on to explain what she'd told me.

"But we don't even go to the same school!"

"I know, but she'll be coming here again with her mom. Let's really try to be friends."

Janelle, her face a cloud of doubt, regarded her friend. "Okay. But it won't be easy."

They were coming here? Why hadn't John mentioned anything to me?. That old familiar nagging feeling returned.

That evening, at dinner, John said he'd like to invite Lilith and Roxanne for dinner. "I've been there several times. I guess we should have them here."

"Do you want to invite them for Sunday dinner?"

"Yeah, let's do that."

I dreaded the day. I knew my attitude was silly, but I just couldn't help myself. I considered fixing dinner, then making other plans so I wouldn't have to be there. But that would be awkward for John. I resolved to act as natural as I could.

When the day arrived I was proud of Leslie, of her effort to make Roxanne feel welcomed. "Roxanne, would you like to go horseback riding?"

"Not really."

"We have a gentle horse you could ride. We can just take it easy, ride around here."

"Roxanne," Lilith said, "you should try it."

"W-e-l-l-l-l..."

"Let's go out and saddle her up for you." Leslie headed out the door.

I glanced at John. He looked pleased with Leslie's effort.

Later, when I looked out the kitchen window, I saw the two girls riding slowly by the house, Roxanne hanging on for dear life, Leslie looking a bit pained, but hanging in there.

Janelle came over after dinner and the three girls went to Leslie's room. Janelle had brought a new board game and I heard laughter, shrieks and groans. They seemed to be having a good time. I was so proud of Leslie for making this effort to make Roxanne feel a part of things. At one outburst from upstairs, John chuckled and shook his head.

After dinner I visited for a bit, then retreated to my room with a good book, a book I held in my hands, but couldn't really concentrate on enough to read. John and Lilith watched television for awhile, then went for a walk around the place. I saw them holding hands as they walked toward the horse corral.

The sight was unsettling, a sort of left-out feeling. My stomach churned. But that was silly. What did I expect? I was doing what I came here to do, what I was hired to do. I had made my position on that topic perfectly clear. Still...

Wade was spared the whole ordeal. He and Teresa had gone to Yakima. Wade had told me, a bit dramatically, that he was going to ask Teresa's father for permission to marry his daughter.

"Do people still do that?"

"I guess. Darrell said he did. Dad said I should."

"Well, I think it's a nice thing to do. How about if her dad says no?"

He grinned. "We'll elope."

They took the horse trailer. Although her family didn't actually farm or ranch, they had acreage, and Teresa and her sister had horses. They would bring back Teresa's horse to stay here.

"Teresa's horse will be living here before she does," Wade said.

13

Wade, Leslie and I sat at the breakfast table. John had eaten earlier and he and Randy had gone off on some errand.

"Wade," Leslie said, "have you *ever* been in trouble with Dad?"

"Oh yeah."

"Really? I don't remember hearing about it."

"You were just little. Anyway, we took care of our business in the barn."

"So...what did you do?"

Wade sighed and looked down, apparently trying to decide whether to tell us.

But then he spoke. "Before Janelle Peterson's family moved here, another family, a guy and his two sons lived on that ranch. I think they rented the place. Kenny, one of the kids, and I were friends. I was twelve and he was a couple of years older than me, and not a very good influence. Dad didn't like me hanging out with Kenny, but didn't really say I couldn't."

Leslie looked disappointed. "That's it?"

Wade chuckled. "No. One day Dad told me to move some cows, just a few head, something I could handle by myself. I rode out to do it, but didn't, and just kept going. To Kenny's. Kenny and I got to fooling around and I didn't get home until almost dark.

"I knew I was in trouble, but I was a pretty cocky kid. I could handle it. Dad was in the barn when I came straggling in."

Leslie and I were in rapt attention.

"He told me that he'd given me a job and that he counted on me to do it. Those cows needed to be moved because their water source had dried up. Besides that, I left the ranch without permission or telling anyone where I was going. He gave me a hell of a whipping with his belt." Wade shrugged. "I had it coming. That was the first, and last, time he ever needed to do that."

"Oh, wow! He's never even spanked me."

Wade snorted. "Not that you didn't have it coming."

She made a smart-aleck face.

He rolled his eyes. "But there was another time and for me it was a lot worse. Dad and I had gone to some kind of stockmen's program at the grange. After the meeting Dad was talking to some of the other men, and I was fooling around with some kids that were there. After awhile Dad called to me and said, 'Time to go home.'

"I said something really stupid, like 'Yeah, an old man needs his rest.'

"The place got really quiet. Guys looked to Dad, then to me. Dad just turned and left and I followed him. He didn't say a word, all the way home. When we got home he said, 'Go to the barn.'"

Leslie took in a breath and I leaned forward.

"I thought I was really going to get it, but we just talked. He said, 'Your talking to me like that showed a real lack of respect. Wade, that's something those men and boys won't forget.'

"I apologized, but it was too late. Oh, Dad accepted my apology, but I know he was right. Those guys probably never forgot it. The damage was done. I'll never forget the hurt look on his face. I grew up that night. I've never given him, or at least tried not to give him reason to think I don't respect him."

"Geez, Wade, that's an awful story," Leslie said.

He nodded.

I said, "Your respect for him is obvious. It was one of the things I noticed when I first came here."

"That's good to hear, Maureen."

* * *

On a sunny Saturday John asked Leslie if she'd like to go with him to a neighboring ranch. "I'm thinking of buying a couple of bulls from Ken Stroh."

"Sure! Is Wade going?"

"Not today. He and Randy have to fix that water line in the heifer pasture."

"John," I asked, "why can't you just not castrate your own bulls and breed them?"

"Because that causes in-breeding problems, like dwarfism. Stroh runs a purebred operation. Ranchers come from all over the country to buy his bulls."

"Do you get all your bulls from him?"

"No, not all, but most of them."

I nodded. There was so much more to cattle ranching that I ever would have believed.

They left and I had a quiet house. I don't think city people realize how quiet life can be in the country. Although I occasionally heard mooing from the cattle, and sometimes a horse's whinny, my world was mostly one of peaceful silence. When I lived in Seattle I got used to the cacophony of city life. But now that I had a taste of this peace, I loved it.

John and Leslie returned sooner than I expected, both strangely quiet. I wondered if they'd had an argument. Leslie spent the rest of the day in her room. When she came down for dinner, she seemed preoccupied, sort of dreamy.

At dinner that night Leslie asked Wade if he knew Sloan Stroh. John's head jerked up.

"That albino-looking guy? I don't know him. Know who he is." Wade glanced up at his sister, then his father. "Why?"

"Oh," she said with what seemed like forced nonchalance, "I just wondered. I met him today at Stroh's. Sloan's their nephew."

Wade helped himself to another pork chop and potatoes. He smashed down the roasted potatoes and drowned them in gravy. "He's about my age, too old for you."

Leslie sputtered. "I didn't ask you how old he is, just if you knew him. Geez."

"Did he ask you out?"

"Wade!" She glanced at her father.

"Did he?" Wade's fork hung suspended as he watched her, waiting for an answer.

"W-well..," Leslie stammered.

"Leslie," John's voice was dead serious, "don't even think about it. The answer is no."

Leslie looked at her father in shock. "Why? How can you say something like that without even knowing him?"

"I know the type."

"What happened to our agreement to talk things over?"

"We're talking it over right now. The answer is no."

Leslie glared at her father, but she wisely said nothing further. John's set jaw and flashing eyes would silence anyone.

I couldn't stand the tension. "Well," I said, "we have apple pie for dessert."

Wade grinned at me. "Got any ice cream to go with that pie?"

Later, as we cleaned up the kitchen, I asked Leslie about Sloan.

She sighed and smiled. "Oh, he's tall, maybe six feet. He's stocky, really strong looking. He has almost white hair–not gray, just white. And white eye lashes.

"Dad saw him talking to me. I think we left early because of it." She shrugged. "He said he thought Sloan was coming on to me. I don't know what his problem is. We were just talking."

"And he's about Wade's age?"

"I guess."

"At your age, that's quite a difference."

Leslie looked at me with impatience.

As he usually did, Jordan called that evening. Their conversation seemed shorter than usual. Afterwards, as Leslie climbed the stairs, I saw her shake her head.

We were gearing up for spring roundup. John was more uptight than usual because Randy had missed a couple days of work. Pearl had given birth to another little boy. Not only that, she was hemorrhaging and confined to bed. Unfortunately, both Karen and Curtis had strep throat. Pearl and Randy so far had escaped it, but Randy had his hands full.

Talk at the dinner table on Friday was all about roundup. Pensive, John turned to Leslie. "Honey, I need you to help Pearl and the kids. I really need Randy out there."

Leslie's face fell. "I was going to work roundup with you this weekend! I've been waiting all week to do that. I even have my homework caught—"

"I know, but Randy's a top hand. I really need him. You can keep your distance from those kids, but see that they don't get near the baby or Pearl. I need Maureen here to feed the crew."

"Dad, I don't want to go there to babysit!"

"But that's where I need you, Leslie. Can I call Randy and tell him you'll help out?"

Silence.

"Leslie?"

"Dad, I... Fine. I'll *babysit*." Her shoulders drooped in disappointment.

John left the table, called Randy, and returned nodding. "He says that will be great."

"Of course it will be great," Leslie said with dripping sarcasm.

I was always amazed at how silent Wade could be in these situations. He always seemed to know when to keep quiet, not take sides, no matter his personal opinion.

The next morning Leslie was ready to go at six, according to her dad's instructions. "Maureen I can't believe I have to do this. Of all the people in the world, why am I stuck with Pearl and those snotty kids?"

"It is too bad, honey. I wish you didn't have to. But I can understand—"

"Oh, I can understand it, Maureen. Dad doesn't think I'm worth any more than a babysitter! Certainly not a *top hand*."

John entered the kitchen just as she was finishing her rant. Leslie looked up at him and just shook her head. John showed no expression at all. "Leslie, I'll run you over in the truck, I have to move some equipment around anyway."

"Fine."

They drove off. My heart went out to Leslie. Really, babysitting Pearl's kids couldn't have fallen on a more reluctant person.

I performed my usual spring roundup insecticide routine as the cattle went through the chutes, but also spent much of my time in the kitchen. At the end of the day everyone came dragging home. Leslie, tired and discouraged, hardly spoke at dinner. I told her I didn't need help with the dishes and she immediately went to her room.

After Leslie left the kitchen, John and Wade remained. "I took Randy home and picked Leslie up," John said. "Leslie said the funniest thing. She said, 'Dad if you plan to have grandkids, they'll have to come from Wade. I'm *never* having kids!'"

Wade smiled. "What did you say?"

John shook his head. "I said, 'Rough day, huh?' She didn't answer. But this morning she said something about not even liking Pearl. I didn't know that. I asked her why, but she just shook her head. I wonder what's going on there?"

"She hasn't since she was little, when I first came here," I said.

"Really? Has she said why?"

I shook my head. "Never, but I've sure wondered. When I've asked, she just shrugs."

The next morning it was the same thing. Six o'clock and Leslie was ready to go. We ate breakfast in a deadly silent kitchen. I couldn't think of anything cheerful or comforting to say. When John came into the kitchen to get her, Leslie looked up at him. "Dad, I don't intend to miss a day of school to take care of *them*."

"No, I don't expect you to, honey. Randy said the doctor's instructions were that after three days of taking antibiotics the kids won't spread strep throat."

"What perfect timing," she said, shaking her head.

John glanced at me, but to Leslie said, "Okay, ready to go?"

All day I ached for Leslie. Two days in a place where she didn't want to be was an eternity. Really, I didn't think I would have been happy in that messy house for two days, either. But knowing Leslie, she'd probably cleaned it up, resenting every minute. I wondered how she managed with Karen and Curtis. She had never played with them, never shared a joke or experience. They were like strangers.

Much to my amazement, Leslie came home in fine spirits. Joyful, even. John left her at the house and drove off in the truck. She bounded into the kitchen. "After dinner, Maureen, let's go to my room. I have something to tell you."

I couldn't wait.

Dinner was a little late with finishing roundup. "Just a few odds and ends to go," John said. He was in good spirits, too.

As we sat down at the table, John and Wade watched Leslie out of the corner of their eyes, no doubt wondering about her change of attitude. She asked about roundup, but not with the bitterness she'd displayed earlier.

Gone too, or possibly just overshadowed, was Leslie's dreamy demeanor that she'd had recently, at least before her babysitting obligation.

Dinner dishes were done in record time and Leslie hurried to her room, looking over her shoulder at me as she left the kitchen. I nodded, indicating I'd be right up.

Her bedroom door stood open and I entered her room to see her bright eyed, sitting cross legged on her bed. I closed the door, took her desk chair and turned it around to face her.

"Maureen, I had the best talk with Pearl."

"Really! How did that come about?"

She shook her head and grimaced. "The first day, Saturday, was awful. The kids were crabby 'cause they still weren't feeling very well. The house was a mess, as usual. I really worked my butt off trying to clean it up. I just did my job, but managed to not really talk to Pearl. I even bathed the baby."

"I'm surprised she let you do that."

"I've bathed Janelle's little brother."

I raised my brow, surprised. "I didn't know that."

"Janelle's mom was standing right there. She offered to let me do it. A little scary, but fun. Anyway, Pearl's baby really needed a bath. While I bathed him, Pearl took a shower, then we changed her bed." Leslie shook her head. "I've never seen sheets so bloody, even though she kept a towel under her. But I guess that was because of the hemorrhaging. Anyway, I managed to do all that without saying anything except what I really had to. Like, she'd say, 'thank you', and I'd say, 'you're welcome.'"

"It must have been awkward though. Did Pearl say anything about your silence?"

"Wait."

I nodded.

"So, today Dad dropped me off again. Boy, Randy couldn't *wait* to get out of there. But the kids were in a better mood and, after I cleaned up the kitchen, I sat them down at the table with games and coloring stuff. Randy had told me that Pearl hadn't had any breakfast, but all she wanted was cold cereal and coffee. So I fixed up a tray and took it in to her. She looked a lot better, too, and said that the hemorrhaging had pretty much stopped and she could actually sit up."

I could not imagine what Leslie would say next. I was so thankful we had this kind of relationship, that she felt free to talk to me.

Leslie continued. "I straightened their room and started to leave when she said, 'Please stay, Leslie. We need to talk.' I'd never heard her use that tone. I said some lame thing like I had to check on the kids, but she said they were fine and please sit down. They have a rocker in their room. So I sat on it. Pearl set the baby up to breast feed, which I'd never seen before, either.

"Then she said that for years she has known something was wrong, that no matter what she tried to do, I avoided her. Well, I just wanted to leave. I didn't want to hear any more, didn't want to ask, didn't want to talk. So I started to get up, but she said, in a really determined way, 'please stay.' So I sat back down. There was this long awkward silence and I finally said, 'I'm sorry if I've been rude.'

"Pearl said, 'You haven't been rude, Leslie, but there has been something bothering you, for years. We need to talk about that.'"

"Oh, my gosh," I said, "that must have been hard for Pearl to say."

"And hard for me to hear. I didn't know what to say. There was this long silence. My stomach churned, I could hardly see straight. Really, I thought I was going to explode. But suddenly I just blurted out 'You weren't nice to me after my mom died!'"

I gasped. "Really? She wasn't nice to you?"

Leslie shook her head. "I didn't think so."

"What did Pearl say to that?"

"She was in tears. But I was so mad I didn't care. Then she said she was so sorry, but I couldn't let it go. I said I was only six years old, even younger than Curtis, and my *mother* had just died. Then I started crying. Maureen, it was so awful. But then Pearl said the most amazing thing. She said she couldn't be sorrier, she had been wrong to act like that. But did I know that at that time she was a year younger than I am now, only sixteen? Maureen, I didn't know that! To me she was an adult."

I was astonished, too. My mouth dropped open. I had no idea Pearl was that young.

"Then she told me about her life. She's the third of seven kids. Her dad had a drinking problem, was abusive, and couldn't keep a job. They moved around a lot, usually when the rent was due. Her mom was worn out with having so many kids, never having money, putting up with her husband's rages. Then, when she was fifteen, Pearl was raped by a friend of her older brother's, a guy she didn't even like. But her brother accused her of coming on to the guy. She got pregnant, with Karen. She was afraid to tell her mom who was already a mess, and was afraid if her dad found out he'd kill her. Finally, when she was four months along and starting to show, she told her mom. Pearl had to quit school, leave her friends, and go to Yakima to live with her mom's older sister."

"Oh, the poor thing," I said. "She's never told me any of this."

"But now comes the good part. She met Randy. He'd just gotten out of the army and was living with his folks, next door to her aunt, until he found a job. Randy's about ten years older than Pearl. Did you know that? She said Randy was the kindest, gentlest man she'd ever known. He could drink just one beer. He knew how to listen. Pearl said Randy was the first person she could ever really talk to. Maureen, Pearl's eyes really glowed—I'd never seen that before, in anyone. She said that Randy believed in her. He wanted to get married so Karen would have a father." Leslie smiled. "She said that Randy's old-fashioned that way. Then, right after Karen was born, my mother died."

I waited for more.

"They saw an ad in the Yakima paper that Dad needed a hired hand. I guess the one he'd had got married and moved away. Anyway, for the first time Pearl had the nicest house she'd ever lived in, with a washer and dryer, but now she couldn't stay in it with her new little baby, she had to take care of me. Well, during the day, anyway. For pay, of course, but she still resented it. She just wanted to care of her new little baby, but now she had to take care of me, too. She admits she was impatient with me, wasn't a good housekeeper or cook. She'd actually had never done those things before.

"Pearl said she's ashamed to admit it, but she was jealous of me. I had a closet and dresser full of nice clothes that were new when I got them, my own room, a father and brother who loved me. She said her dad couldn't even keep one car running. She said she knew she wasn't doing a good job with me. I guess I cried a lot and wasn't eating like I should. Grandma didn't like her, Pearl said. She was relieved when you came, Maureen, so she could stay home, be a mom to her own child and learn how to cook and keep house—or try to.

"But she always knew that she hadn't done right by me. She said she tried to make it up, but I would never let her get close to me." Leslie shrugged. "I guess that's true."

"Once she brought it up, did you remember those things?"

"Vaguely. I probably felt it more than actually remembering it. But after she told me, I felt light as a feather. I could have floated across the room. I thanked her for telling me and apologized for being such a pain. But she said it wasn't my fault, I shouldn't have to apologize.

"Maureen, have you ever noticed Pearl's eyes? They are so beautiful! She has horrible teeth, and her hair is stringy, but she has beautiful eyes. I'd never noticed them before."

"I have noticed her lovely eyes. What a story," I said. "I'll keep all this confidential, but I'm so glad you told me. I'll appreciate Pearl more. And Randy. What a gem! Thank you so much for sharing this with me. I wonder if your dad knows all this."

"No. Pearl said no one besides Randy does. Just me." She smiled, a little smugly.

Then she sighed with gusto and flopped back crosswise on her bed. "I'm exhausted. I'm going to take a shower, go to bed and read."

* * *

A few days later Pearl phoned, asking for Leslie. After she hung up, Leslie told me that Pearl wanted to get involved in Karen's 4H group, and that she needed a babysitter. Unfortunately, the 4H meetings were on Wednesdays after school, the time and day of Leslie's piano lesson, so she knew Leslie wouldn't be available. Pearl asked Leslie if she thought Roxanne could handle taking care of Curtis and the baby for a couple of hours on Wednesdays. Although Leslie was glad to be asked, I think she felt a little jealous having to share Pearl with Roxanne.

"But," I said, "Pearl must have a lot of confidence in you to ask your opinion."

"I guess. Anyway, I gave her Roxanne's phone number. She could ride the school bus to Pearl's, then Pearl will take her home. I'll bet Roxanne will be happy."

"I'm sure she will," I said. "It will give her something to do, plus she can earn a little money."

* * *

The following Monday Leslie surprised me when she phoned after school. "Hi, I'm at Pearl's. I just wanted you to know so you wouldn't worry. I'll be home in a little while."

Normally, right after school Leslie practiced the piano. Rarely did anything interfere with that. It was nice though that she and Peal were developing a new relationship. I'm sure it took a lot of nerve on Pearl's part to dredge up all that history, but it apparently opened the door for friendship.

By the time Leslie got home, she only had about a half-hour to practice before dinner. She again had that preoccupied air about her, in a world of her own.

The same thing happened Tuesday after school. On Wednesday she had her piano lesson and drove the SUV. Thursday and Friday she again stopped at Pearl's.

Over the weekend Leslie and John worked together moving cattle from one pasture to another.

When they came home Leslie told me, with great excitement, that her dad had agreed to talk to Sloan. "Once Dad talks to him, we'll be able to go out!"

"He said that?" I was surprised. John's objection to Sloan had seemed so strong.

"Well...no, not exactly. He said he'd decide after they talked. But I'm sure, after he knows Sloan better, we can go out."

I wasn't so sure, but there was no point in sharing my opinion. "What about Jordan?"

"What about him?" she snapped. "We're not mated for life, Maureen."

I dropped the subject. I realized I had no idea how kids dated these days.

One day that next week, I brought up the subject of Sloan. Leslie was in school and John, Wade and I were having lunch.

"John," I asked, "do you know this Sloan fellow?"

He shook his head. "I've known about him. He's been coming and going to his uncle's over the years."

Wade took a swallow of milk. "What's he like?"

John shook his head, disgusted. "When Leslie and I were over there, I saw him across the pasture, just standing around, giving Leslie the once-over. I said something to Ken Stroh like, 'I see your nephew's back.'

"Ken turned his back to Sloan and said, 'If he wasn't my sister's kid, I wouldn't put up with him. He doesn't do much, comes and goes as he pleases, but expects a paycheck.'

"About that time Sloan moseyed up to Leslie, but I couldn't hear what they were talking about. All I knew was that I needed to get her out of there."

"I wonder what Les sees in him," Wade said.

I chimed in. "Girls are more mature than boys of their same age. So when a man notices her, pays special attention to her, she's flattered."

John stopped eating. "But a guy like that has only one thing in mind. Can't she see that?"

"I doubt it."

"This is exactly what I was talking about when I wanted her to go to Rosemount."

Both Wade and I started to object. John held up his hand. "I know, I know. I'm just saying...."

"The more resistance she gets," I ventured, "the more attractive he'll seem."

"Jesus Christ," John muttered.

Leslie again called from Pearl's after school on Monday. On Tuesday she took the car so she and Roxanne could shop for paints and poster board for some project they had going on. The next day she again drove to her music lesson. On Thursday after school Leslie slammed into the kitchen, a little later than usual, and stormed directly up to her room. Wade followed, as soon as he parked his truck. He looked steamed.

He sat at the table and flung his hat on a chair. "Did you know Leslie has been getting rides home from school with Sloan?"

"No! I thought she was riding the bus, then going to Pearl's."

"She had that jerk drop her off at Pearl's."

"How did you find out?"

"I've thought for the last week or so she was acting sort of strange. It finally occurred to me what was going on, or might be. I waited in my truck at Pearl and Randy's, out of sight, and sure enough they came driving up in his old beater truck. They hadn't come

227

directly from school either—they were almost an hour late."

"Uh-oh."

"Dad's going to be really pissed."

"You'll have to tell him, of course—"

"No, she has to tell him. Tonight. If he hears about this from someone else, she'll be mincemeat."

Later, I called Leslie to set the table and make a fruit salad. She was sullen and quiet.

John came home from town in wonderful spirits. I could hardly stand seeing his cheerful demeanor, dreading how angry he would be by the end of the day. At dinner John said, "Leslie, I spoke to Lilith this afternoon and she told me how you stuck up for Roxanne at her school when you picked her up the other day. I guess the kids were giving her a hard time and you acted like a real friend. It meant the world to Roxanne, and to Lilith, too. I'm proud of you, honey."

Leslie shrugged. "Kids can be mean, especially at that age."

"What were they doing?" I asked.

"Roxanne was standing in front of the school waiting for me and a bunch of girls surrounded her. I couldn't hear what they were saying, but Roxanne looked like she was going to cry. I came up to them, ignored the other kids and said, 'Roxanne, do you want to go shopping for art supplies today?' We took off and those girls just stood there, wondering what happened." Leslie glanced at her brother.

John glanced at both of them. "What?"

Wade looked expectantly at Leslie.

"Nothing, Dad," Leslie said. "I need to talk to you after dinner."

John looked around the table. We were all totally occupied with our meal. "Okay."

John finished his dinner and went into his office. I excused Leslie from helping me with the dishes.

Leslie closed the door, but I still heard a loud "You what?" from John.

After cleaning up the kitchen, I joined Wade in the living room. "I thought you were going to Teresa's."

"I am, but wanted to see what's left of Leslie after she tells Dad about Sloan."

It wasn't long before Leslie left the office, carefully closing the door behind her.

She joined us in the living room and plopped down on the couch. "I'm grounded for two weeks."

"Well, that's not so bad. I was expecting worse," Wade said.

"Just today I told Sloan that I wouldn't ride with him again until he talks to Dad. And I meant it. I told Dad that. I think that helped."

"Good for you, Les."

"You came along right after that. What did you say to Sloan, Wade?"

Wade just shook his head.

"You won't tell me?"

"No."

She sighed. "I have a date with Jordan Friday, tomorrow night! What am I going to tell him?"

"Just say you can't go," Wade said. "It's none of his business why."

"That will be so awkward, though. We've gone together for quite awhile. He'll wonder."

"Just tell him that you had an argument with your dad and he grounded you for two weeks. You don't need to go into detail."

Wade left for Teresa's and I turned on the TV to watch the news. John joined me after awhile, but we didn't discuss the incident.

Being grounded on a large ranch isn't what most kids would call grounded, but it did mean Leslie couldn't go to Janelle's, and except for her music lesson she came straight home from school. It also meant she was given extra chores—cleaning stalls, scrubbing down the instrument room in the calving shed, and the patio concrete. On Saturday John sent her to ask me what she could do to help and I had her weed a section of the garden. She did it all with a minimum of grumbling.

The following Friday she came home from school and sat at the kitchen table to have a snack. "Maureen, Wade said I took advantage of Pearl's friendship by having Sloan drop me off there. It wasn't really like that, I just wanted to talk to her." She paused. "But I guess there's some truth to what Wade says." She searched my face with anxious eyes.

"I'm afraid it might look like that to Pearl. Why don't you talk to her about it right away? Don't let this get in the way of your new friendship with her."

Saturday morning at breakfast Leslie ate early with her dad and brother. "Leslie," Wade said, "I need your help today. Randy has the day off, they're going on a picnic, and we've got to move a bunch of cows off that south pasture. Let's get to it right away."

Leslie nodded.

John asked if I needed anything from town; he needed to get fencing supplies at the hardware. I imagined he would stop to see Lilith when he went to town.

As Wade and Leslie left the house I heard her ask Wade, "Could I get saddled up and then ride over to talk to Pearl for a few minutes?"

I saw him look down at her anxious face. "Okay. Make it quick."

Relieved, she said. "I need to talk to her about...you know."

"Good. I think you should."

When they returned at noon I asked Leslie how her talk with Pearl went.

"I'm so glad we talked! Randy was outside washing their truck, the kids were getting ready to go, and Pearl was nursing the baby, so we had a little time to ourselves. She said she was getting worried about me and Sloan, didn't know what to do, and was relieved when Wade showed up." Leslie giggled. "She said when Wade swung his truck around, blocking Sloan's, she thought it was going to be a 'real fur flyin' event.'"

I laughed. "She really does have a lot of funny expressions."

"But Pearl understands. She said she was glad we talked about it though, and she's glad I'm not sneaking around."

I nodded my approval. Leslie was maturing so fast, I could barely keep up. I was so proud that she stepped right up to make things right with Pearl.

14

*T*wo invitations arrived in Friday's mail, one addressed to the Cahill Family and one to me. We had all been invited to Darrell and Sally's wedding. I usually picked up the mail, sorted out the junk, gave the kids anything that might be theirs, and put the bills and other Cahill mail on John's desk. My invitation remained on the kitchen counter.

John tapped on my invitation. "I wonder why they sent you a separate one."

"I think it's nice they did since I'm really not 'Cahill family.'"

He frowned. "I think of you as family."

Like a sister, maybe. But, in fairness, I had discouraged any type of personal relationship, even avoided it. I still maintained that any relationship other than why I was hired would interfere with my purpose here and would add complications, even heartache. Almost all of my social life, such as it was, was with my own friends, mainly women from our bridge group. In any event, Lilith was in the picture now, though it was hard to tell how serious John was.

Earlier that week, one evening during dinner, Leslie had come right out and asked her dad if he and Lilith were going to get married. He paused, then nodded. "It's looking that way." In my opinion, he hadn't shown a lot of enthusiasm, but that was typical of John.

Wade sprang up from his chair and pumped his dad's hand. "That's great Dad. I'm happy for you."

Leslie put forth a good effort to do the same, with a hug instead of a handshake, but it didn't sound as genuine as Wade's.

John looked mildly surprised at their reaction. "Nothing's for sure yet. We have things to work out."

"Like what?" Leslie asked. Wade gave her an exasperated look, but she ignored him.

"Oh, I don't know. How it will work with her banking career, that sort of thing."

Now John tapped the invitation on the counter. "Do you suppose we could all go together to this wedding?" His voice sounded a little defensive, maybe a bit challenging.

"Sure, that sounds fine, but I think Wade and Teresa will go earlier since they're in the wedding party. Wade's best man and Teresa's the maid of honor." I paused. "I imagine Lilith received an invitation, too."

Clearly, John hadn't thought of that possibility. He actually looked a little wild-eyed.

A few days later I suggested that we invite Teresa, Lilith and Roxanne to Sunday dinner. Leslie seemed more comfortable with Roxanne as they found more things in common. Roxanne's interest in art seemed to help bridge the gap. That late afternoon, soon after Lilith and Roxanne arrived, Roxanne asked Leslie to play the piano.

As Leslie sat down at the piano, I slipped from the kitchen into the living room so that I could see Roxanne's and her mother's reaction. When Leslie began to play I thought Lilith was going to fall off her chair. "Oh, my!" she said. "John said you played, but I had no idea."

"Mom, be quiet! I want to hear!"

I returned to the kitchen, feeling rather smug. I'd always been pleased with myself that I'd taken the initiative to start Leslie on her path to music. It had proven to be a mainstay of her life.

Teresa arrived, and Wade and John came in from gathering strays that had wandered onto neighboring property. The men took quick showers and dressed for dinner.

I think with just the two of them, Lilith and Roxanne lived more casually than a regular family might. I couldn't imagine what their meals would be like, but it seemed as though they might each fend for themselves. I called everyone for dinner and they all filed in, Wade, Teresa, Leslie, John, Lilith and Roxanne. Roxanne immediately took a roll out of the basket, slathered it with butter, and took a bite.

I'd forgotten, or taken for granted, that since I'd joined them many years before, the family always waited for me to be seated before anyone started eating, or even served themselves. Lilith quietly said, "Roxanne, shall we wait for everyone?"

"Oh." The girl's face reddened.

I quickly sat down and began passing the serving dishes next to me.

Lilith took her first bite of food. "This is marvelous, Maureen. I can't imagine the joy of coming home to this every night."

Wade and Leslie's head's popped up simultaneously to look at me, then quickly looked away. John didn't look up from his plate. It was an uncomfortable moment followed by an awkward silence. John and Lilith had apparently talked about whether or not I'd remain here if they married. What would it be like to have her live here? Flustered, I said the first thing that came to mind and reached for the closest plate. "Would you have more peas?"

I'd always been good at covering up my feelings and I managed to bluff my way through dinner. Afterward, Lilith and the girls helped clear the table and I quickly filled the dishwasher. "Thank you, ladies. Girls, go ahead with what you were doing. Lilith and Teresa, why don't you keep John and Wade company in the living room. I'll just put away these leftovers and I'll be done here, too."

Afterward I retreated to my room. But I didn't read; I just sat in my chair, my mind a swirl of dark thoughts. I couldn't imagine another woman in the house. Of course, John had every right to remarry. But where would I fit in? I would probably lose this room, my room. My life would never be the same.

I'd managed to hold at bay these fears for a long time. But now the inevitable rushed in. What I had feared was becoming reality.

I had felt an obligation to Leslie, had always made myself available to her. She still had almost two years before she left for college. My job wasn't done!

Or maybe it was.

* * *

Marvin Cole, world-renowned pianist, just back from a concert series in Europe, was coming to Chewack High School, as unlikely as that sounded. Through Leslie's piano teacher Mr. Shaffer's efforts, many Washington schools would host the famous pianist. As it happened, Mr. Cole's parents lived in Washington and he was honoring his home state with these concerts.

Leslie had been asked to introduce Mr. Cole at a student-body assembly. She was honored to be asked. Even though by this time she had played in front of many audiences through her private lessons and school programs, she was all aflutter about the honor bestowed upon her. We shopped for a special outfit for her to wear for the occasion, a green and blue wool plaid skirt and a beautiful green cashmere sweater.

The day of the concert she appeared at the kitchen door for breakfast wearing her new outfit, her hair perfectly coiffed, a big grin on her face.

My heart filled with pride. "John, doesn't Leslie look lovely?"

"This is your big day, huh? John said. "You look beautiful, honey."

About the same time, I heard Wade bellow from the hall. Often, when Leslie tied up the upstairs bathroom, Wade took a shower downstairs. But what was he hollering about?

Suddenly a wet hairy arm reached into the kitchen, snatched Leslie almost off her feet and she disappeared with a shriek. John and I stared at one another, trying to figure out what was happening.

"Wade, stop it! WADE!"

"Do you like this? Well, I don't either!"

John and I scrambled from the table into the hall. From the open bathroom door I saw Wade, grim and silent, holding Leslie under what was obviously a cold shower. She sputtered and yelled, "Wade, stop!"

For someone who can wrestle a 250-pound calf to the ground, Wade didn't find Leslie's give-or-take a hundred-ten pounds much of a strain.

"Wade!" John's voice thundered, "what are you doing?"

Wade pulled Leslie out of the shower, dripping wet. Water seeped across the floor from both of them. "How do *you* like a cold shower?"

"Look what you've done!" she sputtered. "My new skirt and sweater! Look..."

John took in the scene, his eyes widening at Wade's soaked briefs, which, when wet were almost transparent. "Wade, for god's sake!"

Wade glanced down, snatched a towel off the rack and wrapped it around his waist. He glared at Leslie. "Why don't you tell them how much fun it is to take a cold shower?"

Leslie, hair dripping into her shocked eyes, looked first at her father, then at me. "Maureen," she almost whispered, "look at my new clothes. What will I do?"

I grabbed a towel from the bathroom cupboard, wrapped it around her shoulders and led her out of the bathroom and up the stairs.

"Leslie," I said, "what in the world happened?"

"That stupid bas...."

"Shhhh. We'll take care of it. You have other clothes."

I heard John and Wade's heated conversation downstairs.

I helped her peel off the wet clothes, put on a bath-robe, and dry her hair.

In bits and pieces, Leslie admitted that she heard Wade taking a shower and she slipped into the bath-room and turned off the hot water faucet under the sink, leaving him with a cold shower. This was apparently the second time she had done it and at least one too many times, as far as Wade was concerned.

Unfortunately, it all happened on Leslie's big day. The timing was awful, even though she had caused the ruckus in the first place. While Leslie put on dry underwear, I found another skirt and sweater and handed them to her.

She snatched them from my hands. "That stupid Wade ruined my new clothes!"

"I don't think they'll shrink. The water was cold." I couldn't help but smile.

"I don't think this is one bit funny."

"No, I'm sure you don't." I gathered the wet clothes and left her room.

Leslie again entered the kitchen, totally avoiding looking at her brother. "Dad, I'll need to take the car today. I've missed the bus."

John shook his head. "Maureen's car's in the shop, and she needs the SUV today. Wade will take you."

Wade's head jerked up from his breakfast.

Leslie was appalled. "What? Why?" She turned to me. "Maureen, will you take me?"

John, though obviously disgusted about the whole thing, spoke in a calm voice. "Leslie, sit down and eat your breakfast."

"I'm not hungry."

"Just have a piece of toast. Here." He buttered a piece of toast and handed it to her. "Here's Maureen's good peach jam."

Leslie, sullen, spread jam on her toast and took a bite. Then another.

She again went to her room to finish getting ready for school, then returned to the kitchen. "Dad, please take me to school. I don't want—"

"Leslie, Wade's going to take you." He looked at both of them, his face stern. "I want this resolved."

Neither replied. "Wade, do you hear me? I want this resolved."

Wade sighed. "Yes, sir."

"Leslie?"

"Dad, I don't—"

"Leslie, come here."

She went to her father, looking so forlorn my heart went out to her.

John stood. "I'm sorry this happened today. You look nice, honey. You've been honored, and I'm proud of you. Just put this behind you and make your presentation like you've practiced. And I want this business between you and Wade resolved. Okay?"

She sniffed. "Okay."

Wade stood by the door and opened it as she flounced by. He started to take her arm, but she jerked it away.

"Oh, boy," I heard him mutter. He turned to me. "Maureen, I'm sorry about the mess. I'll clean it up when I get back."

"Don't worry about it. I'll just use that water to mop the floor."

Wade softly closed the door.

"Lord knows there's enough of it," I added.

John snickered.

We stood at the kitchen window as they made their way toward Wade's truck. He actually walked around to open the door for her. Without even looking at him she stiffly climbed in, staring straight ahead.

John turned to me. "I can't believe that whole thing happened."

I just shook my head, and sat at the table. A little giggle escaped. I glanced up at John, sure that to him there was nothing funny about it.

A chuckle rumbled from his lips. "Poor little wet hen."

I laughed harder and he joined me, collapsing on his chair at the table.

Before long we were laughing so hard we could hardly catch our breaths. Wiping my eyes, I gasped for air. "And those skivvies!" I covered my eyes so I wouldn't see it again.

John threw back his head and guffawed, slapping the table. We'd calm down, then start all over again.

Suddenly John put his big, work-worn hand over mine. I was so surprised, I stopped mid-laugh.

"Have you ever been sorry you came here?" He was serious; his dark eyes bored into mine.

"*Never.* These have been the happiest years of my life."

His eyes turned from questioning to relief, to something else...

The phone rang.

As Leslie claimed, when John talked to Lilith on the telephone, his voice seemed different. "No, that's okay. Today? I have a dentist appointment at 10:00. Could we make it around 11:00 or so?" After a pause, "Okay, see you then."

I had stayed in the kitchen, cleaning up after breakfast. After the phone call, John stood in the kitchen doorway watching me for a moment. I briefly looked at him, but continued filling the dishwasher.

"I'll be having an early lunch in town today," he said.

"Okay."

He returned to his office for a few minutes, and I began cleaning up the bathroom mess. I heard him return to the kitchen, go on through to the laundry room, and put on his boots. The back door opened and closed.

I sat on the closed lid of the toilet, numb. My mind was a jumble. What I had avoided thinking about for years now crowded my mind. Why now? Has John's relationship with Lilith brought on these feelings of regret? If so, that wasn't fair. Not to anyone. Why is everything happening at once? For years we worked side by side in harmony, but now everything seemed different. I could see it in John's eyes, too.

Tears flowed. My life here was done. There was no way I could live here with John and Lilith. *What will I tell Leslie? How will I go on? What will I do?*

I forced myself to get back to work. That bathroom had never been so clean. I even took down the curtains to wash and iron.

Wade's truck returned, but he didn't come to the house, much to my relief. I didn't feel like talking to anyone.

John returned to the house and dressed for his dental appointment and lunch with Lilith. I occupied myself in another part of the house.

Wade came in for lunch and I managed to carry on a decent conversation with him, just chit-chat.

That afternoon I attended a meeting at church. It was wasted on me. My mind was consumed with my jumbled life.

By the time Leslie returned home from school I had calmed down, but nothing had been resolved in my mind. I'd keep my thoughts to myself until it became clear what I must do.

Leslie burst through the back door. "Maureen, the concert was wonderful! That's what I want to do, give concerts to high school kids. Wow, Marvin Cole is soooo good."

"Did you have a chance to talk to him?"

"I did! I told him I played and that's why I had the *honor* of introducing him."

"How did it go with you and Wade?"

"Okay, but you know what that Wade did? He drove to within about three blocks of the school and parked! He wouldn't leave until we *resolved* our differences."

I laughed. "Wade follows orders."

Leslie laughed too. "But it wasn't funny this morning. I told him I'd be late and he said we were gonna sit right there until it was resolved. Geez. He started though, said he was sorry he was so rough and that he hadn't remembered it was my big day.

"I told him again that I was going to be late, but he just sat there. It was too far for me to walk by then, I'd really have been late." She sighed. "So I said I was sorry. It was a dumb prank, and I wouldn't do it again. He put the truck in gear and off we went. I got to school right on time."

I nodded. "That's good you guys got it settled."

"Yeah. I don't like it when someone's mad at me. Boy, he was mad, wasn't he?"

I chuckled. "I'd say so."

"Well, it was a dumb thing to do. Sometimes I wonder what I'm thinking."

"Welcome to the club."

"Oh no, not you, Maureen. You always have things under control."

*O*n Saturday of the second weekend of Leslie's restriction, the doorbell rang as she practiced piano. The front door was so rarely used, it even startled Leslie. She answered the door. "Oh, hi!"

I heard a gravelly male voice and from the kitchen door I saw a burley white-haired fellow, about Wade's age, standing, his hat in his hand. The excitement in Leslie's voice showed her pleasure as she invited him in. She excused herself and found her dad in his office. On her way back to the living room, she swung through the kitchen and whispered to me, "Maureen, it's Sloan!"

I stepped into the living room. When Leslie saw me, she said, "Sloan, this is Maureen."

I smiled. "Hello, Sloan."

He gave me a brief nod.

"My dad said he'll see you now, Sloan. He's in his office." The two made their way through the kitchen to the office. Leslie emerged, wide-eyed, after closing the door.

She sidled up to me and whispered. "I'd love to have stayed in there, but dad 'excused' me. Oh, my gosh! What are they talking about, do you suppose?"

"I wonder. Maybe about what he does for a living, that kind of thing."

"I don't know what to do with myself."

"Why don't you play the piano? Sloan has never heard you play, has he?" I seriously doubted if Sloan could begin to appreciate Leslie's talent. He looked more like the honky-tonk type to me.

"Okay, but my hands are so sweaty I don't know if I can keep my fingers on the keys."

Oh, young love is so painful. And really, I didn't like the looks of him. I agreed with Wade and John. But Leslie was an intelligent girl, surely she could see what low-life he was.

Soon Sloan came out and found Leslie at the piano. Without a word to her about her musical ability, he said, "Your dad wants to see you. I'll wait here."

This suspense was killing me. Soon Leslie popped out of the office and rushed into the living room. "We can go riding, here on the ranch."

"Riding!" he boomed. "I wanna take you to town!"

"Well, Dad says this first time he just wants us to be closer to home." She didn't mention that she was still grounded and couldn't leave the ranch.

He sighed loudly, then muttered something I couldn't hear.

Leslie slipped on her riding boots. They made their way to the barn and I watched out the kitchen window as Leslie gathered two horses–Polly and another for Sloan, a big roan called Ben. Soon they emerged, walking the horses, then mounting. Sloan handled his horse much rougher than any Cahill would. Leslie apparently noticed and looked around to see if Wade saw.

Wade had walked out behind them, Dutch at his heels. As Leslie and Sloan started out, Wade commanded Dutch to follow, pointing them out to the dog. The dog ran after them. I had to lean over the sink to see, but saw Leslie point toward the barn, sending the dog back. Wade called out to Leslie, apparently to take Dutch because the dog immediately ran back to them again.

A few minutes later, John came into the kitchen, raising his eyebrows as Wade joined us.

"I gather you and Sloan had your talk," Wade said.

John nodded. "I don't like him." He turned to me. "What did you think?"

"I think he's a sleaze." It popped out without my giving it a lot of thought.

John sighed. "I felt I should let her spend some time with him. As long as I resisted, I was afraid he'd seem that much more appealing to her."

I spoke up. "He wasn't happy with riding here. I heard him say he wanted to take her into town."

"I'll bet he would," John said. "Wade, did she tell you where they were going?"

"To McClellan's Bluff. I thought I'd mosey up there in just a bit. I sent Dutch with 'em. Dutch was with me in the barn when they came in and the minute she saw Sloan her hackles rose and she gave him her icy stare."

John nodded. "That was good thinking, sending Dutch with them. I don't know what I'll do the next time Leslie asks."

"I know what you mean," Wade agreed. "Just looking at the guy makes me want to punch him out."

"I doubt there will be a next time," I said. "Once the pressure is off and it's her choice, I think she'll be able to see what a loser he is."

Leslie and I had ridden to McClellan's Bluff. It was a name the family had given to a steep bank that overlooked McClellan Road that runs along the east side of the ranch. There's an intersection there, the place where Barbara Cahill was killed in the car accident. It was probably two miles from the house.

It wasn't long before I saw Wade walking his horse, Dusty, out of the barn. Randy walked out with him. I saw Wade look into the distance and stiffen. I knew something was wrong and stepped out of the house to see for myself.

Leslie, on Polly, tore down the slope toward home. She was going awfully fast for that uneven terrain. I feared her horse might trip in a gopher hole, but she barreled on. No doubt there was some sort of emergency. She would be in trouble if she rode a horse like that under normal circumstances. My heart hammered.

In the distance I could see Dutch bounding toward home, jumping over small brush. Leslie and her horse slowed, then skidded to a stop near Wade and Randy. Leslie jumped off. Randy gathered both hers and Wade's horses and Leslie ran toward the house, Wade at her heals. As she neared, I could see a rip in the sleeve of her plaid shirt.

Leslie brushed past me and burst into the kitchen. The screen door slammed behind her. As Wade and I followed, I heard her pounding up the steps leading to her room.

Without giving it a thought, I followed Wade up the stairs. She'd slammed the door to her room, but Wade opened it without even knocking. "What, Leslie? What happened?"

John hurried up the stairs.

Leslie sat on her bed, wide-eyed.

"Did he hurt you?" John bellowed. He sat on the bed next to her, forced himself to be calm, and gently reached for her shoulder.

"No, Dad. Not really." She took a breath. "Sloan killed Mom."

"What?" John and Wade said in unison. My mouth dropped open.

"We went to McClellan's Bluff. You know, that guy's a loser. On the way he told me that he was leaving, he has a good job waiting for him in Arizona. He wants me to go with him." She shook her head. "He was bragging that he could always find work, always had money. Yeah, I thought, that's why he drives a beater truck." She looked at Wade. "Did you see how rough he was with that horse?"

Wade nodded.

"He was like that the whole time, jerking poor Ben around."

"Leslie, what happened?" John said.

I was afraid my wobbling legs wouldn't hold me up any longer, and sat in Leslie's desk chair.

"Yeah, okay. I'm just trying to tell you that I already realized I couldn't stand the creep. We got to the bluff overlooking that intersection and he actually told me that about ten years ago he and a buddy were going to his uncle's for summer work, but they were in a bad accident. They were both drunk; Sloan was driving. When the accident happened, both the guys were thrown out of the car, which they stole, by the way. They landed in ditches on either side of the road. Sloan could see right away that his buddy was dead. Sloan was hurt, a broken arm and banged up ribs, but managed to walk away before anyone came. I asked some questions and I'm sure the car they hit was Mom's. He even said he saw in the Spokane paper— that's where he ended up, Spokane— that it was some rancher's wife and that the driver of the other car was not identified. So nobody knew that Sloan had been the driver."

"Dad," Wade said, "that has to be it. The car that killed Mom was stolen."

"That's right, it was. From some guy in Montana. And there *were* two in that car, instead of just one, like we all thought."

Wade's cell phone rang. John looked at him impatiently.

"It's Randy," Wade said. "Yeah," he said into the phone. "Okay, good." Wade walked over to Leslie's window. "Yeah, he's leaving."

Wade turned to his dad. "Randy just called to say Sloan brought Ben back and that he's leaving. Randy said he was waiting for him and watched as he rode down the hill. Sloan didn't look him in the eye, just dropped the reins and walked to his truck." Wade shook his head. "Bastard." He returned to his place to lean by the door, arms crossed, scowling.

"Okay, go ahead, Leslie. Does Sloan know it was your mother who died?"

"No, I'm sure he doesn't. Once I realized it, I was careful not to say anything. By this time, all I wanted to do was get away from him.

"He got off his horse and wanted me to get down. I started to say, no, we'd better get back, but he took Polly's reins in one hand and reached up to pull me off. I was afraid if I refused, he'd get suspicious, so I got down. He immediately grabbed me. He was really rough. I tried to get away. That's how my shirt got torn."

"That damn son of a bitch." Wade turned to leave the room.

John reached out. "Wade, hold on. Let's be careful about this. There's time. Go on Leslie."

Leslie turned to Wade. "You know, sending Dutch was a good idea, although at the time I didn't think so.

The minute I yelled, "Let me go!" Dutch sprang into action and bit his thigh."

"I wish she'd bitten his dick," Wade said.

"Wade." John shook his head. "Go ahead, Leslie."

"Then Dutch grabbed his pant leg and wouldn't let go. Sloan shook his leg and hollered at me to call her off, but I just climbed on Polly and took off." She looked at Wade. "I hated to leave her, but I had to get away."

"She can take care of herself," Wade said. "She was right behind you. You were smart to do what you did. She probably let go of Sloan as soon as you were on your way home."

Leslie looked at each of us in turn. "But that's not all. When he grabbed me and I fought back, he said, 'Oh, I see you're gonna be a little prick teaser like that bitch Tracy.' I'm sure he's the one who raped Tracy. Once, when he picked me up after school he asked if I knew Tracy and he even described her. He said he liked her long hair and he wanted me to grow mine long. I told him I didn't know her very well, but that someone had raped her."

"What did he say to that?" I asked. My stomach roiled realizing the danger Leslie had been in.

"Just, 'Oh, yeah?'"

"Okay," John said. "Let's think about this." He looked at Wade. "I know you'd like to tear him apart, but let's do this right. We need to talk to Sheriff Ellis. It's been ten years since the accident, so I'm not sure what the law can do about that. If he's your age, he would have been only sixteen or so, a minor. But they would have taken DNA samples from Tracy. Maybe there's something they can do there."

Leslie stirred around on her bed and sat with legs crossed, yoga style. "Dad, I'm sorry..."

"Leslie, that was a dangerous situation. But it seems to me you handled yourself well out there." He patted her knee. "I'm just glad you're safe. We need to talk about keeping you that way, safe from Sloan, until we can do something about this."

"But he's such a loser," she wailed, "and I didn't even see it."

"But you *did* see it when it really mattered," John said, "and next time you'll spot it even sooner. It takes experience, Leslie, to recognize those traits in people."

"When he bragged about how much he moved around, went where he wanted, when he wanted, I thought of how hard you guys work keeping this place running. Really, he has nothing and he's your age, Wade." She shook her head. "Boy, he's strong. He knew all the moves—blocked my kicks, held my wrists. If it hadn't been for the dog, I don't think I could have gotten away." She looked at Wade and nodded. "I'm glad you sent Dutch."

"Yeah," Wade agreed, "she's a pretty good judge of character. We should run all your boyfriends past Dutch before you go out with them."

"She's a better judge of character than I am, anyway. I don't know what I ever saw in him. Oh, yuck. I just want to take a shower." She shuddered.

John stood. "Okay, you do that honey." He looked at us. "We need to talk, see how we're going to handle this."

While Leslie showered we sat at the kitchen table. I started to pour cups of coffee.

"You know what? Wade said. "I'm going to have a beer. Dad? Maureen?" I declined.

John ran his fingers through his hair. "Yeah, me too. God, I hate that guy. I couldn't stand him before, but now..."

Wade handed his dad a beer. Neither drank that much, but there was always cold beer in the refrigerator. "So, how do you want to handle it?"

John took a swallow. "I think the first thing we should do is talk to Sheriff Ellis, maybe make a list of everything Leslie told us."

"You know," I said, "I'll bet this isn't Sloan's first time around. He may have a record in other states, maybe even a warrant."

"That's right! The sheriff can check into that," Wade said.

John called Sheriff Ellis, who was actually a friend of his, but learned the sheriff would be out of town until late Tuesday night.

John sighed. "Well, that's too bad. I don't want to talk to anyone else. I have a lot of respect for Dan Ellis, and I don't want this getting around until something can actually be done about it."

"Yeah, I agree," Wade said. "Let go see him Wednesday. Are you going to talk to Sloan's uncle? Poor guy. He probably can't stand him either."

"That's going to be touchy. I'm not sure what I'll do. Maybe just wait until we talk to the sheriff."

We discussed ways we could keep Leslie safe until then. Leslie joined us in the kitchen, fresh from her shower, hair still wet, clean clothes, and a relieved smile.

"Leslie," her dad said, "let's not tell anyone, not even Janelle, until we've had a chance to talk to the sheriff. I think it's important that Sloan doesn't suspect we know anything. All he needs to know is that you're not going to have anything to do with him. Okay?"

"Okay. He'll think it was because he was so rough."

The next morning, Sunday, Leslie went to church with me, allowed even though she had one more day of restriction.

As we passed Stroh's long gravel driveway, Leslie glanced down it. "What a jerk."

"Yes, he is. Well, I'm just glad you weren't hurt. Physically, I mean. I know your feelings were hurt."

Her voice was full as she fought back tears. "I am disappointed. And now I've blown it with Jordan. He knows about Sloan—not all about him, but that I was seeing him. Jordan used to call every day and now he never calls at all."

"How about when you see him at school inviting him over for dinner next Sunday?"

"I don't know if he'll come."

"Tell him we're having apple pie."

Leslie laughed. "That'll get him." She ran her finger along the car's window sill. "Jordan isn't very exciting, but I like him a lot, and I feel safe with him."

"You have the rest of your life to find someone exciting. Dependability is important, too, and Jordan is certainly that." I pulled into the church parking lot. "You may have to make the first move with Jordan, Leslie. His feelings are probably hurt too."

The next morning Leslie assured her dad that after school she would wait with the other kids for the school bus. She was officially off restriction, so she thought she'd stop by and talk to Pearl, but she'd call from there.

Monday, when she returned home after talking to Pearl for only a few minutes, she told me that Sloan had stopped by the school to pick her up, but that she'd just called to him, "No thanks." He signaled her over to his truck, but she just turned her back to him to talk to Janelle. Janelle, who hadn't known Leslie had ridden with Sloan, asked what was going on. Leslie said, "I just told her that he came to the house, but I decided I really don't like him."

"What did she say?"

"Oh, that she didn't think he was my type anyway. She didn't ask anything more about it."

On Tuesday, Leslie came home right after school and practiced her piano, then started her homework. At dinner she reminded her dad that she had her piano lesson the next day and was it okay for her to take the car?

John thought a minute. "Okay. We'll probably see Sheriff Ellis tomorrow, so we'll have a better idea of what to do."

On Wednesday John finally got through to Sheriff Ellis and made an appointment to see him at four o'clock that afternoon. John would have preferred to see him earlier, but since the sheriff had been gone for several days, his calendar was full.

After her lesson Leslie called and said she was out of shampoo and would stop at Rite Aid, then come straight home. John and Wade had left shortly before for their appointment with Sheriff Ellis.

I began to get nervous when Leslie didn't come home when I expected her to. My skin felt prickly. Something was wrong. I'd looked out the window hoping to see her car when Pearl pulled up, hurried toward the house, all three kids in tow.

I frowned. *How odd.*

They burst into the kitchen without even knocking. "What?" I said. "What's wrong?"

Pearl held the baby close, then sat at the kitchen table. "Sit down, Maureen."

"What? What is it?" My mouth went dry.

"Sit down."

I sat. Pearl's beautiful eyes seemed twice their normal size. I couldn't imagine what she was going to say.

"Now let me tell you everythin'," she said, "before you get all riled."

"Okay," I whispered.

"I was takin' Roxanne home after she babysat while I went to 4H with Karen."

Oh, God, I can't stand this. But I kept my mouth shut.

"We was on Marble Street, at the stop light, when Roxanne said, 'Look, there's Leslie. Whose truck is that?' Then she said, 'Pearl, she's sayin' help!'

"I looked when Roxanne first saw her. Leslie was in that Sloan's old beater, in the lane right next to us. I didn't see it, but Roxanne said he looked over at Leslie and pushed her head down."

"Oh, my god!" I said, suddenly standing. *Our worst nightmare!*

"Hold on, now. Maureen, sit down." She waited while I sat. "The light changed and Sloan drove off, fast. I gave my cell phone to Roxanne and told her to call 9-1-1. Maureen, she done good. She was calm. She told 'em that it looked like Leslie Cahill was bein' kidnapped, that Leslie'd said, well mouthed, 'help' to her.

"I followed Sloan and told Roxanne just where we was, and she told the Sheriff, or whoever it was she was talkin' to. Pretty soon though he was goin' too fast for me. I couldn't take the chance with the kids in the car. But the 9-1-1 person said the Sheriff was on the way.

"The next thin' we knew, we heard the sirens and the Sheriff's car tore past us. Then we saw Wade and John in Wade's truck, right after 'em. Wade's hazard lights was flashin' away."

She stopped talking.

"And?"

"An' that's all I know."

"Where's Roxanne?"

"I took her home on my way back to town before I came here."

"Oh, Pearl, you did all the right things. But we don't know what's happening now!"

"No, we don't. But with the Sheriff and Wade and John after him, that Sloan don't stand much of a chance."

Randy saw Pearl's car by our house and came to the door, wondering what was happening. Pearl filled him in and he joined us at the table. I couldn't sit still. I paced the kitchen floor, sat down, then paced some more. We barely spoke, just looked at our watches and each other.

Pearl pulled out a breast and fed the baby. "When they catch up with Sloan, can't you jus' see the Sheriff tryin' to peel Wade off a that loser? It's a satisfyin' thought."

About an hour later the SUV pulled up and John and Leslie climbed out. Wade pulled up in his pickup a couple minutes later.

With shaking hands I jerked open the door. They all filed in. We crowded around the kitchen table and all three answered as we fired questions at them.

"Did you get 'im?"

"Oh, yeah," Wade said.

I looked at Leslie. "What happened to your eye?"

She shrugged. "Sloan hit me. Wade said I'll have a shiner. Just what I need."

What I gathered from their stories, told in bits and pieces, was that Wade and John were in the sheriff's office when a call came through. A lady at the Rite Aid parking lot said she thought a girl was being kidnapped. The caller described the SUV Leslie had started to get into, but then was wrestled into an old scrubby truck. The girl hollered for help as the guy forced her into the truck. The lady gave the sheriff's department the direction they were heading. The sheriff called for one of his deputies to give chase.

The three of them—the sheriff, John and Wade— were just going out the door when 9-1-1 got the call from Roxanne, using Pearl's cell phone, saying they saw Leslie in Sloan's truck and that Leslie had mouthed 'help.' The sheriff in his cruiser and Wade and John in Wade's truck went screaming out of town in chase.

They saw Sloan's truck and were closing in, but Sloan got turned around and passed them, going the other way. They turned around. Sloan took a curve too fast and landed in a ditch with his truck on its side.

The sheriff made Wade and John wait while he climbed into the ditch, gun drawn. Sloan had a gun in the glove box and was trying to reach it, fighting against gravity since the driver's side of the truck was on the down-side of the ditch. Leslie held the glove box closed and that's when he hit her with his fist, trying to get his gun. When the sheriff opened the passenger door, Leslie told him Sloan had a gun and the sheriff reached in with one arm, pulled Leslie out and handed her to Wade, who by this time was half way down the ditch. Wade handed her to John.

"I was so surprised to see Dad and Wade there!" Leslie shook her head.

The sheriff got Sloan's gun, handed it to the deputy who had just arrived, and they hauled Sloan out of the truck, swearing like a mad man.

"He called me some awful names." Leslie shook her head.

Sloan apparently made a fool of himself, calling Leslie a lying bitch, among other things. The sheriff had his hands full trying to keep Wade away from Sloan.

Wade shook his head. "If Sheriff Ellis had let me at him..."

They finally put that jerk in the sheriff's car and the deputy stood guard. It looked like Sloan was in deep trouble. I was right, too: they learned he had outstanding warrants in Oregon and Idaho. My stomach finally settled down, now that we had our girl back safe and sound.

I'd fixed a big pot of stew, thinking we'd have it for dinner, then I'd freeze the rest for another day. We all ate together. The table was quiet — we were all in a state of wearied relief. Leslie snuggled between her dad and brother. Her eye got steadily blacker. Poor thing. The kids at school would make a big deal out of that. Actually, I thought Leslie took the whole thing well. Everyone told her she did just the right thing. Calling for help probably saved her. Pearl's quick thinking confirmed the emergency and provided directions. And John and Wade's happening to be at the sheriff's office when it all unfolded was a lucky break, too.

Later Roxanne and Lilith stopped by and we all made a big deal of the role Roxanne had played in Leslie's rescue. I could tell Roxanne was pleased to have had an important part in this scary event.

"And the 9-1-1 lady said my voice was calm and clear and she could hear every word. She said that's unusual." Roxanne looked around as we all agreed that it was indeed unusual, and that many people would have panicked.

John shook her hand. "Thank you, Roxanne. You had a big part in saving Leslie from...God knows what."

"You're welcome." She solemnly shook his hand, obviously proud to have such recognition.

The next day John met Leslie at school and they went together to give Sheriff Ellis a statement. The sheriff was appreciative of the information about Tracy and would pursue it further. As for causing the death of Barbara Cahill, he would talk to the county prosecuting attorney, but likely there was nothing that could be done, especially since Sloan had been underage when the accident occurred. Leslie didn't want to press charges. She just wanted him out of her life. If there was a trial, she would have to see him and the whole incident would be made public. What with the rape and the warrants from other states, he would be out of commission for a long time.

16

O ur lives finally settled down, especially once Sloan was taken to jail at the county seat in Spokane. His life was now in the hands of the law. Thank God.

My personal life, however, seemed unsettled. I kept myself busy running the household, but my nights were again interrupted by doubts and my recurring feelings of emptiness.

Nothing new seemed to be going on between John and Lilith. I occasionally was aware when they talked on the phone, and John had lunch in town occasionally. But their relationship didn't seem to be growing any stronger. It seemed like a long time since they'd even had dinner together. Finally, I couldn't stand it any longer and mentioned to John just before dinner that I'd like to speak to him that evening. He looked ominous. "Everything okay?"

"Sure, John."

Leslie came into the kitchen, and noticed our serious faces. "Oh, am I interrupting something?" She started to back out.

"No, honey," I said. "That's fine."

"Maureen, do you have time to go over a book review?"

"Sure, just leave it here. I'll do it after dinner."

During dinner I glanced at John's anxious face. I worried that I'd had a glum expression when I mentioned we needed to talk. I think Wade noticed, too, but, typical of him, he said nothing.

After dinner, Wade returned to outside work and Leslie cleared the table while I filled the dishwasher. When Leslie left the kitchen, John stood in the doorway, waiting for me. I dried my hands and followed him into his office.

I had absolutely no idea where to start. "John," I said. He looked at me with dread. I simply couldn't think of what to say next.

"What, Maureen?"

"I...I..."

"Maureen, what is it?" Although his voice was gentle, I could hear his anxiety.

"John, I'm not sure...." I swallowed.

"Oh, my god. What?" He'd reached the end of his patience.

"I'm not sure if I can stay if Lilith's here."

He sat back in his chair. He simply looked at me for a long time.

I sat still as a statue. I tried to keep anxiety out of my face, but I doubt I was successful, especially not with someone as intuitive as John.

"Well," he finally said, "at this point I'm not too sure what's going on there. Lilith is a professional woman, very good at her job. But for a long time I've thought that she wouldn't be comfortable as a rancher's wife. Her career is important to her. She's asked if I would consider living in town."

"Would you?"

"Of course not. You know, Maureen, this situation with Lilith just sort of spun out of control. For both of us. Neither of us had dated other people once we were single again. We just let the momentum of the thing carry us along. I think Lilith is a wonderful person, but..." He shrugged. "It had been so long since I'd dated...."

"When did you start seeing her?"

"We met when I went to the bank to get our household account set up with your name. Lilith is the person I talked to. Then, whenever I went into the bank she usually stopped what she was doing to come over and talk. That went on for years. In the meantime she divorced her husband. We didn't really start seeing each other until just before that Fourth of July party we had. Even then it was just lunch now and then."

He ran his fingers through his hair. "After awhile it seemed we might have a future. We'd talked about marriage, but I never got the feeling that she would be happy living out here. She's a city girl, used to having things convenient. She goes to business meetings some evenings. I think she always thought I'd change my mind. Maybe commute between town and here."

I swallowed hard. "The other day when they were here for dinner, she mentioned something about coming home to meals—"

"I know, but..." He looked down, pensive.

A heavy silence settled between us.

I finally ventured, "I've been worried that it would be awkward having two women in the house."

"I think it would, too."

"Then the natural thing would be for me to leave." My voice sounded thin and reedy. My heart pounded in my ears.

John shook his head. "I don't want that. And I don't think you do, either."

We stared at one another.

"No," I whispered, "I don't. For one thing, I don't feel like my job here is finished."

"Maureen, can we hold off on this? Please don't make any decisions right now. Can you do that?"

"Okay." Relief began edging its way into my soul. But really, I reasoned, nothing has changed. Has it? Now it's just not me who's confused; John is, too. I stiffly left his office.

I forced myself to concentrate on Leslie's book review, made a few suggestions and finished cleaning the kitchen. I read for an hour or so, and then, for some reason, maybe simple emotional exhaustion, I slept better that night.

The next morning after breakfast, everyone went elsewhere. Leslie was off to school, Wade hand fed the stock with Randy, and John had gone to Stroh's, wanting to clear the air with Sloan's uncle to assure him there were no hard feelings between the two ranchers.

Lilith called, asking for John. She left a message for him to call her as soon as possible.

When he returned, I gave him the message and he went into his office and closed the door. When he emerged, he again put on his hat and said he was going into town and that he wouldn't be home for lunch. He turned as if to say something more, but apparently thought better of it, and left.

Something was in the air, but I simply could not anticipate what.

It was a crisp, bright sunny afternoon and I didn't know what to do with myself. I tried to go riding at least once a week, decided there wasn't a better time than right then, and left a note on the kitchen table saying I would be riding to McClellan's Bluff and that I'd be back in the late afternoon. I had a spaghetti sauce made. All

I would have to do would be to cook the pasta, heat the garlic bread, and make a salad.

I saddled Dixie and in just a few minutes the sense of peace riding brought washed over me. I loved my serene life here. Well, granted, it wasn't always serene. I let out a long breath. I cherished these moments when all I could hear was the clop of horse hooves and the occasional ping when a metal horseshoe glanced off a rock. Birds chirped to one another. No traffic noises marred the country-quiet of expansive acres. My mind darted to John's and my conversation, but I wouldn't allow myself to dwell on it.

I pulled my knit hat down over my ears, then pulled up my heavy jacket collar to cover more of my neck. There isn't much warmth to be had riding horseback. The horse's heat doesn't permeate the saddle and a rider is completely exposed to the elements. Pretty soon I'd dig out my long johns to wear under my jeans. I'd noticed that Wade and John didn't bundle up as much as I did in cold weather. No doubt their more strenuous activity kept them warmer.

We'd had a lovely fall, but it wouldn't be long before snow fell and winter would settle in. Now, as we made our way through a pasture at the higher elevation, grass crunched, and we left a trail. We crossed a small stream and Dixie's hooves crushed a thin layer of ice. Condensation chuffed from her mouth as she climbed the bank.

John was home when I came back from my ride. He met me at the door. "Your sister Sue called. You're to call her right away."

He looked so serious and worried, I asked, "Did she say why?"

"Your sister Diane died. I'm sorry."

My mouth dropped open. "Diane? Really? How?"

"Maureen, call Sue."

I went into my room to use the phone. I dialed and Sue answered. Diane had died of a stroke, at the age of forty. She had divorced her second husband and had been living in Seattle. For two days Sue had been trying to call our sister, but with no success. Concerned, Sue and her husband Bob had gone over to Diane's house. She lay on her bed, on top of the bedspread, dead for probably two days.

I didn't feel sorrow. I didn't feel anything.

"The memorial service is next Saturday," Sue said. "I doubt if many will attend, the family and maybe a few family friends. Will you come?"

I didn't give it much thought. "No, Sue, I won't. Diane has been out of my life for a long time. I don't need to say good bye." Then, as a second thought, I asked. "Do you need me? I'll come if you need me."

"No, I don't need you, but I wish you'd come."

"I'll visit you after things calm down, maybe in early November."

We left it at that. I'm glad it was Sue I'd talked to rather than my brother. Roger would have been angry that I wasn't coming. He could never accept Diane's and my long-standing rift. I thinned my lips. *Well, it wasn't him she screwed over.*

Joining the family in the kitchen. I stepped over to the stove and gave the spaghetti sauce a stir, put the water on to boil, and popped the garlic bread into the oven. Without being asked, Leslie had made a salad.

They all sat at the table, stunned, I guess, at my "business as usual" attitude.

Leslie broke the silence. "Maureen, I'm sorry about your sister."

"Thank you, honey."

"Yeah, Maureen," Wade added, "I'm sorry, too. Is there anything we can do?"

Leslie nodded. "When is the funeral?"

"It's a memorial service. Next Saturday." I didn't bother saying I wouldn't attend. A few minutes of silence filled the kitchen. I forced myself to sound normal. "Time to get washed up for dinner."

We sat down at the dinner table. I could feel the family's eyes on me. I think they expected sorrow, but it simply wasn't there.

"How was Ken Stroh? I asked John.

"Mad as hell at Sloan for coming here and involving him in this. He appreciated my stopping by. It might be good if you could invite Doreen over for coffee. I think they're both embarrassed." He thought a minute. "No hurry on that though. When things settle down for you."

"Sure, I'll do that."

Wade spoke up, breaking an awkward silence. "Dad, Randy's been giving Curtis jobs, cleaning out stalls, raking up the corral, that kind of stuff. Should we be paying him?"

"How old is Curtis now?"

"He's seven, almost eight," Leslie said.

"No, his dad should handle that. It's probably time for Randy to get a raise though."

I thought seven, even eight, was pretty young for chores like that, but I guess it's not unusual on ranches and farms. "What's Randy like with Curtis out there?"

Wade took another slice of garlic bread out of the basket. "He doesn't take any crap and when he tells Curtis to do something he follows up to see that it was done right. Today he made Curtis go back and rake the coral again."

John nodded. "Randy's a top hand, an important part of our operation. I'll catch up with him this evening and talk to him about a raise. If we're lucky, Curtis will follow in his dad's footsteps."

John cleared his throat. We all looked up, expecting some kind of announcement. I figured it would be something about my sister.

"I just wanted to tell you guys, Lilith and I are not getting married. It was never a real commitment anyway. It had been mentioned, but..." He shrugged. She's been offered a bank manager's job at a Seattle branch, and she plans to accept it."

"Really?" Leslie looked up, her fork suspended. "They're moving? Geez, I was just getting used to Roxanne."

John smiled at Leslie and nodded. "I think your friendship with that girl gave her the self-confidence she needed."

"And maybe a decent hairdo," Wade added, which made us all laugh.

Leslie looked at her dad. "How are you with all this?"

My heart warmed. What a lovely thing to ask. It showed how Leslie thought of others, of their needs.

We all looked expectantly at John. He glanced up and looked around. "I'm fine. Relieved, actually. Lilith was never cut out for ranch life."

A sense of relief rushed over me. I arose from the table, but could hardly concentrate on cutting slices of chocolate cake. "Leslie, would you dish up ice cream?"

"Sure. Who wants ice cream with their chocolate cake? Just Wade?"

After dessert, Leslie cleared the table and left the kitchen. Wade wandered into the living room. John remained at the table. I noticed him there, but wasn't quite sure what to do. I started to fill the dishwasher.

"When will you be leaving?"

My heart dropped. I'm sure my face fell. "Leaving?" I croaked, afraid to look at him.

"For the funeral. Don't you need to leave soon to spend time with your family?"

"Oh, that. I'm not going."

"What? Not going? Of course you're going to your sister's funeral."

"It's not really a funeral, it's a memorial—"

"I don't care what the hell you call it, you need to be there!"

"John, I didn't have anything to do with Diane when she was alive, why would I—"

"You're not going for her, you're going for your family!"

I wondered where Wade and Leslie were. Other parts of the house were strangely quiet. "I told Sue I'd try to get over sometime in November."

"That's unconscionable! I don't care what you thought of Diane, she was your sister! You need to be at that family gathering."

I sighed and shook my head.

"How about if I drive you over?"

I turned to face him. "John, why would you do that? I don't need—"

"Because I think you should go." He hesitated. "Because I want to."

I was so shocked, I was speechless. "John—"

"Please let me take you. This is Tuesday, we could leave Thursday, give you a couple of days before the service."

"How can you get away? I don't think—"

"Wade and Randy can handle things here. I could use a break."

I nodded numbly.

17

*A*t the breakfast table the next morning John announced to Wade and Leslie that he and I were going to attend my sister's funeral.

"Memorial," I said.

"Whatever. What's the difference?"

"A funeral is with the body present; a memorial is without the body." I didn't go into the Celebration of Life so popular now. In any event, I'm not sure my family could have put one together for Diane. She wasn't that popular. I couldn't imagine anyone talking about the good times they'd had with her.

"Was your sister married, Maureen? Did she have kids?" Leslie asked.

"Twice divorced. No kids."

"I don't think I ever saw this sister, did I?"

"No. We weren't close."

Leslie's eyes grew big, but she remained silent. Wade, as usual, made no comment.

"So you guys can take care of everything here?" John looked at Wade, then Leslie.

"Sure," they said almost in unison.

"How long will you be gone?" Leslie asked.

"Probably until Sunday," John said.

Wade looked up at both of us in wonder, then took another piece of toast.

Leslie glanced at her brother.

Things were moving so fast, I barely had time to reflect on what was happening. I only had one day to prepare if we were leaving Thursday. I lined up easy meals for Leslie to fix, writing down dinner ideas. I had several prepared dishes in the freezer. I made a dash into town to buy lunch fixings so Leslie could make her school lunches, and for Wade to fix for himself. Pearl might invite them over, but I thought they'd prefer to manage on their own.

John had asked me to call Abbie, just to let her know we wouldn't be home, in case of emergency.

When I called her, she expressed sympathy for my loss. I didn't go into any detail, just thanked her.

"You say John is going with you to the memorial?"

"Yes, isn't that nice?"

"Uh, yes, and surprising. Did he know your sister well?" Her voice was full of doubt.

"Not really. I think he's going for my sake."

"Ohhh." Silence, then, "Well, I hope things go well. Thanks for letting me know." The excitement in her voice didn't go unnoticed.

We would take the SUV and I'd leave my car for Leslie.

Wednesday night we both packed. I opened my bedroom door to John's knock. It was hard to read his expression; I'd never seen that particular look.

"Do you want me to dress western or straight?"

"Western, for sure. *All* western. Boots, Stetson, the works."

He chuckled. "Yes, ma'am."

I again answered a knock at my bedroom door. Leslie stood, holding her dad's boots. "Wade and I are going to shine dad's boots. Do you have shoes that need a polish?

"Sure! That would be great." I handed her my good black shoes, glad to have the help.

The next morning as I prepared a quick poached eggs-over-toast breakfast, I glanced out the window. My heart warmed when I saw Wade and Leslie putting the finishing touches on washing the SUV.

When they came in for breakfast, I said, "You guys are the best. Thank you so much!"

"Sure," Wade said. "Maureen, you've done stuff for us for years. We hardly ever get to do anything for you."

"That's right," Leslie chimed in.

John looked out the window, then at each of them. "Thanks, guys."

We left right after breakfast, dropping Leslie off at school. She seemed to be fighting for a calm voice. "I'm not sure what to say." She thought a minute. "I hope everything goes okay."

I smiled at her. "That will do it. Funerals aren't fun, so the best we can hope for is that it goes well."

"Memorial," John said.

I smiled. "Right. Memorial."

After dropping Leslie off we settled into the long ride. We chatted about what time we should get there, where we'd stay. He said if it was awkward, he could call his cousin and stay there. I mentioned that between Sue and Roger, there would be room.

We enjoyed a comfortable silence.

"So," John said, "what happened between you and Diane?"

I waved my hand dismissively and shook my head.

"Maureen, you know just about everything there is to know about my family. You've seen us through thick and thin, sickness, health, even death. Fights and laughter. The whole thing. I know virtually nothing about your family."

"Sure you do. You know Sue and Bob, Roger and Ellen."

"I know who they are, barely. I didn't know Diane at all, never saw her except for the time you kicked her off the ranch—"

"I didn't kick her off the ranch!"

John looked at me, his expression clearly saying, "Come *on*."

"Well, okay, I guess I did. I didn't want to have anything to do with her."

"Why?"

I should have known I would have to tell him. Although my family and close Seattle friends knew why, I had never told anyone else. Had never intended to. Even though I'd tried to bury it, it was like a festering sliver, surfacing every once in awhile through the years.

"Diane had an affair with my fiancé." My insides felt like jelly.

John didn't look shocked when he glanced my way. He simply studied me. "That must have been terrible for you. How did you find out?"

"We were to be married in about six months. Supposedly, Diane went over to Tom's to discuss some 'surprise' for me, something about an engagement party." I took on a sarcastic voice. "'Things just got out of control,' they said. 'It was nothing we planned. We just couldn't help ourselves.'" I couldn't keep the bitterness out of my voice. "Their affair had gone on for about three months. I never suspected a thing." I shook my head. "When they finally told me, Diane said she was pregnant with Tom's child."

John shook his head. "What a mess."

"Actually, I never knew if the pregnancy part was true or not. She apparently lost the baby, had a very early miscarriage. Actually, to me it didn't matter if she was pregnant or lying about it. The fact is, they'd had an affair, which ended Tom's and my plans to marry."

"Did Diane and Tom marry?"

"Oh, yeah." I shrugged. "They married even before the date Tom and I were to be married."

"Did it last?"

"Less than a year."

"Did Tom ever marry again?"

"Once, but it only lasted a couple of years. He's never had children."

"I can see why you and Diane weren't close. Did she ever try to apologize, try to make things right?"

"They both did. I told them both they were out of my life. I wouldn't speak to either one. They'd call, and I'd put the phone down, not hang up, just put it down. Tom called once at the ranch, with the same treatment. He finally stopped trying. Diane, always wanting to have her way, never stopped trying."

"Had you been close at one time?

"Diane was about ten years younger than me and I was thrilled when she was born. But it was soon apparent that she would be spoiled. My parents doted on her. I think by this time they'd mellowed, weren't nearly so strict with her, their fourth child. They had more money by then and they pretty much bought her whatever she wanted. My folks, Mother especially, expected everyone to give in to her. She couldn't stand to hear Diane whine or cry, which she did often to get her own way."

John nodded. "I can understand that, but it's not right."

"The thing is, Diane couldn't stand not to have what everyone else had. If I got something new, she had to have the same thing, even if it didn't make sense."

"What did Roger and Sue think about the deal with Tom and Diane?"

"They were furious. Roger really stormed around. Sue was in tears for days. My parents were heart-broken, too, and mad at Diane. But after a time, they thought we should forgive and forget. Well, they knew I couldn't forget, but at least forgive. She was my sister, after all."

"But you couldn't."

"No. I couldn't. Wouldn't." I know my voice sounded hard. I didn't care.

John pulled off at a rest stop. We went into our respective bathrooms. I knew my face was red and blotchy. I splashed cold water on it. When I came out, John was sitting in a sunny spot on a picnic table, feet planted on the bench. He patted the place next to him. I climbed up.

"Maureen, you've been carrying this a long time. Probably for at least fifteen years."

"Yep." Bitterness still tinged my voice.

"She's gone now."

"I know." I was horrified when my voice caught.

"Let her go in peace."

The dam broke. The old, tired dam that I'd kept in check for so many years finally cracked and gave way. John put his arm around my shoulders.

"I'm sorry." I fumbled in my purse for a hanky. I simply could not stop the tears.

John reached into his pocket and brought out a clean handkerchief, one of his good ones I had ironed, and handed it to me. "That's okay. Just let it out, Maureen. You've kept this bottled up all these years. Let it all out now. It's done."

We still had a long way to drive. John's patience surprised me. I finally mopped up what I hoped was the last of the tears.

Once back in the car we were able to talk about other things. Although John had known I'd worked at my father's insurance agency, had later taken care of my aging parents, and that after their death I had worked at a large insurance company, he asked me particulars about those things. It seemed so strange to talk about something other than the ranch. John surprised me with his interest, his knowledge of business, his compassion.

I couldn't believe how quickly the time passed before we arrived at my sister's. When I'd called the day before Sue suggested we stay with them, that the kids would double up so John could have their son's room and I would sleep in their guest room. John knew Sue and Bob, and fit right into the family, but at times I felt a little awkward. I had never been in any situation with John other than at the ranch and occasionally brief kid-related things away from home. We were getting acquainted on another level. At Sue's he seemed bigger than life. When I looked at him, everything else faded away. I could see Sue's mind whirling away, but she didn't mention it, only showed her appreciation that he came.

On Friday, I showed John the house where I was raised, the schools I attended, and the building which once held my father's insurance agency. We even drove by the apartment building where I had lived just before I'd come to the ranch.

We drove around the University of Washington campus where John had gone to college. He had lived in a dorm the first year, an apartment building with two other fellows the next three years. He couldn't find the apartment building. "I guess it's been torn down."

We drove to the University District and I showed John the big Safeco building, the corporate offices, where I had worked as a programmer/analyst after my parents passed away.

"I'll bet you were good at that job." John pulled into a parking space and shifted the SUV to park. He looked up at Safeco's tall building.

"I was," I agreed. "They offered me a supervisor's position, but then I saw your ad."

John looked into my eyes for a long minute. "I can't imagine how we got so lucky. You gave up a lot to come to us, Maureen."

"It didn't seem like that to me. I needed a change, a new lifestyle, new scenery. I needed to think of something," my voice cracked, "other than what I had lost."

He studied my face, then pulled onto the busy street. "Boy, I don't know how people can stand this traffic."

Friday night we were invited to my brother's for dinner. Roger and Ellen were fun and friendly, and seemed especially pleased that John had come. We returned to Sue's for the night.

The next day I would be saying my final farewell to Diane, to the person whom I had allowed to fashion much of my adult life. My emotions seemed to toggle from relief to....to what?

18

*O*n Saturday, the day of the memorial service, a few cousins came to town, a couple from Tacoma, another from Enumclaw, a family from Spokane and family friends from right there in Seattle. In all, I suppose fifty people attended the memorial, more than I expected.

Up to this point John had worn good jeans, western-cut shirts and his better riding boots. But for the memorial service, he wore a suit, a soft rust color with a subtle western flair, and a white shirt. His good boots shone to a fare-thee-well. I thought he looked particularly handsome. I wore my navy-blue pant suit with a white blouse, an outfit I often wore to church, and low heels.

Heads turned as John opened the car door for me and took my arm as I climbed out of the car. People whispered and craned their necks. I loved their reaction.

John took off his Stetson as we entered the building and hung it on a hook in the foyer.

We sat with Roger's and Sue's families, near the front. Sue had arranged the service and, typical of my sister, it was well organized. A minister, a friend of the family, gave a short sermon. He didn't have much to say about Diane, he'd barely known her, but rather spoke of the family. There was a time for people to stand and speak about Diane, but only a few did: Sue, Roger, and a couple of our cousins with childhood memories.

During the service I glanced around, though I couldn't see much since we sat so close to the front. Later, at the reception where Sue had ordered refreshments, I had more opportunity to see familiar faces. As I looked around, it occurred to me that John was by far the best-looking man in the building. Dashing, even. Strong and fit. He constantly stayed by my side, leaving only to refill my coffee cup.

In the brief moment John was gone, a paunchy middle-age man started toward me. Tom. He had just approached when John returned with my coffee. It occurred to me to simply turn my back on Tom, but I knew John wouldn't approve.

"Tom." I shook his extended hand. "Hello." He clung to my hand, brought it up to his chest. I thought of jerking it back, but suddenly realized it didn't matter any more. "I'd like you to meet John Cahill. John, this is Tom Nelson, Diane's first husband." I tried to keep all trace of bitterness from my voice. John handed me my coffee cup. Tom had to let go of my hand so that I could accept the coffee and so he could shake John's offered hand.

John acted as though he knew nothing about Tom and Diane's affair, simply shook his hand and nodded. I saw Tom's eyes widen at John's firm handshake. I'm sure John noticed Tom's soft hand.

"How have you been, Maureen?" Tom asked. He looked as though he might cry.

"Fine. Thank you." I turned to John. "I want you to meet my cousins before they leave. Good to see you, Tom."

We went on to briefly visit my cousins, and then talk to some family friends and neighbors who had come to pay their respects. Out of the corner of my eye I saw Tom lurking in the background.

All in all, the whole ordeal had been quite pleasant. I felt fulfilled, accepted. For years when around these people I had often felt sympathy, even pity, which I hated. Now I felt whole again with a sense of belonging. I loved the admiring glances John got from the other women. Even men gave him a second glance.

We had taken the SUV to the service, leaving room in my brother's and sister's cars for their families. As we pulled out of the parking lot, I said to John. "You were right. It was good that I came. My not being here would have been awkward for the family."

"How about for you? Was it good for you?"

I thought for a moment. "Yes. I feel like the whole subject is closed, put to rest. And you got to meet Tom. Geez. What did I see in him?"

John laughed. "He apparently still sees something in you."

I shrugged. I fully looked at John, watched as he expertly skirted the SUV around a traffic jam. "I was proud to introduce you to my family and friends."

He glanced at me. "I'm glad."

We needed to leave early Sunday morning. For John to be gone this long from the ranch set some kind of record. In the years I'd been at the ranch he'd only been gone overnight maybe a dozen times, mostly hunting trips. During roundup he'd been away from home, but that happened when they'd been too far away gathering the herd, necessitating they camp at remote places on the ranch.

We set out right after an early breakfast. "John, thank you so much for bringing me. I really appreciate your taking the time to be away from the ranch this long."

"You're welcome. I've had a good time too, despite the fact that it was a funeral."

"Memorial," I said. We both laughed.

We chatted about the various people who had attended the service, about Roger, Sue and their families. The miles rolled by. Snoqualmie Pass was especially beautiful with sun shining on sparkling snowy mountain peaks. John braked for a deer and her fawn crossing the highway. He mentioned that he wanted to go hunting with Wade in the fall, put some venison in the freezer.

I sighed. "It was good seeing Seattle again. I'm glad I could show you where I lived and worked. But I'm always happy to get out of the big city."

"I can't imagine living in a city all my life. When I went to the University it was kind of fun at first, but I got tired of all the noise, of the rush." He mentioned Lilith's request that they live in the city. "She just doesn't understand ranching, that it's a way of life. Not being there would kill me. It just isn't a nine to five job."

"No, I'm sure she doesn't understand. You have to live it to understand that. Do you have regrets about breaking up with her?"

"No. I really didn't have strong feelings toward her. I think it was the novelty of being with a woman again."

A few minutes passed, then, "Maureen, have you ever thought that we, you and I, might get married?" He glanced at me, then back to the road.

My heart pounded. "It's crossed my mind."

"I've tried to ask you out but you always have excuses. I've wondered if you didn't like me....in that way." I could feel John's eyes on me, waiting for my response.

We drove a distance before I answered. "I haven't wanted to confuse our working relationship with a social one. It could just cause....confusion."

"Why? Why would there be confusion?"

I closed my eyes and tried to breathe normally. I wondered how I could express my feelings to make him understand.

"Why, Maureen? When things come up, like going to Abbie and Bob's, why won't you do those things with me? Or even go to a movie, or out to dinner? You always find reasons not to go."

"I haven't wanted that kind of pressure between us. I didn't want to push you into something you might not want. Other people would jump to conclusions when they saw us together. I was afraid it would bring our relationship to another level, one that you might not necessarily be comfortable with. Then later you were with Lilith."

He pulled off the highway onto a little dirt road, and turned off the engine. I looked around to see why we'd stopped.

"I don't want to get us in a wreck. I need to concentrate." He unbuckled his seat belt; I did the same.

"But you didn't seem to want to do things with me even before Lilith was in the picture."

"Because if we did social things and it didn't work out between us, it could put my position, my reason for being here, in jeopardy. It could become awkward and I'd have to leave. When I first came, I made a vow to myself that I wouldn't let the family, especially Leslie, down. You'd been through so much...."

"How would you let us down?"

"Well, it might not work out." I felt like a broken record.

"What might not work out? Maureen, we've lived together for nine, almost ten years! We've done all the hard stuff, the daily grind. You know about all there is to know about me. You know that I'm not the easiest man to live with. You know that the ranch and its stock has to come before almost everything. And I know you, but," he smiled, "other than your really bad sense of direction, I know that you're easy to get along with, you're helpful, generous. I've loved living with you...."

I started to object. "Well, we haven't really lived togeth—"

"Yes, we have lived together. That's what marriage is, Maureen. The inconveniences, the squabbles, the crazy hours we keep. You've worked your tail off for us, cleaning up after us, cooking, doing our laundry—"

"But you've given me a home, complete run of the house. It hasn't been all 'give' on my part. John. It's been wonderful, being on the ranch with you and your family."

Cars swished by. John turned to face me fully.

"Do you love me, Maureen? Do you want to live with me the rest of your life?"

My breath hitched. I vaguely wondered if he could hear my pounding heart.

He didn't give me a chance to answer.

"I love you Maureen. I want to be with you. I want more of you than to give you the responsibility of the house, I want to give you my love and affection. I want to take you places, to have fun. Life can't be all work, although on a ranch it mostly is. But I want more. I want you, Maureen. I can't imagine not having you in my life. I want to marry you." He took a breath. "Will you marry me?"

I looked into his eager, pleading eyes. What in the world was I worried about? Here is the most wonderful man in the world asking me to marry him, and I'm afraid it won't work out? What won't work out?

"I do love you, John. I've just been afraid to admit it, even to myself. I really can't imagine living without you, either." I took a deep breath. "I'd love to marry you. YES!"

His smile, his obvious relief, his sparkling eyes all showed me his love. He reached over for me. We kissed, long and hard. I melted into the smell of him, the feel of his strong arms around me, his closeness. It was as though I'd come home at last. This was what I'd been afraid to imagine all these years.

He pulled away and looked into my eyes. "You've made me a happy man."

I sighed. "I don't think I've ever felt such peace."

"When do you want to get married?"

"Soon. I'd like a church wedding. Would that be all right with you?"

We untangled ourselves, and John started the car, fastened his seat belt, and slipped the car into gear. With a big grin, he backed out of the little dirt road and merged onto the highway.

"Sure," he said, "that's fine. I know it's important to you."

"It is. I don't want a huge wedding, just a few friends and my immediate family."

"That sounds fine."

We chatted, more relaxed with one another than we'd ever been. I felt dreamy, as though I were floating.

In Yakima, we stopped at a little diner for lunch.

"I'll bet you're anxious to get back. You've been gone for a record length of time, for you."

John nodded. "I have, but I'm not worried. Wade can handle anything that comes up."

We gave our lunch orders, then sat back, relaxed.

"Wade has been clearing that land for his house. Do they have house plans yet?"

"No, but they're talking about it. That's something you and I need to talk about. Wade's thinking about putting in a double-wide, mostly because of the money. I'm not that crazy about the idea, so I want to propose to him that the ranch pay to have a regular house built—we'll make some sort of financial arrangement with him and Teresa. Depending on what they say, I think a three-bedroom house would be good. Then, when they start their family, they could move into the main house and we'd live in the smaller one. That would save you work keeping up that big place, and give them more space."

I moved my arm so the waitress could pour more coffee. "That sounds like a great plan. It's probably a few years down the road."

"Oh, yeah. But I need to talk to them about it before they put in a double-wide."

I smiled.

"What?"

"I can't wait to see Wade's and Leslie's expressions when we tell them we're getting married."

John smiled, a relaxed, contented smile, and nodded. He paid the bill and we continued our journey home.

Going through Chewack, I suggested we buy a pizza so I only would have to heat it up. "I should call Leslie first, make sure she hasn't something planned for dinner."

Leslie was so glad to hear from us, to know we were close to home. She'd taken steaks out of the freezer and planned to bake potatoes. "I like your pizza idea better. I'll put together a salad."

John pulled into the SUV's parking place and Wade was there to open my door and give us a nice greeting.

Later, as we munched pizza at the kitchen table, John casually said, "I've told Maureen I want my bedroom back." He reached for my hand.

A stunned silence enveloped us. Then Wade let out a cattleman's whoop, which made Leslie jump. The expression on Leslie's face was at first puzzled, then with Wade's whoop, her eyes and mouth formed matching "O's." To my amazement, tears sprang to her eyes.

"Leslie." I stood, alarmed.

She scraped her chair back and rushed into my arms. "It's what I've always wanted!"

She reached for her dad and we had a three-way hug.

Wade was next in giving me a hug. "I'm really happy about this." He shook his father's hand. "I can't say I'm surprised. When you two got out of the car you were both glowing like neon lights."

John laughed. "Nothing gets past you!"

"Not if I can help it. I've learned from the best." He grasped his father's shoulder.

They stood, looking into each other's eyes. Man to man, father to son. They smiled and nodded.

John stepped over to me and put his arm around my shoulder.

Leslie stood back and beamed at us. "I am soooo happy. When's the wedding? Wow, we have two weddings in the works. I hope you guys don't do something embarrassing, like have a double wedding."

I laughed. "We'll try not to embarrass you, Leslie. We plan to have a small wedding, maybe in three months or so, right here at Calvary Baptist."

* * *

It was the lovely wedding I'd always hoped for. One invitation led to another and about a hundred people attended. My brother Roger gave me away and my sister Sue served as my matron-of-honor. Wade was John's best man. Randy and Bob Peterson were ushers.

Leslie greeted people in the foyer and made sure they signed the guest book. Later, she cut the wedding cake. The ladies from church served refreshments and Teresa poured coffee and tea.

During the ceremony and even through the day, I kept having to remind myself that what we were doing was real. At times I fought tears of happiness. I'd find John looking at me as though he, too, was afraid he was just dreaming. My family glowed in their happiness for me. All in all, it was the wedding of my dreams.

* * *

The end of Leslie's junior year quickly approached. "Maureen," she said, "there's a mother-daughter tea at school on June 3rd. Will you come?"

"I would love to, Leslie." What an honor, I thought, to participate in a mother-daughter event. Leslie and I shopped for new dresses for the special occasion.

The tea, an elegant affair, was after school on a Friday. Leslie waited in the hall with the other girls ready to greet their mothers and escort us into the library where the tea would be held.

Several teachers greeted the guests and one of Leslie's favorites, Mrs. Wurth, walked toward us.

"Mrs. Wurth," Leslie said, eyes sparkling and with a big grin, "I'd like you to meet my mother, Maureen Cahill."

My heart swelled with happiness and contentment when Mrs. Wurth reached to shake my hand.

"Welcome, Mrs. Cahill."

About the Author

*M*ary E. Trimble, award-winning novelist, lives with her husband on Camano Island, Washington. Their family, most of whom live in the Northwest, play an important role in their lives.

Trimble has written two memoirs, *Sailing with Impunity: Adventure in the South Pacific*, and *Tubob: Two Years in West Africa with the Peace Corps*, and has been a frequent guest speaker to groups interested in those topics. Her previous three contemporary-western novels have met with acclaim.

A prolific writer and author of 400-plus magazine and newspaper articles, Trimble draws on personal experiences including purser and ship's diver aboard the tall ship, *M.S. Explorer*, two years with the Peace Corps in West Africa; a 13,000-mile South Pacific sailing trip aboard their 40-foot Bristol, *Impunity*; and extensive overland RV trips. She recently retired after serving 20 years as a volunteer with the American Red Cross. The author is an active member of Women Writing the West and Pacific Northwest Writers Association, and is also a member of The Authors Guild and Electronically Published Internet Connection.

For the latest information on my writing and blogging, please visit my website:

www.MaryTrimbleBooks.com

Made in the USA
Lexington, KY
29 July 2017